SAFE AND SOUND

Books by Fern Michaels:

Sweet Vengeance
Holly and Ivy
Fancy Dancer
No Safe Secret
Wishes for Christmas
About Face
Perfect Match
A Family Affair
Forget Me Not
The Blossom Sisters
Balancing Act
Tuesday's Child
Betrayal
Southern Comfort
To Taste the Wine
Sins of the Flesh
Sins of Omission
Return to Sender
Mr. and Miss Anonymous
Up Close and Personal
Fool Me Once
Picture Perfect
The Future Scrolls
Kentucky Sunrise
Kentucky Heat
Kentucky Rich
Plain Jane
Charming Lily
What You Wish For
The Guest List
Listen to Your Heart
Celebration
Yesterday
Finders Keepers
Annie's Rainbow
Sara's Song

Vegas Sunrise
Vegas Heat
Vegas Rich
Whitefire
Wish List
Dear Emily
Christmas at Timberwoods

The Sisterhood Novels:

Safe and Sound
Need to Know
Crash and Burn
Point Blank
In Plain Sight
Eyes Only
Kiss and Tell
Blindsided
Gotcha!
Home Free
Déjà Vu
Cross Roads
Game Over
Deadly Deals
Vanishing Act
Razor Sharp
Under the Radar
Final Justice
Collateral Damage
Fast Track
Hokus Pokus
Hide and Seek
Free Fall
Lethal Justice
Sweet Revenge

Books by Fern Michaels (Continued):

The Jury
Vendetta
Payback
Weekend Warriors

The Men of the Sisterhood
Novels:

Truth or Dare
High Stakes
Fast and Loose
Double Down

The Godmothers Series:

Getaway (E-Novella Exclusive)
Spirited Away (E-Novella Exclusive)
Hideaway (E-Novella Exclusive)
Classified
Breaking News
Deadline
Late Edition
Exclusive
The Scoop

E-Book Exclusives:

Desperate Measures
Seasons of Her Life

To Have and To Hold
Serendipity
Captive Innocence
Captive Embraces
Captive Passions
Captive Secrets
Captive Splendors
Cinders to Satin
For All Their Lives
Texas Heat
Texas Rich
Texas Fury
Texas Sunrise

Anthologies:

Mistletoe Magic
Winter Wishes
The Most Wonderful Time
When the Snow Falls
Secret Santa
A Winter Wonderland
I'll Be Home for Christmas
Making Spirits Bright
Holiday Magic
Snow Angels
Silver Bells
Comfort and Joy
Sugar and Spice
Let It Snow
A Gift of Joy
Five Golden Rings
Deck the Halls
Jingle All the Way

FERN MICHAELS

SAFE AND SOUND

KENSINGTON PUBLISHING CORP.
http://www.kensingtonbooks.com

KENSINGTON BOOKS are published by

Kensington Publishing Corp.
119 West 40th Street
New York, NY 10018

ISBN 978-1-64385-194-5

Prologue

There were those who referred to the Circle, a property in a residential area of Virginia, as an oasis. Others questioned why there would be an oasis in an area populated by an average number of human beings and a few four-legged creatures. The queries gradually died a natural death as the years passed because, to put it simply, no one cared enough to keep questioning something that didn't matter to them one way or the other.

The truth of the matter was that the parcel of land in question was circular—a thirteen-acre plot of land with three homes on each side of the Circle. The bottom half of the Circle consisted of a massive hydraulic gate with a retina scanner to which one had to submit in order to gain entrance unless one had a key to the gate. The message was clear: If you don't belong here, go away. Dead center, at the top of the Circle but beyond its perimeter was a long, low, sprawling, one-story structure constructed of aged pink brick and covered in ivy. A small, burnished-brass plaque near the wide mahogany double doors that might have been at home on the castle side of a moat in ancient times spelled out the words ELEANOR LYMEN AMERICUS INSTITUTE. More often than not it was simply referred to as ELAI.

The Eleanor Lymen Americus Institute hosted gifted children, all of whose IQs were off the charts. These were children who, at the age of ten, had graduated from high school and immediately gone on to college. The Institute had working arrangements with a number of first-rate colleges and universities, including the University of Virginia, the College of William and Mary, and Johns Hopkins University, which allowed its students to take online courses that instructors at the Institute supervised, thus allowing the Institute's students to obtain higher-education degrees without suffering the adverse social effects of living on a college campus with people in their late teens and twenties. At the Institute, there were youngsters who had their MBAs at twelve, and others with PhDs at the age of fifteen. It was evident to anyone who examined the situation that most of the children were smarter than their instructors, including those at the aforementioned colleges and universities.

The ELAI was, architecturally speaking, a beautiful building inside and outside, though its sterile appearance, once inside, was not to everyone's taste. No expense had been spared to make its form and structure as good an example of modern utilitarian architecture as one could find. A five-star chef prepared meals for the students and staff. The outside campus was exquisite, with just the right amount of flowers, shrubbery, and trees, all of which were precisely maintained by someone with manicure scissors. Every blade of grass matched its neighbor. No branch, twig, or leaf dared to outgrow its neighbor. Colorful benches and chairs were scattered over the grounds alongside flower-bordered walkways. The campus, however, was all for show, because no child, instructor, or house mother ever wandered over the spiky grass, no one ever sat with a book on the colorful benches and chairs or ate lunch in the beautiful setting.

The six McMansions that dotted the sides of the Circle were magnificent Tudor-style homes ranging from eight thousand to ten thousand square feet each. Three of the McMansions were currently inhabited, one by the owner of the Circle and the other two by the owner's two best friends. All three houses sat next to one another on the left side of the Circle facing the Institute. The three McMansions on the opposite side were uninhabited. No one among the public knew why, because no one cared enough to ask. The center of the Circle was a flower garden maintained by the same person who maintained the ELAI campus. It was a beautiful rainbow of color even in the winter, when there was snow on the ground and scarlet poinsettias—artificial, of course—dotted the dead winter grass, along with some bright green Astroturf.

The Circle was just there. A place. To be talked about or not to be talked about.

The truth was, no member of the public seemed to care about the Circle. But one person and her friends cared, the founder of the Circle and the ELAI, Eleanor Porter Lymen, whose inherited railroad wealth allowed her to create the Circle and fund it unto eternity, as she was fond of saying.

Eleanor Porter Lymen had given one interview to a pesky young reporter named Maggie Spritzer when construction began. She never granted another, even when the Circle was completed. Nor would she grant an interview when the ELAI opened to admit its first students.

It wasn't that Eleanor Porter Lymen was a recluse.

She wasn't.

Eleanor Porter Lymen was a woman with too many secrets, secrets that she didn't want pesky, pushy, obnoxious reporters ferreting out, and the best way to prevent that from happening was simply to ignore any and all requests for anything pertaining to herself or the ELAI.

Thirteen years after the Circle had been built, the ELAI and the six McMansions were all but forgotten by the press and anyone else who might have been interested enough to ask about them.

The Circle was just that.

The Circle.

Chapter 1

Isabelle Flanders Tookus picked her way carefully through the beautiful autumn leaves as she made her way to a park bench to eat her lunch with her new best friend. She carried her lunch in a small take-out bag. It was a simple lunch—pastrami with spicy brown mustard on rye along with two equally spicy garlic dill pickles. And one peanut butter and jelly sandwich, just to be on the safe side. Two bottles of Snapple iced tea, along with napkins and two wet wipes, completed the contents of the bag.

Isabelle loved autumn's crisp air, the magnificent colored leaves, and the scent of smoke in the air to go along with all the fall decorations. She closed her eyes for a moment to allow conjured-up memories of childhood to appear behind her closed lids—visions of pumpkins, scarecrows, and haystacks.

She was partial to this little park because it allowed her to see what Realtors referred to as the Circle, the enclave she had designed early in her career as an architect. She never got tired of looking at it. She had also designed the little park she was sitting in at the moment. Because she loved the area so much, she had located her offices a block behind the enclave, so she could still enjoy gazing at the fruits of her labor whenever she chose to do so.

Weather permitting, she brought her lunch every day, usually from home, and spent a quiet hour doing nothing but people watching and devouring her lunch. It was also something she did alone, never inviting anyone to join her, because this hour of the day was hers and hers alone. Until six months ago, that is.

Isabelle looked down at her watch. He was late. A first.

He was never late. More often than not, her lunch date was early and waiting for her. It wasn't always that way. In the beginning, when she first met him last spring, he would simply wave and move on. Waving became "hi," then a few words here and there. Each encounter was for no more than a few seconds. Gradually, over the past six months, those few seconds slid into minutes, to be followed by an exchange of identities. First names only. So far.

A worm of fear crawled around Isabelle's stomach. She wondered if something was wrong. She'd been crystal clear when she issued the luncheon invitation. Lunch on Friday—a first. Twelve noon. He'd nodded in agreement. Seeing no watch on his wrist, she wondered if he would be on time. She smiled now when she remembered how his eyes had lit up and sparkled like bright blue jewels at her invitation. It was a sign that their relationship was safe and moving to another level. Something she totally understood.

Isabelle shifted on the bench as she strained to see down the many paths in the little park that led to another circle, then back to the main entrance. She could see two young women jogging in their brightly colored spandex outfits that screamed, *Hey look at me, I'm exercising*. Two elderly gentlemen were wearing gilly hats and getting ready to set up a chessboard for their daily game. And a young couple was strolling along, holding hands.

It was such a beautiful day, so inviting, so golden and bronze that Isabelle was surprised the park wasn't jammed with office workers taking advantage of the nice weather to eat their lunch outdoors. In a few weeks, these days of Indian summer would be nothing more than a memory.

Isabelle chewed on her lower lip as she stared down at her watch. Eight minutes late.

And then she saw him, pedaling his bicycle as fast as his eight-year-old legs could pump the pedals. "Hey, Izzy! I'm sorry I'm late! I had to help a lady catch her dog. I caught him, and he was *fast*." The little boy beamed happily. "Look, she gave me five dollars! I didn't want to take it, but the lady insisted. I didn't want to insult her, so I took it."

"It's okay, I just got here myself. That's wonderful about catching the dog! You ready for lunch?"

"I am. What are we having, Izzy?"

"Something you told me you have never eaten before, a pastrami with hot mustard on rye bread and some really good pickles. Snapple."

Ben Ryan slid off his bike and propped it up against the back of the bench before he skedaddled around to sit down next to Isabelle, his only friend in the whole world.

"If you don't like it, you don't have to eat it. I also brought a peanut butter and jelly sandwich, just in case."

Ben grinned from ear to ear as he waited for Isabelle to hand over his sandwich and napkin. "I am sure I'll like it. I have a discriminating palate." He chomped down on his sandwich.

Isabelle had trouble not laughing at his final comment before starting to eat. She nibbled on her own pastrami sandwich as she studied her new friend. She was obsessed with the little guy, who was so skinny she worried that a strong wind would blow him away. Childless herself, she simply assumed what she was feeling was some kind of motherly instinct. She knew so little about him. She understood his original reticence about not talking to strangers. But months of hand waves, short greetings, and short conversations meant they'd moved to a place where the young boy felt safe and comfortable around her. And yet he was still aloof to a fault. He had never volunteered any information about himself; nor had he asked her anything about herself. As much as she wanted to quiz him, she'd restrained herself, afraid that if she did, she'd drive him away.

She saw him three days a week, Tuesday, Wednesday, and Friday. Five months into the friendship, Isabelle found herself scheduling her appointments earlier or later so as to always be available at the noon hour to spend time with the little boy. She couldn't explain it to herself, much less explain it to her sisterhood friends or her husband, Abner. In a way, it was her special secret, one she wanted to keep to herself. She couldn't help but wonder if Ben had told his parents about her. For some reason, she thought it unlikely.

Ben Ryan was an endearing little boy. His dark, curly hair was too long. His bright blue eyes confused her because, at least in her opinion, they were the eyes of an adult. He had a cute little pug nose and chipmunk cheeks, and there was a gap between his front teeth. Endearing. Something about Ben suddenly stirred in Isabelle. It was something she was all too familiar with: fear. Now why would a little eight-year-old be fearful? He was well dressed. Just because he was whippet thin didn't mean he wasn't fed. He had a bicycle, and it was relatively new. Obviously, he was allowed to be out and about on his own, so he wasn't being held a prisoner anywhere.

"Is this your lunch hour, too?" Isabelle blurted.

"In a manner of speaking. This is a very good sandwich, Izzy. You were right when you said I would like it. I like the tea, too. Sometimes I get tired of drinking milk."

Isabelle decided it was time to take a gamble. "Are you homeschooled, Ben?"

Isabelle froze in place as Ben grew still and stopped eating. She instantly regretted asking the question and wished she could take it back. She knew instinctively that she'd crossed some invisible line. It made her want to cry. "Never mind, that's none of my business. So," she said, as cheerfully as she could, "are those pickles everything I said they were?"

"They're very good. I guess you could say I'm homeschooled. See that building with all the ivy growing up the front? I go there on Mondays. The rest of the week, I do my studies at home and turn it all in on the next Monday. Sometimes, I have to go during the week to be tested. Usually from one o'clock till six o'clock."

"You go to the Institute?" Isabelle asked in stunned surprise.

"I do."

"That has to mean . . ."

Ben grinned. "One of those wussy geniuses who go there." He grinned again. "What grade do you think I'm in?"

Isabelle blinked. "Well, let's see, you said you were eight, so I guess either the fourth or fifth grade."

Ben hooted with laughter. "I finished high school in May. Now I'm a college freshman." The grin left his face. "Knowing that, do you still want to be my friend?"

Isabelle was stunned. "Of course I do. What kind of a question is that?"

"Most people are uncomfortable around me. I guess you figured out by now that I don't have any friends. I try to act like the kids my age, but I can't manage to do it. Normal kids my age make fun of me. The instructors, the doctors, stress to all of us who go to the Institute that we're not normal. My IQ is so far off the charts that they're not sure exactly what it is. That's why I'm registered at the Institute. The instructors call me Mr. Ryan because, in their eyes, I'm their equal. Actually, Izzy, I'm smarter than every single one of them. Please understand, I'm not bragging about that. It's just a fact. And you can't argue with facts, now, can you?" He grinned that endearing grin, and Isabelle laughed.

Isabelle fought the urge to hug the little boy, who was already a college freshman. "No, you can't argue facts. And I'm honored to be your friend. I hope I measure up. I'm . . . ah . . . pretty much just normal, to use your word."

"Oh, you do. I made up my mind about you a long time ago, Izzy. What's your story?"

"Huh?"

"You know, your story. Your *schtick*. Like what do you do? Are you a mother? What makes you tick? When you told me I could call you Izzy, I knew we could be friends because only friends allow friends to call them by a nickname. I think that's a fact. At least I hope it is.

"That's why I told you to call me Ben. I thought you would laugh if I told you I was Mr. Ryan. No one ever called me Ben except my grandmother."

"What do your parents call you?" Isabelle asked uneasily.

"That's another can of worms. I don't have any *real* parents. My mother died when I was two years old. I don't know anything at all about my biological father. My mother was smart like me. My mother married Connor Ryan, and he adopted me. After my mother died, I lived with my grandmother for a few years. Then, two years after my mother died, Connor Ryan married a woman named Natalie."

Ben threw his hands in the air. "So, no real parents. But to answer your question, they call me Benjamin most of the time. Okay. Now it's your turn."

"Uh-huh. Well, I'm an architect. In fact, I designed the Circle. And the building where you go every morning as well as the six houses on the Circle. I'm very proud of that. I'm married to a great guy named Abner. If you ever want to meet him, I can have him stop by on his lunch hour. He's very smart, too. You two would probably have a lot in common. We don't have any children, so no, I'm not a mother. I wish I were. I have quite a few friends, all nice people. My office is over there," Isabelle said as she waved her hand in the direction of the Institute. "I bought a building there just so I could come to this park and see the Circle. Weather permitting, I come here every day."

"That's a valid reason," Ben said. "I pretty much surmised something along those lines."

Isabelle blinked. She had to remember this was an eight-year-old she was talking to. "Do you live near here?"

"I do, but behind the Institute. I used to live on the Circle until my mother died, but I was only two, so I don't remember much about living there with my mother and my stepfather. But until I was four, I lived with my grandmother. At first, Connor moved into an apartment. I'm not allowed to ride my bike there because Connor hates my grandmother. I come here for the same reason you do, to look at the Circle and hope to get a look at my grandmother. I used to sneak in to see her, but I got caught, and they told me if I did it again, they'd make me live at the Institute. See, I'm smart, but not that smart. I got caught."

Isabelle suddenly felt sick to her stomach. "Ben, is your grandmother by any chance Eleanor Porter Lymen?"

"Yes!" Ben shrieked, his voice rising in excitement. "Do you know her?"

"Yes, I do. Very well, in fact. I don't understand. Why aren't you allowed to visit her?"

"Because Connor hates my grandmother. Shortly before Connor married Natalie, my grandmother took him to

court to get custody of me. The lawyer told my grandmother that he thought she had a chance to win because
Connor had let me live with her for the past two years, he
was not related to me by blood, and I was her daughter's
son. Once Connor married Natalie, the judge said because
Connor had adopted me and had a stable family life, I had
to stay with him and Natalie. I told the judge I wanted to
stay with my grandmother, but he said I was just a kid,
and he knew better than I did what was good for me. Connor, Natalie, and I moved into the house that my mother
had purchased before she married Connor, when I was
about seven months old. Apparently, she intended for us
to live in it, but for some reason she never got around to
moving before she died. Now I own the house because the
deed was in my mother's name and my name. They also
said that my grandmother has to give all my mother's money
to Connor. He gets some every month now, but he wants
it all.

"That happened before I was tested, and they found out
how smart I was. Can you find out where my grandmother is, Izzy?"

"Isn't she home in her house?"

"No. She's gone, and so are Rita and Irene, her two best
friends who live next to her. Rita lives on the right and
Irene lives on the left. They do everything together. Grandma told me they are both my godmothers."

"How long has your grandmother been gone, Ben?"

"Six months! Almost seven. Just before they left, Connor had gone back to court and told the judge Grandma
was a bad influence on me. He was mad at her because she
won't turn over my mother's money to him.

"Grandma showed me where she kept a key, and I
sneaked over there and went into the house."

"You mean in the birdhouse up in the tree?" Isabelle in-
terrupted.

"Yes. I cried when I went into my old bedroom. Big boys aren't supposed to cry, but I cried anyway. And I didn't care. Everything looks the same, but she's gone. All the electrical plugs were pulled out. There is no food in the refrigerator. The water still runs, and the lights still come on. The whole foyer is full of mail the postman drops through the slot. I checked Rita's and Irene's houses, too, but only by looking in the windows. All three of them are gone. Can you look into it for me?"

Isabelle swallowed hard. She nodded. "I can try."

"I have to go now. Connor said if I take more than an hour, he'll ground me."

"Then by all means go. I'll see you on Tuesday. I'll see what I can do over the weekend. Would you have any objections to my asking my friends to help?"

"Do you trust them?" Ben asked as he fastened the strap under his helmet.

"With my life." Isabelle reached out and hugged the rail-thin little boy. She held him tight, and he didn't object. "Ben, do you have a cell phone?"

"That's good enough for me," Ben said when she finally released him. "My grandmother used to hug me like that. I miss the feeling. You can hug me anytime you want to. And no, I don't have a cell phone. Grandma was going to get me one, and it was going to be our secret. But Connor said I don't need one."

"You may not have one, but I want you to have my business card, so you can get in touch with me if you need to." Isabelle took out a pen and scribbled something on the back of the card. "I just wrote my cell phone number on the back. You can call me at any time of the day or night if you need me. Okay."

"Thanks, Izzy. I really have to be going now."

Isabelle's eyes burned. All she could do was nod as she watched the little boy with the old man's eyes pedal away.

She smiled when he bellowed over his shoulder, "Thanks for lunch, Izzy."

Isabelle sat back down on the bench and kneaded her hands. Her head felt like a beehive. What to do? She closed her eyes, hoping a bolt of lightning would strike, showing her what her next move should be. When nothing happened, she gathered up the remnants of her and Ben's lunch. She was about to bag it all up when she noticed two fat little squirrels watching her. She scattered the peanut butter and jelly sandwich and the crust from her sandwich. Before she knew it, there was a whole family of plump little squirrels chewing away. *Must be the peanut butter,* she mused.

Isabelle pulled out her cell phone and called her office. "I'm running late, Carol. Cancel my one-thirty appointment. The Sinclairs are nice people, they won't mind. Reschedule at their convenience. I'll work around them."

Isabelle slid to the opposite end of the bench so as not to startle or disturb the squirrels, who were contentedly dining on their unexpected meal.

The park was full now, something she'd barely noticed while she had been with Ben. Runners, joggers, and mothers pushing baby gear filled the paths and benches. Isabelle picked her way down one path, crossed over another, and found her way to the monster gates that led to the enclave, her pride and joy. She leaned down to allow the retina scanner to identify her. When the gate opened, she walked through as if she belonged there. Since all the houses were empty, at least according to Ben, there was no one to see her. Unless someone at the Institute was watching from one of the ivy-bordered windows. And if someone was, she felt confident she could talk her way out of any kind of confrontation given her background and credentials.

Isabelle looked around as she made her way to Eleanor

Parker Lymen's house. The Circle didn't look deserted; it just looked quiet. The shrubs were pruned and clipped, the lawns were mowed, the fall flowers were watered, probably by the same person who maintained the Institute's campus.

Isabelle didn't bother going to the front door of the Lymen McMansion. She walked around to the back of the huge house. She stopped at the edge of the terrace and looked up at the beautiful sycamore tree, whose leaves were unbelievably gorgeous. She could clearly see the one-of-a-kind birdhouse she'd designed as a special gift to Eleanor when she'd finished the project. It was a mini replica of the McMansion, right down to the cedar-shake shingles on the roof. She smiled when she remembered how Eleanor had clapped her hands and said it was the perfect spot to hide her house key. But, she had said, "I'll need you to install a pulley of some kind, so I can raise and lower it." Isabelle had complied, and Eleanor clapped her hands again, then hugged her.

Isabelle had to poke through the Virginia creeper crawling up the tree, which hid the pulley completely. When she found it, she frowned. For some reason, she remembered its being higher. Stupid. Of course Eleanor would lower it so her grandson would have access to the key. She released the pulley, and the birdhouse slid downward.

Isabelle stuck her hand in the small opening and withdrew the key to Eleanor's house. She looked around to see if anyone was watching. She couldn't *see* anyone, which was understandable, given all the foliage that surrounded the immense backyard. More importantly, she couldn't *feel* anyone watching her.

Isabelle was inside the house within seconds. Lightning-fast, she locked the door behind her, then clutched the key tightly in her hand. What was she doing here? What did she hope to find? Did Eleanor, Rita, and Irene leave of their own accord, or had someone taken them. Taken them, as in kidnapped?

Ben was right, she noticed, all the plugs were pulled. The coffeemaker, the toaster, the blender, the refrigerator. She looked inside. A box of baking soda to absorb odors. Otherwise, totally empty.

Isabelle walked through the rest of the house, noting that lamps were also unplugged as well as the various television sets, which seemed to be in every room. She looked around, poking here and there, not even sure what she was looking for. Clues. Clues to what? She simply did not know.

Isabelle made her way to the second floor and Eleanor's suite of rooms. She almost laughed out loud when she entered the huge bedroom decorated in polka dots. Eleanor loved polka dots in her furnishings as well as her clothing.

As Isabelle checked dresser drawers and the walk-in closet, she had no idea what, if anything, was missing. There was some of everything in the drawers, but none of them were full, so some garments might be missing. It was the same thing with the closet. There were tons of clothes, coats, jackets, rain gear, dresses, slacks, formal wear in plastic dry-cleaning bags. Shelves held shoes and handbags. There were empty slots, so it was perfectly possible that some items were missing. Not very many, though.

All indications were that the owner had left of her own accord and would return at some point. The question was when?

Isabelle sat down on the side of the bed and looked around. *What am I looking for? What?* Her gaze went to the little desk in an alcove by the huge bay window. Would Eleanor leave anything important in her desk? Knowing the woman as well as she did, she was absolutely certain that the answer was no, she wouldn't. Probably anything important was in the hands of her battery of lawyers. She made a mental note to identify the firm who handled legal matters for her. She corrected the thought. She would have Abner look into it.

Still, she went through the small desk, but she found nothing that could help determine where Eleanor had gone or why she had left.

There was a safe. She'd had her crew chief install it, that much she remembered. She had to squeeze her eyes shut to try to remember where it was situated. In the bathroom, in the linen closet. Eleanor had been exceptionally pleased when she'd explained how it all worked.

Isabelle made her way to the large luxury bathroom and the linen closet, which was the size of a small room. She opened the door to the scent of lavender. She slid a pile of thick snow-white towels bordered with black-and-white polka dots to the side. She pressed down on the shelf, then stood back as the shelf holding the piles of towels slid to the side. It was a large safe with a digital locking mechanism. And she did not have the combination. She doubted Ben had it. Annie would be able to open it if it came to that. Annie was proud of her safecracking abilities.

Isabelle stared at the safe, wondering what Eleanor kept in it. Her thoughts were all over the place. She couldn't help but wonder if there was a clue inside that would tell her who Ben's biological father was. She sighed as she pressed the shelf to slide it back in place. She closed the door to the linen closet and left the room.

Isabelle walked down the stairs to the front foyer, where she stared at the mountain of mail that was all over the floor. Hundreds and hundreds of glossy catalogs, piles and piles of flyers and brochures, all addressed to either Occupant or Resident. As she sifted through the mail, she realized that there was not a single piece of mail that was personal in any way. There were no electric or water bills. No insurance notices, no bank statements. No bills of any kind. She supposed Eleanor did all that online the way so many people did. The only problem with that theory was that Eleanor was an admitted Neanderthal when it came to anything electronic. She did carry a cell phone called a Jitterbug. She knew how to dial 911, and that was the extent of her usage. Isabelle knew this because she'd had many, many conversations with her employer concerning the convenience. Eleanor had retorted that there was no need for anyone on this earth to have to be able to get in touch with her twenty-four/seven. In the end, Isabelle had given up, consoling herself with the old saying that you can lead a horse to water but you can't make it drink.

Isabelle picked her way through the mess of slick paper till she was standing by the front door. The mail was piled as high as the slot. She swept at it with both hands, sending it toppling and scattering far and wide. Who knew that six months of mail could look like what she was looking at right now.

Isabelle looked at her watch. She'd been here almost an hour. Time to go. Time to put the key back in the birdhouse and secure the pulley and the Virginia creeper vines, so no one would know that anyone had been here. On the assumption, of course, that someone periodically checked the property.

A bust. A total bust. Still, she was glad that she'd come here and walked through the house. At the kitchen door, Isabelle took one last look around before she closed and locked the door behind her. Outside, she noticed that the sun was gone, and gray clouds were scudding across the sky. The temperature had fallen, too. She shivered when she adjusted the one-of-a-kind birdhouse in its nest in the old sycamore and hid the chain in the Virginia creeper. Perfect.

One last look. Nothing had changed since she'd gotten here except the weather.

Time to head back to the office to think about young Ben's plea to find his grandmother.

Where are you, Eleanor?

Chapter 2

Isabelle let herself into the old pickle factory that her husband, Abner, had meticulously converted to their living quarters. They lived upstairs, while the first floor of the building was used to store Abner's fishing skiff, his jet skis, the family Mercedes, his Silverado truck, and Isabelle's Range Rover. The space was so large that there was still enough room to house four more vehicles. She noticed right away that the Mercedes was missing, which meant Abner wasn't home. Yet. Usually, he made it home before her, especially on Fridays.

The space was sterile-clean and neat as a pin, with bright overhead fluorescent lighting. Custom-built shelves her husband had built himself covered one wall and were full of cans of paint and other items used for repairs in a household, all neatly lined up. A second wall was made up entirely of a huge pegboard and held every tool for inside and outside known to man. Isabelle smiled. Abner loved gadgets, loved working on things in the house when he wasn't doing what he did best, hacking.

She made sure the door was locked behind her before she made her way to the elevator that would take her to the second-floor living quarters. Originally, the elevator was just a platform that was hoisted up and down with pulleys. Abner had installed this one all by himself. It hummed soothingly as she rose to the top, where, when the door slid open, she emerged from the elevator to stand in a small foyer. She set the elevator to full stop, which meant no one could get to the second floor if they broke into the building. Any intruder would need to know how to override the stop function, and only she and Abner knew how that worked.

Abner wasn't home. That had been obvious the minute she stepped into the lower level because the Mercedes was gone. Strange, because today was Friday, and Fridays were pizza nights. Three months ago, Abner had insisted on installing a real pizza oven because he loved pizza. There had been a lot of mishaps and horrible-tasting pizza, which she had bravely consumed, until he finally perfected his recipe. These days, she looked forward to Fridays and the special pizza.

Isabelle kicked off her shoes, tossed her keys into a little bowl on the foyer table, and slid her briefcase under the table.

In the kitchen, Isabelle looked at the clock. Ten minutes past six. Abner was late, but then, so was she. Usually, he called if he was going to be late. It hit her then. She'd turned off her cell phone in the middle of the afternoon when she walked into a meeting with four prospective clients, and she had forgotten to turn it back on. She fished her phone out of her pocket. Sure enough, six texts from her husband, one from Kathryn Lucas, and two from Maggie Spritzer.

Isabelle made her way to the bedroom, where she shed her business suit, hung it up, and pulled on an old pair of sweatpants and a fleece-lined sweatshirt. She poked around till she found what she called the fuzzy rabbit slippers that Abner had given her as a gag gift. She absolutely loved them.

On her way to the kitchen, she stopped to adjust the thermostat to raise the temperature since it had started to get noticeably colder. Isabelle carried the wine bottle and wineglass into the living area and poured herself a glass of wine. She knew before she even looked at the texts that there would be no Friday-night pizza. She settled down into the most comfortable sofa on earth. She propped her slippered feet onto the coffee table and looked at her messages. Abner first. He was on his way to Vermont. *No pizza tonight, babe. Be gone at least a week. I'll call you tonight. Or not. If not, first thing in the morning. Don't forget to water the Christmas cactus.* And the last one: *I love you.*

Isabelle finished off her glass of wine and poured another. *Might as well drink my dinner,* she thought. *Darn, I was really looking forward to pizza and a fun night with Abner. Oh well.*

Kathryn's text was curt. *Will be in town for three days on Monday. Call me.*

Maggie's texts were just as short and curt. *How about lunch tomorrow and we do a little shopping? Need to pick up some catnip for Hero. Call me.*

Isabelle leaned back into the downy pillows and closed her eyes. She needed to think. Her eyes flew open. Thinking, serious thinking, required a clear head. Two glasses of wine did not generate a clear head and serious thinking. *So I might as well go for a third, then maybe take a nap for a few hours.* She knew her own routine, which was what she was well into now. When Abner was gone, she didn't sleep well, so she worked at night and caught up on her sleep during the day. Schedule permitting.

Two glasses of wine at any given time were Isabelle's limit, but here she was about to polish off a fourth, which would empty the bottle. In her whole life, she'd never consumed a whole bottle of wine on her own. She wondered if she was drunk. It didn't feel like she was drunk. She supposed the true test would come if she tried to stand up. *Well, screw that,* she thought. She plumped up the pillows, snuggled down for a nap, and didn't wake up till fifteen minutes past midnight.

She knew instantly that yes, indeed, she had been drunk. She also knew instantly what had transpired during the day and the time it took to drink a full bottle of wine. She wasn't groggy, but she did have a headache. She made a promise to herself to never, as in ever again, drink a full bottle of wine all by herself.

In the kitchen, she poured herself a glass of tomato juice that she liberally dosed with Tabasco sauce and a dash of hot pepper flakes. She downed the concoction in two long gulps, shivering and gagging as she did so. "Serves you right, you lush," she chastised herself aloud. Then she popped two Advil and returned to the foyer for her briefcase, which held her laptop. She carried it back to the comfortable sofa. She cleared the coffee table, refusing to look at the wine bottle and glass. In the end, she could not avoid their lingering presence, so she trotted out to the kitchen with them and made coffee.

Back in the living room, she turned on the gas fireplace. She looked around. Good to go. Or she would be as soon as she got some coffee into her belly.

Where to start? With Eleanor Lymen, obviously. Eleanor was key, as was Ben. Somewhere down in the garage, she had a full file folder on Eleanor, but it was a business folder. In the two years she'd worked on the Circle project, their business relationship had turned personal, and they had become good friends. She was also friends with Eleanor's two best friends, Rita and Irene.

It wasn't the kind of friendship that led to a sharing of secrets. Although more than once, Isabelle remembered thinking that Eleanor was harboring some dark secrets, secrets, Isabelle was sure, that Eleanor shared only with Irene and Rita. And that was okay with her. Actually, she preferred not to know Eleanor's secrets.

Eleanor had had a daughter named Diana. More than a ton of friction there. Isabelle had only met Diana twice, and both times she left with the feeling that there was some deep, dark secret between mother and daughter. Diana, Ben's mother, was a brainiac like her son. That's why Eleanor had commissioned Isabelle to design the Institute. She'd had hopes, high hopes, that Diana would succeed her in running the Institute and somehow magically turn into the person Eleanor wanted her to be.

It never happened.

Isabelle sipped at her coffee, which was rapidly cooling. She didn't care. Coffee was coffee, hot, warm, or even cold.

She rolled her shoulders. There was more. She needed to remember what else she knew. About four years after the Circle was completed, on one of her few trips to the DC area with the sisters, Isabelle had visited with Eleanor again, and at that time there had been a man in the picture. Diana's friend. Diana's *special* friend. Someone Eleanor wasn't too fond of. At least that had been her impression at the time.

The young woman had been a dreamy sort. She didn't interact with others well. Isabelle recalled Eleanor's saying that her daughter's intelligence needed to be channeled, and that's why she wanted to build the Institute, because even if it was too late to help Diana, maybe it could help other children like her. But Diana was having no part of that. And that was the sum total of what she knew about Diana Ryan, née Diana Lymen, Ben's deceased mother.

She had finished the project on time to great fanfare. She'd won awards, basked in her success. Eventually, her friendship with Eleanor Lymen waned because life marched on, and Isabelle had become one of the sisters.

At some point, she'd heard or read that Diana moved into one of the houses directly across from her mother. Again, she'd moved on and was no longer interested in the young woman. And that was the sum total of what she knew about Eleanor and Diana Lymen.

Isabelle's brow furrowed in thought. Obviously, at some point, Diana had married Connor Ryan, Ben's stepfather. That had to mean Diana gave birth to Ben . . . when? Was it sometime after Isabelle had learned about the mystery man? Was the man Eleanor wasn't too fond of Ben's biological father? And who was he? Where had he gone? Had Diana ever married him, or had Ben been born out of wedlock?

And then the unthinkable happened. Diana Lymen Ryan was standing in line at the Sovereign Bank of Virginia, waiting her turn to deposit her trust-fund check, when a robbery took place. According to the newspaper reports she'd read, masked gunmen appeared out of nowhere, guns drawn and firing blindly to gain everyone's attention. Diana was hit by a ricochet and died before she could be transported to the hospital.

Isabelle rubbed at her temples, which were suddenly throbbing. She recalled how she'd been out of the country with the sisters and hadn't heard about the tragedy until months later, when they were back in Washington on a mission. She had immediately gone to see Eleanor Lymen and was stunned to see the tormented shell of the woman she'd once known so well. She recalled being told that her grandson was at his father's that day, visiting him, but that he was living with Eleanor. She did not recall ever being told his name, which was why she had not made the connection between Ben and Eleanor until earlier today—actually yesterday.

Isabelle remembered how they'd talked over tea, with Rita and Irene fussing over Eleanor. It was Irene who explained that Connor Ryan had packed up and moved out of the house on the Circle into an apartment. Unable or unwilling to care for Ben on his own, he had let his stepson stay with a very willing Eleanor.

After the boy, Ben, had lived with Eleanor for two years, Eleanor decided that it was time to make sure that Connor Ryan never gained custody of Ben and she sued for permanent custody. She had filed a lawsuit, according to Ben. Isabelle made a mental note to speak with Maggie tomorrow . . . today, actually, and ask her to do some digging to see where things currently stood. Little Ben might know some things about what had happened, but it was doubtful he would know all the nitty-gritty details.

Isabelle leaned back into the cushions and let her mind run wild. The Eleanor Lymen she knew, the woman who, despite the state of her emotions after the death of Diana, had taken in Diana's son to live with her, would never leave her grandson and take it on the lam to protect her own interests. The Eleanor she knew would fight for young Ben until hell froze over; and then she'd continue to fight on the ice. Ben was all she had left of her daughter. No, Eleanor would never leave Ben unless . . . unless . . . what? Maybe she had an agenda no one knew about. Like maybe finding the mystery man in the hope he would return and claim Ben from Connor Ryan. And the money, of course. No way would Eleanor turn her daughter's trust fund over to Connor Ryan. That had to be when she disappeared, but not before she made sure the trust fund was safe from Connor.

Who was Eleanor's lawyer? She should know, but she didn't. At least not right this minute. But down in the garage in one of the many footlockers that held rolls and rolls of blueprints, she was certain she could find the name of the firm.

Where are you, Eleanor?

Isabelle's gut told her Eleanor's lawyers would know. Eleanor would never leave for more than six months and not let her attorneys know where she was. Business had to be taken care of. She would not allow decisions only she could make to be made by others. Lawyers were a close-mouthed lot, and Isabelle was sure they wouldn't tell her anything. Confidentiality and privacy were the name of the game. Trickery would definitely be called for. That was something she couldn't do on her own. Time to call in the sisters, and that's exactly what she would do after she talked to Maggie later on today. With Kathryn coming back to town, that meant all the sisters would be available to kick this case, and it was a case, into high gear.

Isabelle looked down at her watch. It was three-thirty in the morning.

She bolted upright. Did Diana Lymen have a will? If she did, was it drawn up before or after she married Connor Ryan? She scribbled a note on a yellow pad next to her computer, along with the other reminder notes she'd penned earlier.

Isabelle felt her eyes start to droop and knew it was time to go to bed. She fluffed up the pillows, reached for a colorful throw to cover herself, and curled up. Her last conscious thought before drifting into a deep sleep was that of a skinny little boy with a head full of curls and an endearing gap-toothed smile, pedaling away from her.

Isabelle woke to the sound of her phone chirping in her ear. She reached for the phone, clicked, and heard Maggie's shrill voice saying she was about to call someone to check on her. "Why haven't you answered my calls or texts, Izz?"

Isabelle brushed her hair out of her eyes, cleared her throat, and said, "It's complicated, Maggie. What time is it anyway?"

"Almost noon."

"Noon!" Isabelle screeched. "It can't be noon!"

"Well, it is," Maggie snapped. "Are we meeting up or not?"

"Yes. Yes, of course. You wanna pick me up? I just need to take a quick shower. Half hour should do it. I'll explain when I see you, okay?"

"Am I gonna like your explanation?" Maggie asked in a more mollified tone of voice.

"Yep. It's right up your alley." Isabelle didn't give Maggie time to respond but ended the call. On the way to the bathroom, Isabelle started to strip down as she clicked on her phone again to see she had eleven text messages from her husband. "Shoot!" She scrolled down to the last one, which would tell her all she needed to know. *Where the hell are you, Isabelle?* Ooooh. *I've been texting you for hours. Are you okay? If I don't hear from you in the next hour, I'm calling the police to check on you.* Whoa.

Isabelle, naked now, turned on the shower after she sent off a text to her anxious husband. *I'm fine. I'll explain later. I drank a whole bottle of wine last night . . . or was it this morning? I slept a little too soundly. Love you.*

"Boy, when you screw up, you really screw up, Isabelle," she mumbled to herself as she washed her hair, then soaped up her body. She was in and out in less than ten minutes. She used up another ten minutes trying to decide what to wear. By craning her neck, she could see out the window that it was a gray, overcast, typical fall day. Which meant it would be chilly. She finally opted for gray flannel slacks and a cherry-red sweater. She then used up another three minutes with the blow-dryer to damp dry her hair. She smeared some cream that guaranteed to make her look ten years younger on her face. Not surprisingly, the guarantee turned out to be a lie, but right now, she didn't care.

Her sneakers and socks in hand, Isabelle raced into the kitchen to make a quick pot of coffee. No way could she start her day, even if it was half over already, without a good cup of coffee.

She was pouring her first cup of coffee for the day when Maggie buzzed. Isabelle ran to the foyer to send the elevator to the first floor just as she pressed the remote that would open the door for Maggie. It wasn't quite Fort Knox, but the comparison wasn't very far off.

Isabelle had a cup of coffee waiting for Maggie, who looked surly and out of sorts. "Who rained on your parade this morning?"

"You! I thought something happened to you. I was worried. You need to answer when someone calls or texts."

Isabelle's head bobbed up and down. "You're right! I'm sorry. I had a fiendish day yesterday. See that empty bottle! I drank it all last night. All by myself. I guess I slept too soundly. Abner reamed me out, too. I'm sorry, it won't happen again."

"Well then, okay. So what got your knickers in a knot for you to drink a whole bottle of wine?"

Isabelle told her. Maggie's eyes popped, growing wider and wider as Isabelle recounted yesterday's events. "Look, Maggie, here's a picture of him. I took it when he wasn't looking. This kid is eight years old and is a freshman in college. Do you believe that?"

Maggie said she did believe that. "So, are you saying this is going to be the start of a mission? If so, this is a good time, because Kathryn is due back in town. Are we going out to lunch, or are we staying here? I can pick up the catnip on the way home, so that's not a problem. If you don't have any food, we can order in. Just so you know, the temperature outside is in the low fifties and the wind is pretty damn sharp. It also looks like rain."

Isabelle grinned. "Okay, you convinced me. We're staying in. What would you like me to order, Chinese, Italian, or deli?" Isabelle asked, pointing to the magnets on the Sub-Zero refrigerator that pinned down brochures with the numbers for more than twenty take-out restaurants in the area that she and Abner used at least once or twice a week.

"I could go with a big, as in big, meatball sub with a side order of spaghetti. We should get a salad, too, don't you think? And maybe like six cannolis."

"Absolutely." Isabelle laughed as she called Anthony's Pizza two blocks away.

Maggie refilled her coffee cup and looked at Isabelle, who nodded that she would also like a refill.

"Tell me where your thoughts are taking you with the boy and the grandmother. I'm getting excited, thinking we can help the kid. A genius at eight years old. Unbelievable!"

"Yes, and his mother was also. That's why Eleanor built the Institute."

Maggie leaned back on her chair, and said, "Okay, start from the very beginning. That means when you were commissioned to design the Circle. Do not leave anything out, no matter if you think it's important or not. I'm almost positive Ted did an article on Eleanor Lymen when the project was finished. I think I did one, too, perhaps earlier, but it's vague in my mind. Nothing memorable for sure, or I would remember it. We didn't know you then, Izzy. Go!"

Isabelle ticked events off on her fingers as she rattled on and on and wound down just as the buzzer sounded down below.

"Now I am excited. I'll go down to get the food. Lunch is on me."

When Maggie returned, Isabelle had the old plank table set for two, using her good dishes and cloth napkins. This was a special lunch. As an added touch, she fired up two blueberry candles in honor of the dim day.

"This sure is a lot of food," Isabelle said.

"Enough left over for dinner if it gets to that," Maggie said, tucking into a meatball sub that was so thick and oozing sauce she had to hold napkins under it to catch all the drippings. "This is *soooo* good."

Isabelle laughed. Everyone knew about Maggie's whacked-out metabolism. If it was edible and could go in her mouth, it was *soooo* good. Even if it was fried octopus in a lemon-lime sauce.

"Do you think the other sisters will view everything I told you the same way you and I are viewing it?" Isabelle asked, her voice anxious and jittery.

"Damn straight they will. I can hardly wait to get started."

"What's your best recollection about what the *Post* might have on file in regard to the Institute and the Circle? I know Eleanor Lymen keeps a pretty low profile. At least she did back when I worked for her."

Maggie pondered the question. "Not a single thing that stands out as memorable. I didn't work that story. I think it might have been Ted and Espinosa, but I'm not sure. My article must have been pure fluff. Filler, that kind of thing. No fanfare. If there was, I think I would remember it. It was a school opening for special gifted children and a Realtor's dream of high-end housing. Like I said, nothing memorable there. I'll check the archives when I get home. I don't have my laptop with me. And Ted is out of town with the boys, so he's out of the loop for now."

"You can use Abner's computer. It's right over there in the office. He won't mind," Isabelle said. "It's his backup. He prefers to work over there," she said, motioning to a cordoned-off area that at first glance looked like something out of a space movie, with all the computers, printers, and miles of cable everywhere. "It's also off-limits to me and everyone else. I don't mind because I don't understand half of what he does when he's over there. I just know he's pulled our fat out of the fire too many times to count."

"No problem," Maggie said, sitting down and flexing her fingers before she turned on the computer and waited for it to boot up.

"Izz, do you suspect foul play with Mrs. Lymen?"

"No, I don't, Maggie. I think she left of her own accord, knowing that Ben was safe, at least for now, because she hasn't turned over her daughter's fortune. As for Ben's trust, she doles that out, or her lawyers do. As long as the money continues to flow monthly, Ben is safe. I think that's how she's looking at it. She would never leave on her own if she thought the boy was in any danger."

Maggie looked skeptical. "Almost seven months is a long time to be gone, Izz. Did she go to ground, or is she on the hunt for something?"

Isabelle sighed. "Both I think. Look, do whatever it is you need to do. I'm going down to the garage and look in the footlockers where I store all my blueprints. I know that I stapled Eleanor's lawyer's card to her set of prints. I do that with all my projects once they're finished."

"Do you really think her lawyers will tell you anything? Attorney-client privilege." Maggie didn't bother to wait for a response before she babbled on.

"Okay. I have Ted's password, so I can access all his files. If he's the one who did the write-ups, we'll know shortly."

Isabelle was halfway to the door before Maggie realized her pal probably hadn't heard anything she had said. She shrugged. *What will be will be,* she thought as she started to pound the keys on Abner's computer.

Two hours later, Maggie looked up and rubbed her eyes to stare at Isabelle, who was holding out a cup of coffee. Maggie reached for it and gulped it down in two long gulps. "There's nothing here, Izz. Well, there's stuff here, of course, but nothing the rest of the world doesn't know. It's fluff. Nothing jumped out at me, which means there's nothing there of any importance. A new school for gifted kids. Yeah, so what? Parents with normal kids don't give a hoot about schools like that for two reasons: Their own kids aren't geniuses, and they don't have the money to send them there to be tested, so why would they care?

"Another high-end oasis for the rich. No one cares because they can't afford to live there, so why torture themselves. Just a story to cover that did NOT grow legs.

"Eleanor Parker Lymen. So she's rich. She endowed the Institute. Big deal. Rich people do that all the time. It's nothing more than a one-day news story. For the most part, no one even knows who she is. Railroad money. Again, big deal. This is a bust, Izz. What, if anything, did you come up with?"

"The name of the law firm. It's possible Eleanor has more than one firm representing her, but I don't think so. For the most part, she's basically a simple person. She likes things to run smoothly, with no problems. Why complicate life with more than one law firm to handle her legal issues? One set of lawyers would do it for her. Did you come up with anything on the daughter, Diana?"

"You mean like debutante stuff? No. Again, a low profile. A birth notice and a death notice. A birth announcement when Benjamin Andrew Lymen was born. That's it. Nothing about Diana's being a gifted child, nothing about any relationship with the Institute or the reason her mother built it. Like I said, a low profile all around. Nothing about any of them, the properties, the Institute, them personally was worthy of the twenty-four-hour news cycle. It kind of makes you wonder why."

"Why indeed?" Isabelle mumbled under her breath. "What about the court case, when Eleanor took Connor Ryan to court for custody of Ben? It's possible the court records are sealed. I'm not saying they are, but they could be. If they are, then Eleanor Lymen or her attorneys have some juice to make that happen. And did you find a marriage record for Diana and Connor Ryan? Remember, Ben said that Connor adopted him. It must be true, because Ben said his name was Ben Ryan. Not Ben Lymen. Obviously, Diana didn't use the biological daddy's name when she filled out Ben's birth certificate."

"Most of that digging is beyond my pay grade, Izz. We need someone like Abner to dig deep if some of this stuff is buried for reasons we might never know. We need someone who knows how to hack into the court records and leave no footprints behind. I don't know anyone, do you?"

"Just Abner's friend Phil. But I don't even know how to get in touch with him. I suppose I could call Abner, but you know the rules—when the boys are on a mission, we do not interfere, and vice versa. We might have to wait till they get back. I don't think this is as dire as I've made it out to be, Maggie."

"But you don't know that for sure, Izz. He's just a little kid."

"A very smart little kid. I gave him my business card, and wrote my cell phone number on the back. I think he'll find a way to get in touch with me if he has to in an emergency, even though he does not have a cell phone. He knows where I work. He could ride his bike there. BTW, he's probably the only kid in the world who doesn't have a cell phone. Or a watch."

"Lots of kids don't have cell phones," Maggie said. "Or watches."

"I know that. I'm talking about genius kids like Ben."

Maggie finished her coffee. "So what do we do? Just wait for Tuesday? Does Ben ride his bike on the weekends? The two of us could show up at the Institute on Monday and be waiting for him."

"I don't know what he does on the weekends; we didn't get that far in our show-and-tell conversation. And I'm not sure we could get into the Institute on Monday. The powers that be might call the police. Ben might get scared. I suppose we could waylay him on the way. But Tuesday is a long way off, Maggie."

Maggie nibbled on a thumbnail, which was already bitten to the quick. "I know. Make some more coffee, Izz. I'm going to try another tack with the court records. You check out the law firm. Find out which members are the litigators, find out everything you can on the firm. I'm sure they have an extensive website."

"Okay. I'm worried, Maggie."

"I know. Something is wrong here. I can feel it. I really can, Izz."

Isabelle shivered at Maggie's ominous words as she made her way to the kitchen to make fresh coffee.

Where are you, Eleanor? Your grandson needs you. I need you.

Chapter 3

At first glance, one would think it was a monk's spartan bedroom. Certainly not the bedroom of an eight-year-old boy. There wasn't a cartoon poster to be seen. In fact, there were no pictures at all on the gray walls. There was a maple twin bed, but it didn't have a kid's coverlet with cars or airplanes on it. It was dark blue. There were blinds on the windows but no curtains. The windows were casement windows and didn't open. An oversize desk was pushed against the wall. It held a desktop computer and a printer. There was also a telephone and a modem because the house had no wi-fi or cable connecting to the Internet. The chair was made of wood, a captain's chair with three cushions and a thick telephone book underneath so the boy could reach the keyboard.

A chair, a recliner, actually, that had seen better days and was also dark blue, sat in a corner, with a reading lamp and small table next to it. Bookshelves lined two walls and were full to overflowing, and all had been read by the room's occupant. A coat tree held a rain slicker, a windbreaker, and a puffy winter jacket, along with a long gray scarf and matching woolen hat.

The closet held a few clothes, not many. A suit, a jacket, three pairs of trousers, and four shirts on hangers. Printer paper, binders, folders, pencils, pens, paper clips, and the like filled the shelves in little boxes. Everything was military, neat. Shoes and sneakers, along with a pair of rubber boots that were a size too small, were neatly lined up on the floor.

A maple dresser that matched the twin bed held the boy's daily clothes, jeans, shorts, tee shirts, and two sweaters. There was a light jacket, which he never wore, that, along with his socks and underwear, completed the contents.

There was no skateboard, no roller skates, no hockey stick, baseball bat or glove. No mementoes of any kind could be found in the sterile, institutional-looking room. It was the sort of room one might expect to find in a state-run orphanage of the kind Isabelle and Abner had occasionally lived in when they were children, perhaps one located in a county that prided itself on the accommodations it provided its orphans.

This was the room in which Benjamin Andrew Lymen Ryan lived.

Benjamin Andrew Lymen Ryan had had another room in another house that he had once lived in. BTCT. Before the court trial. That room was a real boy's room. It had everything a young boy could possibly want. Colorful cartoon murals on the walls. Every toy, train, truck, car known to kids the world over, all battery-operated, filled two overflowing toy chests. There was a skateboard, skates, baseballs, bats, gloves. Snapshots and framed photos of the boy's mother were everywhere. And, of course, Freddie. So he wouldn't forget. It had all been played with and used. And for two years it had.

The bed in the shape of a racing car had a coverlet with racing cars stitched all over it. It was colorful and inviting. Like the oversize chair that just begged to be curled up in.

He'd curl into it almost every day before he'd had to leave that house on some judge's orders.

The room also held books, duplicates of the ones in the sterile institutional room the boy now lived in. But Freddie, his beloved panda bear, was nowhere to be found in that sterile room. For some reason, he had not been allowed to take it with him. Later, when he'd asked, Connor told him that it was because his grandmother had forbidden him to take it. He couldn't argue with that, so he hadn't. He knew that his grandmother never did anything without a good reason. It was just something he'd have to figure out on his own.

Ben Ryan was sitting at his computer, searching for everything he could find on his new best friend, Isabelle Flanders. He liked her a lot, and he thought she liked him, too. It was nice to have a friend, even if that friend was a grown-up. He'd done a search on her before, not on the computer, though. It was on a Wednesday after one of their meetings, when he'd followed her to see where she went after she left the park. For some reason, that particular day it had been important for him to know where she worked. He thought of it as a precaution so that, in an emergency, he could make his way there if he needed help. He'd never defined what kind of emergency would require him to need her help or exactly what kind of help he could expect. Why he thought he needed to take that sort of precaution was not at all clear to him. What he did know for sure was that he could get there on his bike in twelve minutes. In a real emergency, twelve minutes could mean life or death.

Ben turned on his computer and started a search. There was a great deal of information about his new best friend, but there was no home address. He wondered now why he hadn't come right out and asked Izzy where she lived. Maybe because she hadn't asked him exactly where he lived, nor asked for an address or a telephone number.

Ben clicked and clicked. Every site he visited promised a home phone number plus address for $29.95. Well, he didn't have $29.95. All he had was the five dollars the dog lady had given him. And even if he had $29.95, he didn't have a credit card. And then a bolt of lightning suddenly hit him. His grandmother Ellie had credit cards, lots of them. She had so many she had to have two wallets to keep them all together. And he knew exactly where she kept the overflow. But had she taken them with her when she left to go wherever she went, or did she leave them behind? There was only one way to know for sure. Despite the risk, he'd have to make a sneak trip to the Circle.

Today was Saturday, and it was starting off with a bang. Natalie, Connor's wife, was already yelling her head off, and it was only ten o'clock in the morning. He thought about putting earplugs in his ears but decided this particular fight might work to his advantage.

Ben sat up straighter in his chair when he heard his name mentioned by Connor.

"Well, you can't go shopping because you maxed out all our credit cards. Ben's allotment hasn't come in yet. All indications are it isn't going to come in, either. We're going to have to go back to court, and the lawyers want more money, and I absolutely do not have any money to give them. Are you listening to me, Natalie?"

"Take it out of Ben's trust fund. You have the right to do that! You told me you could do that," Natalie screeched at the top of her lungs. Ben winced and shook his head to clear it.

"That was then, and this is now. Now his lawyers look at his account every single day. If I took even a dollar out, they'd be here in a nanosecond. Go window-shopping!"

"Window-shopping! Is that what you said, window-shopping? This marriage isn't working for me anymore. I'm sick of eating fried-egg sandwiches and fast food. I'm not used to this. Nordstrom is having a shoe sale."

"Then leave. See if you can find someone else to pay your bills. This is the situation we're in, and until it's resolved, there is nothing I can do."

A devil perched itself on Ben's shoulder. He bolted from the room and ran down the stairs. He skidded to a stop and looked at his stepfather, then at Natalie. "I need a hundred dollars."

"What?" they both bellowed in unison.

"I need a hundred dollars. I don't *want* it. I *need* it. Mr. Brady said you are supposed to give me a hundred dollars every month. You are now four years in arrears. Mr. Brady said I do not have to account to you what I use it for. I'll take it now. If you don't give it to me, I will tell them at the Institute, when I go on Monday, that you're stealing my money so Natalie can go shopping." *How do you like them apples, huh?*

Natalie was like a wild woman as she whirled around and reached for Ben, but Connor stiff-armed her before she could reach him. She struggled with her husband, calling Ben a freakish little snot.

"Well, this freakish little snot pays for all those clothes you wear and those stupid shoes you can't even walk in," Ben shouted, loud enough to drown out whatever vile invective Natalie was spewing.

"That will be enough of that, young man! And, Natalie, you pipe down, too." Connor turned to Ben, and said, "You never asked for money before. Had you asked, I would have given it to you. I'm aware of the court order."

"I shouldn't have to ask, Connor. I know what a court order is, and I read it. You are supposed to give me a hundred dollars on the first day of the month. You are seriously in arrears. On Monday, I will bring it to the administrator's attention. So get it ready. I'd like it in cash, too."

Natalie jerked free of Connor's arm. "Are you going to let this little snot talk to me like that? Well, are you?" she shrilled when Connor remained silent. Ben, mindful of Natalie's talon-like nails, scooted behind Connor as he dug crumpled bills out of his pants pocket. He handed over five twenty-dollar bills to Ben, who snatched them up so quickly he thought his hands would burn.

Ben ran from the room, yelling over his shoulder that he was going to the park. He knew the two squabbling adults would be at it for at least another hour if things ran true to form. Now he had a hundred and five dollars. What to do with it? He jammed the bills into his pocket and took off on his bike like he was shot from a rocket. His destination, his grandmother's house.

Ben pedaled as fast as his skinny legs would allow. After getting through the gate, he rode around the Circle twice to make sure no one was watching. But really, when he thought about it, who would be watching? No one. That's who. Finally, on his third go-round, he slowed and pedaled to the back of the house. He leaned his bike up against the tree with the pulley, released the chain, and fished the key out of the birdhouse. He craned his neck every which way to make sure no one could see into the backyard. Satisfied, he let himself into the house and locked the door behind him.

Ben looked around and immediately choked up. He tried hard not to cry, but hot tears trickled down his cheeks. He didn't bother to brush them away. He had loved living here, loved watching his grandmother make spaghetti just for him or apple tarts with lots of whipped cream. She'd joke that she had to fatten him up. She had a nice laugh. He always felt really good when she'd laugh and hug him and tell him he was her little butter muffin.

He wasn't sure he wanted to be a buttered muffin, but if that's what his grandmother wanted him to be, then he decided that that's what he would be.

The house smelled just like his grandmother. Like vanilla, lemon, and the purple flowers she filled the house with in the spring. He loved and adored the smell. Just loved, loved, loved it.

Where are you, Grandma? Ben walked through the rooms, checking this and that, poking at things, wondering if she had left a clue somewhere that he'd missed when he was here the last time. This time he was more careful as he made his way to his room. He stood in the doorway and looked around. He remembered the day of the "unveiling," when his grandmother opened the door, and said, "I hope you like it, Ben. I tried to put everything in here that I thought you would like. Did I do okay?"

He'd sighed so loud and melted into her arms. "I love it," he whispered. And he did. For the two years he lived with his grandmother, before sheriff's deputies carted him off to take him to live with his stepfather, Connor Ryan, and Connor's new wife, Natalie. He'd cried. No, he'd sobbed as if his world was ending, and in a way, it was. His heart was breaking. His grandmother had cried, too. So did Rita and Irene.

The deputies kept saying over and over that the law is the law.

Ben stepped into the room and went to the shelf where a stuffed panda bear sat guard over the room. Freddie. It was supposed to be a giant pillow that doubled as a place to put his pajamas. "A perfect hiding spot," his grandmother had told him when she'd given it to him for his third birthday. Quick as a wink, Ben unzipped Freddie's zipper and stuck his hand down into the deep pocket. His face lit up like a thousand Christmas lights when he found an envelope stuffed inside the bear. It was yellow, the size of a hardcover book, and it was packed solid.

Papers, all kinds of papers. He didn't want papers, he wanted credit cards. And then he saw them, a dozen or so with a rubber band around them. Visa, MasterCard, American Express, Discover. He stuck them in his pocket. How well he remembered the day his grandmother told him she was going to retire the cards because all she needed was the black one called Centurion, but the others would still be good.

He supposed he should look at the papers. But look here or take them home to look? Maybe a cursory glance to see what they all were. He decided whatever they were about, it must be important enough for his grandmother to have hidden them in Freddie, knowing that Ben would find them sooner or later. "I should have thought of this before now, Grandma," he sobbed, his eyes filling with tears again. "I'm sorry. How come if I'm so smart, I was stupid about this? If I hadn't met Izzy, I might never have found them. Well, I've found them now," he cried happily.

Ben jammed everything back into the yellow envelope. He didn't have his backpack, so where was he going to stash it? "In my underwear, where else?" he mumbled as he jammed the envelope down his underpants. It crackled a bit but not so loud that anyone would pay attention. Not that Connor or Natalie ever actually paid attention to him. When he got home, he'd go in through the kitchen since that was the one place Natalie avoided like the plague. Connor wasn't fond of the kitchen, either. He could take the back staircase up to his room, and no one would even know he was home unless he announced himself.

Since his bedroom door didn't have a lock on it, he'd have to go into the bathroom and lock that door. He'd curl up in the bathtub and read the papers. *Yep, that's exactly what I will do.*

Where are you? I need you, Grandma. I miss you.

Having arrived home and successfully made it to his bedroom without having been discovered, Ben was just about ready to lock the bathroom door when he heard a crash that sounded like thunder. Check it out or stay put? He opted to check it out. He ran out of the bathroom down the hall, then halfway down the stairs. He had a clear view of Natalie, with a broom handle in her hands, standing in the middle of the dining room, where the contents of the toppled china cabinet lay in smithereens.

"Now look what you've done!" Connor roared. "What the hell is wrong with you? How am I going to explain this to the estate?"

Her long red hair flying every which way, her eyes wild, Natalie brandished the broom handle as if it were a baseball bat or a hockey stick. Her next target was the Bavarian crystal chandelier hanging over the dining-room table. One swipe, two swipes, and crystal flew in all directions. "I'll tell you what's wrong with me. You! You're what's wrong with me. You and that bratty snot-nosed kid of yours. Well, I've had enough!"

"I've had enough of you, too! Pack your stuff and get out of my house. Now! And don't ever come back here. I'm going to change the locks and file for divorce!" Connor snarled.

Ben hugged his skinny knees to his chest where he was sitting on the stairs and watching through the spindles. He felt like yelling, "Yippee!" but he didn't. He'd witnessed this same scene so many times that it felt old hat. Natalie would calm down, Connor would clean up the mess, then he'd find money from somewhere so she could go shopping. Unless . . . unless this was the final straw, the one that broke the camel's back.

He quickly got up and raced to his room when he saw Natalie head for the stairs. Maybe she meant it this time. "I hope, I hope, I hope," he muttered under his breath.

Ten minutes later, he cracked the door to his room to see Natalie dragging a suitcase to the top of the steps. She gave it a shove, and it rolled down the steps to land on its wheels. To Ben's surprise, nothing spilled out. He heard a horn blare. He ran to the window. An Uber car pulled into the driveway. A middle-aged man got out, stashed the suitcase in the trunk, then held the door for Natalie.

Ben watched until the Uber was out of sight. "Please, please, don't come back," he whispered over and over. He wondered what he should do. Go downstairs and act surprised? If he did that, he just might get stuck cleaning up the mess. Should he just ignore it all and stay in his room the way he always did when Connor and Natalie had a fight? But this was different; this time Natalie had left. Connor said he was going to change the locks. That had never happened before.

Before he could change his mind, Ben opted to go downstairs. This, after all, was his house, and as such, he could do whatever he wanted. At the bottom of the steps, he made his way carefully because of all the broken glass that had scattered all over. He picked his way to the kitchen, where he heard Connor on the phone with a locksmith. "I need someone right now. Not tomorrow, not later today, *now*. Double your rate is fine if you come right now."

"Go ahead and say it, Ben," Connor suggested, slamming the phone back into the cradle on the wall.

"Say what? I just came down for a bottle of water. Just so you know, I'm not cleaning up that mess your wife created. And I sure hope you have a boatload of money so you can replace that china cabinet. It's worth a fortune, and the crystal was from Grandma's grandmother and worth a fortune also. You were tasked with keeping things just the way they were when you moved in here. Guess you plan on using my allotment for that, huh? Won't be enough, Connor," he said bravely.

"Natalie was right—you are a bratty little snot. I can't believe I adopted you, and you carry my name. Don't ever talk to me like that again. Do you hear me?"

Ben suddenly felt even braver and wasn't sure why, maybe because of the envelope upstairs under the bathroom rug. Or maybe it was because he knew he could call his new best friend if something went wrong. He jammed his hand in his pocket and felt the comforting card she had given him. Isabelle had said he could call her any time of the day or night. He could feel his backbone stiffen.

He drew a deep breath. "Or what, Connor? What are you going to do to me? If anything happens to me, you are certainly the first person the police will look at. How do you know I haven't told the people at the Institute about you and Natalie and how you treat me? That you don't cook for me, you leave me to fend for myself. How do you know I didn't tell them how you two spend all my money? How do you know you aren't under surveillance? Huh? Aren't you going to answer me?

"Here's something else for you to think about. Don't you ever talk to me like that again. This is *my* house; it is solely my name on the deed after my mother died. Neither it nor the house on the Circle was ever yours. It's *mine*. I'd like pork chops for dinner this evening. Six o'clock will be fine. Oh, and apple juice. I love apple juice."

Connor Ryan stood perfectly still, his mouth hanging open. For the first time in his life, he was totally speechless. And then, red-hot anger raged through him as he fought the urge to snatch the boy and wring his scrawny neck. *God Almighty, how did it ever come to this, with that skinny little shit kid calling the shots?*

Controlling his anger, Connor bent over, picked up the broom, and set to work.

Ben turned on his heel and marched out of the room. At the doorway, he turned around and came back. "I wish you had never adopted me, too, so that makes us even."

Ben ran for the steps, taking them two at a time. In the wide center hall, he looked into the master bedroom that Natalie had taken over as her own. It was what his grandmother would call one unholy mess. He grinned as he scurried into his room, then to the bathroom, where he locked the door. He wadded up a bunch of towels and curled into a ball, comfortable as could be.

This is like Christmas, he thought. *Or one of those game shows in which you have to choose which door holds the big prize.*

What was in the envelope? It was for him, he was certain of that. Otherwise, his grandmother would never have put it in Freddie for him to find. He pulled everything out. There was a thick wad of money with a band around it that said "$5,000." Ben whistled. Five thousand dollars was serious money. His grandmother's will. Okay, he'd read that later. He rifled through the papers until he found an envelope with his name on it. He literally swooned and grew light-headed. It was sealed. He picked it open, doing his best not to rip the envelope. He felt warm all over just holding the letter, which was addressed to him. And then his eyes started to burn as he read:

> *My Dearest Darling Ben,*
> *I wish I weren't writing this to you because it means I'm leaving you alone. When I say alone I mean without me nearby to watch over you. I know you are safe with Connor and that person he married. They will never harm you because you are the goose that lays the golden eggs once a month. I have people*

watching over you. Many eyes, Ben, so feel safe. They know what to do if they even suspect for a second that something is wrong. No harm will come to you. I wouldn't leave you otherwise.

I know you want to know where I am and why I left. Right now I can't share that with you, but it is for your own good that I've gone. You see, I made a serious mistake that I have regretted ever since, and now I have to make it right. No one else can do that but me. Rita and Irene are going to help me. Remember the talk we had when I told you how grown-ups sometimes make mistakes from time to time, and that's okay as long as you learn from the mistake and try to make it right? That's what I have to do. I should have done it a long time ago.

I left for two reasons. That was the first. The second reason, of course, was the lawsuit. I wanted to leave before the judge decided the case. I didn't want them to arrest me for refusing to turn over all your mother's money to Connor and that person he married. Your mother's money is safe, guarded and controlled by some very good people. They're keeping it safe for you.

When I do what I have to do, I will return and hopefully at that time you will be able to come home to me. I count the days, Ben. You, my darling grandson, are the first thing I think about when I wake in the morning and the last thing I think about before I fall asleep.

I was hoping you would remember about Freddie and where I kept the key. And if you are reading this, then you must have. It was my hope that you would remember quickly, so you would not have too many unhappy days. I cry, Ben, for our loss. I'm going to make this right for both of us or die trying.

I love you, Ben, more than all the stars in the sky, more than all the water in the ocean, and more than all the grains of sand on the beach. Be brave, my darling grandson.
Love,
Grandma.
P.S. Rita and Irene send you hugs.

Tears rolled down Ben's cheeks. He reached over for some toilet tissue and blew his nose with gusto, all the while holding his grandmother's letter over his heart with his left hand. If he had tape, he would have taped it to his bare chest.

Ben cried harder. *I'm so sorry, I should have found it sooner.* All these months, and he never knew. He wondered who the people were who were watching over him. He never saw anyone who looked suspicious. Izzy? Was she one of them? And who did all the people watching over him report to?

What kind of mistake did his grandmother make that she had to go away to try to fix it? Did it have something to do with him or Connor? Or maybe his mother? Who?

Ben wracked his brain to try to figure out what kind of grown-up mistake could take someone like his grandmother six months to make right? He read the letter again. The mistake was part one. Maybe she had already fixed it, but part two was still hanging out there. Part two could take forever. Then again, maybe part one was tied to part two, and that was still open.

Ben looked down at the other papers. They looked like legal documents to him, with seals and stamps. His adoption papers. His birth certificate. His mother's birth certificate and her death certificate. Tears flooded his eyes again. What was he supposed to do with all of this? Where was he supposed to keep it? Now that he'd stirred up a hornet's nest with Connor, his stepfather might decide to check out his room. And horror of horrors, Natalie would probably come back at some point. For sure she'd poke around his room, check his computer.

Computer! He'd gotten sidetracked. Ben gathered all the papers and the letter from his grandmother and fit everything back in the envelope. All he needed was one credit card to do what he wanted to do online. He picked a Chase Visa at random, checked the expiration date, and set to work. He opened three accounts, each for $29.95. Isabelle Flanders Tookus, Natalie Kendrick Ryan, and Connor Sylvester Ryan. A window appeared, saying the results would be sent to his e-mail account within twelve hours.

Ben bundled up the rest of the credit cards and stuffed them into the yellow envelope. He kept the Chase Visa. But where to hide it? He finally decided to hide it under the inner sole of one of his dress shoes, which was sitting in the closet.

Ben paced. He knew he had to take the envelope back to his grandmother's house and put it back in Freddie. His gut instincts told him it wasn't safe to keep the contents of the envelope here in this house.

Once again, he jammed the envelope down his underwear and pulled on his windbreaker. He zipped it up all the way. He looked in the mirror to check that no bulges showed. He made his way downstairs. The china cabinet, he saw, was once again upright, but there were deep gouges in the old wood. A few pieces of crystal were on the shelves. Connor was still cleaning and sweeping.

"I'm going for a bike ride," Ben called out. "When you make the pork chops, make mine breaded and fried. That's the way I like them, just the way Grandma used to make them."

Outwardly, Connor ignored him, but he cursed the little boy under his breath.

"Boy, did that ever feel good," Ben mumbled to himself as he pedaled his way to the Circle and his grandmother's house. Because he was a kid, he took his hands off the handlebars and did a wheelie. Then he laughed out loud. "How's it feel, you lying sack of poop?" he bellowed, knowing no one could hear him. Boy, he sure felt good.

He felt so good that he rode the rest of the way with his arms straight out, laughing the whole time.

Chapter 4

The ancient grandfather clock in the foyer, a treasure that Abner had found at a flea market and lovingly restored, chimed eight times as Isabelle and Maggie hugged each other. Both women looked tired, yet exhilarated. "I think we're on to something, Izz," Maggie said. "I also agree to a meeting tomorrow at the farm. Oooh, hold on, I just got a text from Kathryn."

Isabelle could hear her phone pinging from down the hall. She was probably getting the same text Maggie was. She looked at the reporter expectantly.

Maggie laughed. "I was right, it's Kathryn. She said her last stop was canceled, and she's on her way to the farm, so she'll be there tomorrow for our meeting. Sometimes things have a way of working out just the way you want them to. Ever notice that, Izz?" she said, stepping into the elevator.

"All the time." Isabelle giggled. "This way, we'll get an early start on the mission if the others agree to take it on. Drive carefully, Maggie. See you tomorrow."

"Okayyyyy, Mom," Maggie drawled, as the elevator door slid closed.

The loft seemed exceptionally quiet after Maggie left. What to do with herself? Isabelle turned on the television but not to watch it, just for the noise. With nothing else on her immediate agenda, she wandered around the massive loft, wishing Abner were there so they could cuddle on the oversize chair that held them both comfortably. It was the one place in the loft where they, as a couple, confided to each other, shared secrets, and laughed and hugged and kissed. Their space. A simple chair. Who knew? She supposed she could curl up in it, but it wouldn't be the same without Abner there. Better to plop down on the sofa and go to sleep as she watched some mindless TV game show or a rerun of some prehistoric movie she'd already seen a dozen times.

Or . . . she could go out to Target, which was eight minutes away, and do some shopping for the little guy. A cell phone so she could communicate with him. A watch, preferably a Mickey Mouse one, so he would always know what time it was, and so he wouldn't be late. Why not? Mickey Mouse? He was certainly young enough in years to wear one, but with him a college freshman she wasn't sure. Then she hooted with laughter. Annie wore a Mickey Mouse watch and loved it. She knew for a fact that Annie had more than one Rolex and several diamond-encrusted Tiffany timepieces. Yet she wore the Mickey Mouse watch with the leather strap band all the time, even when she was dressed to the nines. But then, Annie de Silva was just Annie.

If Ben didn't like it or thought it was silly, she could always take it back. As to the phone . . . one of those Jitterbugs she saw advertised all the time by that guy John Walsh. This way, if anything ever happened, and Ben found himself in trouble, all he had to do was press the 5* button, and he'd be connected with a help line, and assistance would arrive within minutes.

Without even realizing it, Isabelle had already made up

her mind because she was slipping into a windbreaker and reaching for her purse.

Fifteen minutes later, Isabelle was cruising up and down the aisles of the Target store, looking for the electronics department. There was a whole end of the counter that displayed the phones. Isabelle debated a moment, trying to decide if an eight-year-old boy would do better with the flip phone, even though flip phones were dated, or the one with the plain screen. He'd probably carry it in his hip pocket. Boys that age were careless. Without meaning to, he might crack the glass or drop it. The flip would offer more protection. Now to color. Maybe blue to match his bike. Easy decision. The box found its way into her shopping cart.

She looked around for the jewelry department and saw it three aisles ahead. She beelined for it and once again found the end cap with Disney products for both boys and girls. The watches stood out like beacons in the night. They were brightly colored, had large numbers, and who didn't love Mickey and Minnie Mouse? She snatched one up and looked to see if they came in small, medium, and large as a vision of Ben's skinny arms came into focus. She heaved a mighty sigh when she saw that they did come in sizes. She chose a small one and put it in her cart.

Isabelle stood in the middle of the aisle, wondering if there was anything else she could get for the little boy. It came to her in a flash. A whistle. Every kid needed a whistle. Even a big kid like Charles was never without his whistle. Absolutely. But . . . where in this vast store would they be? She asked a man in a red vest, an employee, she presumed, who pointed her in the right direction.

One whistle coming up.

Isabelle was back home in the loft in just under thirty-five minutes. She smacked her hands together gleefully.

She couldn't remember the last time she'd been more satisfied with something she'd done.

She spread her purchases out on the kitchen table, then made herself a pot of coffee and a ham sandwich.

As she chewed her food and drank her coffee, Isabelle read the instructions for the Jitterbug phone. She loved that all Ben had to do was press the 5* button if he was ever in dire trouble. She programmed in her number and the numbers of all the sisters. She was having a hard time coming to terms with why she was suddenly so concerned about something possibly happening to the little boy. *He's just a little boy,* she thought. He might be a genius in some areas, but he was still a defenseless little boy, a *fragile* little boy in her mind. *Someone has to help him,* she told herself over and over. And since no one else was standing in line for the job, it might as well be her.

Isabelle called the 800 number on the booklet and activated the phone. She made sure the operator understood that the phone would be in the boy's possession even though the bill was coming to her home address. Once she was assured all was well, she slipped the phone, along with the booklet, into her purse to turn over to Ben when she saw him on Tuesday.

Isabelle cursed as she ripped at the stiff plastic packaging around the Mickey Mouse watch. She broke two nails before she dug out the kitchen shears to cut around the watch. She couldn't help but smile at the cartoon character. Maybe that's why Annie wore hers, so she would smile more often. "Whatever works," she muttered under her breath. She set the timepiece by the clock on the gas range. The instructions, once she pried them out of the mangled plastic, said the battery should work for a full two years. Like that was really true. Ben, genius that he was, would figure it out if the watch stopped at some point. She wrapped the watch in a paper towel and dropped it into her purse, along with the phone.

The whistle was next. Once again, she attacked the plastic packaging and broke another nail, but she finally pulled out the whistle and hooked it onto a beaded chain. He could either wear it around his neck or stuff it in one of his pockets. She felt like a little kid again when she brought the whistle to her lips and let loose. She blinked at the shrillness of the whistle. If Ben blew it, people would take notice. She wrapped it in a paper towel and dropped it in her bag to join the watch and the cell phone.

Good to go!

Isabelle looked down at her own watch and was stunned to see that it was already eleven o'clock. Time for bed. She hoped she would be able to sleep.

In the bathroom, Isabelle washed her face, brushed her teeth, and donned her pajamas before she crawled into bed. She missed Abner, hated sleeping alone. She switched up pillows and sighed contentedly when she smelled his scent. She hugged the pillow as she drifted off to sleep.

The next day, the sisters all clustered in Myra's kitchen, hooting and hollering, and high-fiving one another as they laughed and giggled just as Isabelle, the last to arrive, walked through the kitchen doorway.

"Just in time for lunch," Myra said. "Annie has the hot dogs on the grill, and we've been sitting here waiting for you. It's a little too nippy to eat outside, and the wind is kicking up, so we'll have to eat here in the kitchen. Fall to it, ladies!"

The sisters each had a chore before and after a meal, so they fell to it. Within five minutes, the lovingly restored huge plank table was set, coffee cups filled, and several serving pieces were placed in the middle of the table. Condiments were in little bowls on a revolving lazy Susan.

"Pumpkin pie for dessert straight out of the freezer. But it was made by Charles, so it is not store-bought. I personally whipped the cream that goes on top a little earlier," Myra said proudly.

Annie appeared with her favorite food of all time, in one hand perfectly grilled hot dogs with delicious-looking grill marks and a platter with toasted buns in the other.

Between bites, the sisters *oooh*ed and *aaah*ed and complimented Annie, who beamed her pleasure. Who would have thought that Countess Annie de Silva, perhaps the richest woman in the world, would know how to grill a perfect hot dog? No one, that's who.

"I think this is the best hot dog I ever ate, better even than a Nathan's special," Maggie said, as chili, green relish, and bits of onion dribbled down her chin. "The messier they are, the better they taste." She was already on her third hot dog.

"Is this a late lunch or an early dinner?" Kathryn asked as she reached for her third hot dog.

"Both, so eat hearty. It's four o'clock," Annie said. "We could save the pie for later if we get hungry." She turned to Isabelle. "How much time do you need to present your case?"

"At least an hour," Isabelle mumbled around the food in her mouth.

"That means we need three or four hours to kick it around, which will bring us to eight o'clock or thereabouts. I say we save the pie till then," Nikki said. "Do you all agree?" Everyone said that they did.

"More coffee, anyone?" Alexis asked. Seven cups were raised in the air, including her own. Alexis poured generously. She looked over at Yoko, and said, "It's your turn to make the new pot." Yoko nodded her agreement.

Myra sighed as she played with the pearls around her neck. She had no idea how the sisters kept track of who was to do what and whose turn it was, but somehow it always worked out, and even to this day, there had never been one objection from any of them.

The after-meal talk was easy banter, with just a trace of edginess that concerned the weather but disappeared entirely when the subject turned to Halloween and how beautiful the leaves were that were just starting to fall from all the trees. And then somehow, by some unknown signal, the sisters got up as one and started to clear away the remains of Annie's perfectly cooked meal.

Nine minutes and two seconds later, they all laughed out loud. The dishwasher was humming, and the last dish towel had been hung on the handle of the oven door. "Our best time yet, nine minutes and two seconds," Maggie said.

"That's because we used throwaway plates, and there was no silverware to speak of, and no pots and pans," Yoko said.

Annie reached into the cupboard for clean cups. Myra poured.

The room went silent.

Time for business. All eyes turned to Isabelle.

Isabelle licked at her lips. She closed her eyes for a minute as she tried to gather her thoughts. "I'm going to have to go back a ways, about fifteen years, before we all knew one another, to when I designed the biggest project of my young career. So bear with me."

"Take all the time you need, dear. We have all night if need be," Myra said.

"Okay. This lady, her name is Eleanor Parker Lymen. She walked into my office one day with a sketch in her hand. She asked me if I could design it for her. It was a circle with six houses and a park in the middle of the Circle. I said yes. Any first-grade architect could do that. Then she said she wanted me to design a special school for gifted children. She wanted it to be built at the top of the Circle but outside the Circle. I, of course said yes. I think it was something like thirteen acres, possibly a little more, that I had available for what was asked for. So she commissioned me to build six mansions, three on each side of the circle, then the school. I won two awards for my designs.

"Eleanor and I became friends over time. She told me to call her Ellie, which I did.

"Ellie had a daughter. Her name was Diana. At the best of times, their relationship was contentious. Diana was one of those gifted children, what we today call a brainiac, because she was *wayyyy* up there in the clouds, if you know what I mean, but Diana wasn't a child. I only met her twice. It's hard to describe her. She was there, but she wasn't there. It was like she lived on another plane of existence somehow. Ellie wanted her to run the Institute when it was completed. Diana said no thanks. She was sick and tired of her mother's thinking of her as some freak of nature. Which wasn't what her mother thought at all. Diana was brilliant. I'm not sure, but Ellie said she did a lot of drugs and smoked a lot of pot. As I said, I only met her the two times.

"Once the houses were finished, Ellie moved Diana into one of the mansions. She said Diana could live in a tent and not know the difference, that's how far *out there* she was. Anyway, she, Diana, never even showed up when the Institute opened. Ellie had to find people to run it. It's very successful.

"Yesterday, Maggie and I worked at my place trying to gather as much background as we could, which isn't all that much. You see, Ellie and her two friends who live on the Circle next to her are gone. They've been gone for six months, almost seven. But I am getting ahead of myself here.

"Back to Diana. I had not seen Ellie in quite a while. You'll remember we were quite busy those days, and often out of the country or on our hilltop. But when I next met Ellie, Diana had a boyfriend of sorts. From what I remember Ellie telling me, he was like Diana, a dreamer, a free spirit. Then one day, he was gone.

"Almost nine months later, Diana gave birth to a baby boy. Diana wasn't capable of taking care of the child, so Ellie and Rita and Irene took over. Then about seven months after the boy was born, Diana met another man and, to Ellie's dismay, married him. Ellie was certain that he married Diana for her money. Ellie said she knocked on her door one day, and said, 'Meet my new husband. Give me my son.' Ellie had no choice but to turn the seven-month-old baby over to her daughter. Connor Ryan was the name of the man Diana married. Connor adopted the baby and gave him his name. They lived on the Circle in the house directly across from Ellie's house.

"A little more than a year after she got married, Diana was killed. She was in a bank when a robbery went down. She was simply in the wrong place at the wrong time. Ellie was devastated, inconsolable." Isabelle looked over at Annie and Myra, both of whom just nodded that they understood.

"Connor moved out of the house on the Circle into an apartment shortly after Diana was killed. He was unable to take care of a two-year-old child on his own, so Ellie, with Rita and Irene's help, took the boy in. Two years later, at Rita and Irene's urging, Ellie went to court to obtain permanent custody of her four-year-old grandson. She had the best lawyers in the state, but she could not get custody of the child. Connor had adopted him. And after Ellie sued him, he married a woman named Natalie. With an intact family unit for the boy to move in with, and with Connor having adopted the boy, Ellie lost her bid for custody. Grandparents have no rights. Furthermore, in retaliation for Ellie's having sued him, no matter what she did, Connor wouldn't let her have visitation rights. All he wanted was Diana's money.

"Once Ben came to live with Connor and Natalie, monthly child support checks from the trust fund were paid to Connor. But about eight months ago, Connor went back to court, demanding that Diana's trust fund be turned over to him. I suppose the monthly checks were not enough to keep him satisfied. Anyway, the judge agreed with Connor's position.

"Ellie was going to be ordered by the court to turn it over. Since she wasn't about to let that happen, she . . . ah . . . took it on the lam. She's gone. No one has seen or heard from her since, and that was more than six months ago. Before she left, she apparently did some fancy financial deals. All the money disappeared just the way she disappeared."

Isabelle leaned back in her chair and looked around as she sipped at her cold coffee.

Six pairs of eyes stared at Isabelle. "But you found her, and she's the client. She wants her grandson back, and this is to be our mission, is that what you're saying?" Nikki said.

Isabelle sighed. "I wish." Isabelle reached for her phone, moved her index finger until she found what she was looking for. "This is our client if we take on the case."

Everyone in the room gasped as they stared at the smiling, gap-toothed, curly-haired little boy straddling his blue bicycle. "Meet my new best friend, Benjamin Andrew Lymen Ryan. He's our client if you all agree to take on the case."

Even before the last words were out of Isabelle's mouth, six hands shot high in the air. Isabelle grinned and raised her hand, too.

"There's more. I went to Ellie's house. I know where she keeps a spare key. In fact, I built a special birdhouse high in a tree in the backyard as a surprise for Ellie. When I showed her the birdhouse, she was delighted and suggested that it would be a wonderful place to hide a key. Then I had to install a pulley system to lower the cage to get the key. The tree is covered in years of Virginia creeper vines, so you can't see the pulley. Anyway, the house is empty. Ellie planned this. She wasn't abducted, that much I can tell you. Oh, and her two friends, Rita and Irene, are also gone, so they must be with her. That alone tells me that the Ellie I know has no intention of turning over her daughter's money to Connor Ryan.

"I also understand that the house that Connor, Natalie, and Ben moved into after Connor obtained custody of Ben is actually owned by Ben, not Connor. As I told you, Connor gets a check once a month for taking care of him. Ben had no idea how much the check was for, and I have no clue, either. Other than the amount for child support, however much that is, the monthly checks from Diana's trust fund stopped when she died. She was in the bank about to cash one of them when she was killed. And do you believe that Connor fought Ellie to get that check paid? Ellie had the account frozen, so he never got it. I was with you guys out of the country when Diana was killed and only heard about it when we came to DC on a mission. Ellie told me about it when I went to pay a condolence call.

"Ben says he hates Connor's wife, Natalie. He's not particularly fond of Connor, either, but I tend to think Connor treats him okay and doesn't abuse him.

"Ben attends the Institute. He's eight years old and is a freshman in college. He's a whiz kid. He's as cute as a button. It took almost five months before he would talk to me. You all know I go to the park to eat my lunch, so I can stare at the Circle, which is still my pride and joy, especially after the debacle in England, which almost cost me my marriage, thank you very much.

"Ben would pedal past me and smile or wave, then the wave turned to 'hi,' then to maybe a few words, until just the other day we had lunch together. He goes to the Institute on Mondays, gets his assignments, and works at home and turns them in the following Monday. After Thanksgiving, he will be a senior in college. How amazing is that?"

"Pretty damn amazing. What's the plan? A snatch and grab? Then what? The stepfather will raise holy hell, and the fallout will be horrendous," the always blunt-spoken Kathryn said.

"I don't know what the plan is. Yet. First, we need to find Eleanor Lymen. Ben actually asked me for my help. Of course I said yes. *My* plan for the moment is, we all meet up at the park on Tuesday. Tomorrow is out because he has to go to the Institute. I will introduce you and let him talk. Then we make plans."

"How much money is involved here?" Yoko asked.

"Not sure. I saw some of Ellie's financials back when I was designing the project. At the time, I had no idea there was that much money in the world. Millions and millions plus more millions. And from what Ben said, Rita and Irene have just as much as Ellie does, and it was all going to go to Diana, and now Ben, because they have no heirs."

"By any chance do you know what happens to all those millions if something were to happen to young Ben?" Annie asked softly.

"I don't know. I doubt if Ben knows, either. We'd have to see Ellie's will, as well as Rita's and Irene's. No one was expecting Diana to die. Things moved at the speed of light after that. Did the ladies change their wills? I have no clue," Isabelle said.

"We need to assume that young Ben is in danger then. Not immediate danger but danger nonetheless," Myra said.

"We need to ask why Ellie would desert Ben for such a long period of time. Does she have someone watching over him? Who? The people at the Institute? Obviously, she isn't or wasn't all that worried about his safety when she took off. More than six months is a very, very long time," Maggie said.

"I rummaged in my footlocker and found the name of the law firm that paid me my fees when I worked for Ellie. We could go there and talk to them. Ellie must check in with them from time to time. Maybe they can help us. The firm is one of the oldest, most prestigious law firms in the state. We go and plead Ben's case," Isabelle said.

"It doesn't work that way, Isabelle," Nikki said. "Attorney-client confidentiality is in force. The most we could hope for is, we plead Ben's case and ask them to get in touch with Ellie if they can. I'll go with you tomorrow if you can get an appointment that quickly, or we could wing it and just show up. Let's take a vote." Seven hands shot in the air.

"Isabelle, do you have any idea, any idea no matter how far-fetched it might seem, as to where she might have gone for such a long period of time?" Alexis asked.

Isabelle shook her head. "We were friends, but while Ellie spoke of many things, she never got really personal with me. The Diana part was something I could see, and she *needed* to talk about her daughter. I understood that. But to answer your question, she could be anywhere, out of the country, in New York, California, or holed up around the corner. I just don't know."

"Then our best bet is her law firm or Ben himself. He might remember something or have some clue. If he's as smart as you say he is, he might know but is afraid to betray his grandmother. It's obvious he loves her dearly," Yoko said.

"So now what do we do?" Annie asked. It was clear to all at the table that she was itching for action.

"I have an idea," Myra said. Everyone looked at her expectantly.

"The night is long, and we're just sitting here. Why don't we all go to the Circle and check out Mrs. Lymen's house? Seven sets of eyes, fresh eyes. Maybe one of us will pick up on something." She turned to Isabelle. "Do you see any possible problems? It is dark out now, and there's no moon. How well lighted is the area?"

Isabelle pondered the problem. "I have the key to the main gate, but there is also a retina scan. I don't know why Eleanor switched up. Probably because she didn't want to have to get out of the car to get the gate to open. The key works just as well, but, of course, you have to get out of the car to use it. A card swipe would work better for her. You can drive through, but you would need to swipe a card. If you drive in, you take the ring road behind the Circle but are still within the Circle because that's where the garages are. We'll walk it. I don't see any problems. We can park in my office parking lot. I'm game if you guys are."

They moved as one and were out the door in seconds, Myra last as she issued orders to Lady and her pups to watch the house.

"We need two cars," Annie said.

Maggie and Nikki volunteered to drive as each had a four-door sedan.

Forty-five minutes later, the group stood under the old sycamore tree as Isabelle poked around the leaves of the Virginia creeper for the hand pulley.

"This is really clever, dear," Myra said in awe.

"I thought so. Ellie loved it. Don't talk above a whisper

since voices carry in the night. Not that there is anyone around here, but there might be eyes on us. You just never know. Okay, I have the key. Be careful now and walk in single file," Isabelle said.

When the sisters reached the kitchen door, Isabelle fit the key in and opened the door. A small light glowed in a round circle over the kitchen range, but it was still dark. Isabelle and Maggie both pulled small Maglites out of their bags and aimed them at the floor. "We'll split up here. Annie, Myra, Yoko, and Alexis take the ground floor. Be sure to keep the lights aimed at the floor. Nikki, Maggie, Kathryn, and I will take the second floor. Then we'll switch up. You never know what one of us will see or miss."

The sisters went at it with gusto.

An hour later, they met on the landing of the staircase. "Nothing, absolutely nothing!" Maggie said, disgust ringing in her voice.

"It's here. I know it," Isabelle all but cried. "Ellie would never, and I mean never, desert Ben. She left something here for him. He said he came here looking, hoping for the same thing, but he couldn't find anything. He was on the verge of tears, so he wasn't conning me. I think he truly felt, at least for a little while, that his grandmother had deserted him. I don't think he feels that way any longer. It's just a gut feeling."

"If she did leave a clue or something for him, where do you think she would have left it, Isabelle?" Annie asked.

"His room. But we all went over it. Even Ben said when he sneaked in here he went straight to his room, but he ended up crying and left. If there is anything, it has to be in his room. Come on, let's give it another once-over. We can pull up the carpet if we have to. Take the pictures off the walls, strip it down to the bare nub."

"We need light for this," Kathryn said. "Light will still leak out if we close the shutters. Let's take the coverlet and drape it over those two side-by-side windows. Tuck it behind the rod, and it should black it out. A towel over the little window will work. Two would be better."

Thirty minutes later, the room looked like a tsunami had hit it at full speed.

"Nothing!" Isabelle cried dejectedly.

"Not so fast, ladies. It's here. I can feel it," Maggie said as she looked around at the torn-up room. "What kid leaves his junk behind? Look at that shelf. It looks like it belongs in a magazine to tempt some parent into decorating a kid's room like this one. Look at this room! It's a kid's dream. Connor, bastard that he is, or we assume he is, wouldn't he take all these things for the kid to comfort him? Wouldn't Ben have cried to take them? He's only eight years old, for crying out loud. What? They just ripped him out of here, and he wasn't allowed to take anything? That's pretty damn shitty if you want my opinion," Maggie exploded in frustration.

"Sure does look that way. I never even met the guy, and I hate him already. Lots of clothes in the closet. Lots of clothes in the drawers. No false bottoms in any of the drawers," Nikki said. "No messages taped anywhere. No safe either. You'd think someone like Mrs. Lymen would have a safe."

"There is a safe. It's in the linen closet. I checked it when I was here. No point in looking at it since we don't have the combination. We can come back another time, and Annie can take a crack at it," Isabelle said.

It was Myra who reached for the panda bear on the shelf as she remembered her daughter Barbara's favorite bear, which she had called Willie. She hugged the bear to her chest, wondering if Ben had cried himself to sleep because he missed the bear. She wondered if it had a name and what it was.

"Oh! Oh! I found it! I found it!" Myra screamed. "Look! It has a zipper. Kids keep their pajamas in it. They call these special bears, Sleep Bears. I see them advertised all the time. There's something in here, and it certainly isn't pajamas," she said, pulling the zipper down. "We found it, ladies! We found it! The holy grail."

"It would help if you told us what you found, Myra," Annie suggested.

"Yes, yes, yes. Okay, here's a bundle of credit cards. A stash of cash, hard currency. And the Last Will and Testament of Eleanor Parker Lymen. A bunch of loose papers . . . a diary. Entries. A packet of what look like deeds to properties."

"The mother lode, no doubt about it." Annie sighed. "Quick, bundle it all up and we'll take it with us. We'll each carry some under our jackets in case there are eyes on us out there. We've been here way too long as it is. We have to leave. Like right now. Stuff something back inside the bear so it doesn't look so limp. Some of Ben's tee shirts from the drawers. Turn off all the lights, and let's get this room back to the way it was before we tore it apart."

The sisters fell to it the same way they divided up the kitchen chores.

Six minutes later, Maggie yelled, "Done! Six minutes! Move, people, move!"

They moved and were back in Myra's kitchen in exactly seventy-two minutes.

"I think we need the table for this," Myra said, switching on the light in the dining room.

"I'll make the coffee," Kathryn said. "Don't start without me."

"Wouldn't think of it, dear," Annie said as she unzipped her jacket to clutch at everything she'd stuffed inside the

pockets. The others did the same as they waited for Kathryn and the coffee.

Isabelle couldn't take her eyes off the bounty on the
table. "I hope we find some answers here."

"I'm sure we will, dear. I'm sure we will," Myra said, re-
peating herself for effect.

Chapter 5

While the sisters were deep into planning how to help Isabelle's new best friend, Ben was trying to help himself with the aid of his grandmother's credit card and his computer. He watched as the reports he paid $29.95 for rolled out of his high-speed printer, hoping there would be something in the reports that would help him somehow find his grandmother.

Just as the printer beeped to indicate that the printer had finished the job, Ben heard the front door slam shut. He ran to the window in time to see his stepfather, Connor, running to his car. Correction, his mother's car. Ben couldn't decide at that moment if Connor's leaving was a good thing or a bad thing. Normally, Connor didn't go anywhere in the middle of the afternoon, especially on a Sunday. He pondered the problem and decided that with Natalie gone, the habitual behavior of one Connor Ryan was likely to change. That also meant, he supposed, that he was going to have to feed himself, not that Connor or Natalie actually ever *cooked*. Their version of mealtime was either to go out to eat or order in. Most times, Ben was left to fend for himself.

He thought, then, for a few moments, about what he would do for dinner if Connor didn't bring back some takeout. He was pretty good at making grilled cheese sand-wiches, providing, of course, there was any bread and cheese in the house. And he could make ramen noodles with his eyes closed.

Suddenly, the little boy burst out laughing. He could order in now if he wanted to. He had money. Lots and lots of money, and he knew where he could get more if he needed it. He could even ride his bike to several fast-food places and actually sit down and eat pizza, tacos, or burg-ers till he was stuffed. Right now, at this very moment, he decided the world was his oyster.

The house was quiet. Sometimes he liked quiet. Other times he would turn on the small television set in his room just to hear voices. He was lonely, no doubt about it.

Ben ran back to the printer and pulled out the reports he'd paid for. Skimpy at best. Maybe he should have gone for the $59.95 deluxe package. He shuffled the pages and stapled them together. His and Hers. Meaning Natalie and Connor.

Ben started with the report on Natalie, a fairly minimal one, and read through it in warp time. While there wasn't all that much, what there was was pretty powerful in his opinion. He wondered if Connor knew about Natalie's background. The report was rocky road. In his opinion.

The report on Connor Ryan was pure vanilla. He sum-marized Connor with: a lazy, good-for-nothing, idiotic moron. And yet his biological mother had married him, as had Natalie. Maybe women liked lazy, good-for-nothing, idiotic morons. He made a mental promise to himself to research women in regard to their choice in men.

Ben went back to the dark-chocolate report. He read it again, then a third time until he had it memorized word for word.

Natalie Kendrick. Age thirty-one. Born in Tuscaloosa, Alabama. Didn't finish the tenth grade. "Ooooh," Ben said. That certainly explained a lot. Job history was about what he expected. Cocktail waitress, cocktail hostess, bartender. All told, there had been seventeen different employers. Married twice and divorced twice. No mention of her current marriage to Connor Ryan. No children. Two DUIs, both in the two years before she married Connor. Loss of driver's license the second time. Twenty-three different addresses during her life.

Three arrests, two for shoplifting, sixty days for each conviction in the county jail. The third arrest was for solicitation. Ben knew what that meant. He was well versed on the birds and the bees.

And that was it.

Ben wondered what kind of additional information the deluxe $59.95 package would have yielded. Other than not having Natalie's financial records, which he was pretty sure would only show that she had nothing, he didn't think he'd made a bad choice opting for the $29.95 package.

Now the question was, what does he do with the information? Natalie was gone. Maybe the point was moot.

A second later, Ben was off his chair, out of his room, and running down the hall to the master bedroom, where he ripped through it like a tornado. In his life, he'd never seen so many pairs of shoes. There had to be hundreds and hundreds, all colors, all kinds of heels. Lots and lots of clothes, some with price tags dangling from the sleeves.

No way in the world would Natalie leave all this behind, especially her hair. He looked at the dresser and saw long strings of red hair clipped to a Styrofoam head. For sure, she was coming back at some point. He remembered the time Natalie and Connor had had a knock-down, drag-out fight, and Connor reached for her hair to pull her closer to him, and he had ended up with a bunch of hair in his hand as Natalie danced across the room screaming and

yelling. And Connor screamed right back, asking if anything about the person she presented herself as was real.
Ben ran from the room, giggling all the way.

Natalie had probably left because she was mad and
wanted to hurt Connor. Ben felt sick to his stomach at the
thought that she would probably return. Connor was such
a fool.

Ben ran back to his room and sat down at his desk. He
wanted to cry. But only babies cried. So he knuckled his
eyes to ward off his tears.

Ben picked up the report on Connor and read through it
three times until he had it committed to memory. Connor
was thirty-five years old. Born in Reston, Virginia. He attended and even graduated from Catholic University. Married once to Diana Lymen. Adopted Benjamin Lymen, Diana
Lymen's son. He was a widower. He was a potter and a
glassblower. He sold his creations at local flea markets and
on occasion was commissioned to do special projects. No
DUIs on his record. Like the report on Natalie, his marriage to Natalie was not mentioned. Obviously, the reports
that the company compiled weren't up to date. He thought
about demanding his money back. Truth in advertising
and all that. He knew he wouldn't bother, but it was a
thought he stored away. But then he began to wonder if
perhaps Natalie and Connor weren't married at all. But he
just as quickly dismissed that idea since in order for Connor to have won the lawsuit over custody of Ben, he
would have had to establish to the judge's satisfaction that
he was turning Ben over to a married couple and not a single stepfather.

The report on Izzy was next. He scanned it and realized
there was nothing alarming in the report. Car accident.
Lawsuit. He saw it every day on the news or read it online.
Sooner or later, everyone had a fender-bender and ended
up in court. No big deal. Her license had been suspended,

then reinstated. Okay, that happened, too. The fact that she was reinstated told Ben she wasn't at fault. Married to Abner Tookus. Born in Falls Church, Virginia. Grew up in an orphanage. Won many awards for her designs. The biggest awards were for the Circle and the Institute.

Izzy Flanders Tookus was double vanilla.

Now, what he should do with this information was the burning question. Should he show it to Izzy when he met her on Tuesday? She said she would help him find his grandmother, but would this help in the search? Couldn't hurt, was the answer he came up with. He carefully folded the reports and stuck them into one of his books, knowing neither Natalie, if she came back, nor Connor would ever even think of looking at his books.

Ben was surprised when he looked out the window to see that it was dark. It was the end of October, he reminded himself. That meant he was not allowed to leave the house. Once it was dark, and the streetlights came on, he had to be indoors, and until now, he had always followed the rules. That had to mean he was going to have ramen noodles for dinner because at lunchtime he had seen that there was no bread. He'd eaten peanut butter and jelly out of the jars and swigged down a glass of milk that tasted funny.

Or, he could gamble and take a chance and order something from one of the many magnets on the refrigerator. He could use one of the hundred-dollar bills he'd kept from his grandmother's stash. He could do that. Yes, he could. But then what would happen if Connor suddenly came back? He slapped himself upside the head when he remembered Connor had given him five twenty-dollar bills.

Oh, man, he was good to go! He quickly let his gaze rake over the magnets on the refrigerator and chose Enrico's Pizza. He called in and ordered a medium everything pizza, antipasto, and a large bottle of Coca-Cola. He figured that with the salad in the refrigerator, he would have meals for at least another day. "How long?" Twenty minutes was the reply.

Ben's mouth was already watering. Pepperoni, sausage, green peppers, onions, mushrooms, and garlic. His grandmother's favorite; his, too. He busied himself setting the table for one. Then he ran upstairs to get his money to pay for the pizza. He was halfway down the stairs when he turned around and ran back up to gather his dirty clothes to put in the washer. He'd learned the hard way that if he wanted clean clothes, he had to wash them himself. He just wished Natalie had bought better detergent instead of the one where he had to use three times as much in order to get any suds.

Ben stood at the washer and debated about separating the clothes, white versus colored, the way he usually did it because he'd seen his grandmother do it that way, but decided he no longer cared if his underwear turned colors. Time was what was important. He turned all the dials to the right arrows just as the doorbell rang. He banged down the lid of the washer and raced to the front door as he dug in his pocket for the twenty-dollar bills Connor had given him.

The transaction completed, Ben reached for the pizza and was happy to see that it was still steaming. With his hands full and his thoughts on nothing but the delicious pizza, he forgot to lock the front door with the newly installed locks.

Ben dived into the pizza and, before he knew it, he'd eaten the whole medium-size pie and consumed half the bottle of soda. He had no room left for the antipasto and put it into the refrigerator. He couldn't remember anything being as good as what he'd just eaten. Satisfied that he hadn't made a mess, he carried the box out to the garage and put it in the trash can. He closed the soda bottle and set it in the refrigerator alongside the antipasto, then checked the washer. It was down to one minute on the last spin. He waited patiently and transferred his clothes to the dryer. The time on the clock in the laundry room said it was seven o'clock.

The long night loomed ahead of him. What to do? He wished he had a dog or a cat, but Connor said that animals made Natalie sneeze. And that was the end of that.

Ben had one foot on the steps leading to the second floor when he stopped and looked around. He was alone. The house was empty. In a nanosecond, he knew exactly what he was going to do. He turned around and ran down the hall to what Connor called the study, which was off-limits to him.

Inside the room he was forbidden to enter, he walked around, wondering what the big deal was. Why wasn't he allowed in here? Shelves with wall-to-wall books. A fireplace. Two chairs and a sofa. A desk, closer to what was called a secretary. Probably his mother's. All the furniture and other stuff was from the house on the Circle. Nothing new in here. He knew for a fact that all the books on the shelves were his mother's books, because his grandmother had told him so. There had to be more than a thousand books, maybe more. He wished he knew if his mother had read them all. His grandmother said she thought so, but she wasn't sure.

Ben poked around the desk, hoping to find something interesting. He went through the desk slowly and methodically, the way he did everything. Stacks and stacks of unpaid bills. Legal papers. Notices with big red stamps on them saying utilities were going to be turned off. Receipts for the sales of Connor's pottery and glassware. Ben found himself grinning like a monkey when he pulled out a thick wad of credit-card bills. Nordstrom, Neiman Marcus, Saks. He did a quick calculation and came up with $82,000, and that didn't include the American Express bill for $33,433 and a Visa bill for $19,987. He laughed out loud when he saw that the accounts were in Connor's name and not Natalie's. Yep, an idiotic moron. Natalie was off the hook, and Connor was on the hook for the bills. No wonder he wanted Ben's mother's money.

Ben kept rummaging until he found what he was looking for. A record of the amount of money Connor received for Ben's upkeep. He finally found it. He gasped at the amount, $12,000. Each month—$12,000 a month, and he had to eat peanut butter and jelly, ramen noodles, and whatever else he could scrounge up. Time to do something about that. He needed some new clothes: His jeans were pretty worn, with holes in the knees, his socks had holes, and his underwear was too tight. He was also going to need a new winter jacket. He giggled to himself as he thought about how he would confront Connor and how he would threaten him by telling him he was going to file a complaint at the Institute that would then get back to his grandmother's lawyers. And, with any luck, would provide them with enough ammunition to return to family court to get the decision to grant custody to Connor reversed, so he could go live with his grandmother on the Circle.

His jubilation was short-lived when he heard a sound that sent chills up his spine. The front door opened, and the robotic voice announced that someone had opened the door. Every door on the first floor was rigged to alert the owners that someone had opened a door. In a flash, he remembered not locking the door after getting the pizza.

He was doing something he wasn't supposed to be doing in a room he wasn't supposed to be in. Connor would skin him alive. Where to hide? There were no hiding places. No room under the spindly secretary desk. Behind the sofa? He ran across the room just as he heard Natalie's screeching voice. "Yoo-hoo, Connor, your sweet baby love is back. Come out, come out wherever you are! I'm sorry. Come on, sweetie, let me make it up to you. I know you missed me," she trilled as she made her way to the study, in which Ben was desperately trying to make himself invisible.

Ben thought he was going to faint. He hugged his bony knees to his chest, and under his breath muttered, "Shit shit shit," knowing if his grandmother ever heard him, she'd put soap in his mouth. He mentally apologized to her as he suddenly got a whiff of Natalie's overpowering perfume. Secretly, he thought her stinky perfume was what reduced Connor to the state he was in when he was around her because he had to fight to breathe.

"Okay, Connor, enough is enough. Where the hell are you? We need to talk."

Dummy, didn't you see that his car is missing? Ben wanted to shout at her. *Just go already. Go, go, go!* Ben pleaded suddenly.

"Well, you're going to pay for missing my homecoming, you louse," Natalie raved and ranted as she started to stomp around the room.

Please don't look behind the couch, please, please, please, Ben begged silently.

The minute Ben heard her heels tapping their way to the door, he relaxed. And then he started to shake. He had to get out of the room, but first Natalie had to go upstairs in order for him to do so safely. He crawled out of his hiding place and crawled toward the door, careful to hug the wall that gave him a view of the stairway. She was halfway up, her suitcase thumping on each step. He waited, hardly daring to breathe, before he made a run for it, straight to the laundry room, where he saw that the dryer had eight minutes to go until it shut off. He struggled to take a deep breath, slid down on the floor, and hugged his knees. His fervent hope was that if Natalie decided to check the downstairs rooms, she'd see him waiting for his clothes to dry. Nothing for her to get excited about. When the dryer pinged, he sighed again. Wait, or open the dryer and fold his clothes? As far as he could tell, there was no other option.

The front door opened again. Connor was home.

"Shit, shit, shit. And shit again," Ben muttered under his breath. "I know, I know, Grandma, and I'll voluntarily put soap in my mouth, but not now, later."

Ben waited. For what, he didn't know.

He listened to Connor's footsteps. *Please, don't let him come into the* kitchen. *Please, please, please.* Just to be on the safe side, Ben inched across the floor and pushed the door almost closed. He sat back down and waited for whatever was to come.

Ben was trying to decide what to do, which was basically no decision at all. He was stuck in the laundry room. He watched with one eye through the crack in the door. Connor was unpacking his dinner, Chinese food. Ben knew what it was the minute Connor opened the cartons. Firecracker shrimp in a hot sauce, pork fried rice, and egg rolls. He didn't even bother setting the table and just started to eat out of the cartons. He twisted the cap off a bottle of Chinese beer from a six-pack just as Natalie appeared in the doorway.

Ben stared with his one eye and was pleased to see that Connor turned as white as the winter snow. Natalie's face was full of hate. She snatched the beer out of his hand and threw it at the refrigerator. "I can see you really missed me!" she snarled.

Connor recovered and yelled, "How did you get in here?"

"How do you think I got in here? I opened the door and walked in. I live here, too, you know."

"I changed the locks. I asked you a question. How the hell did you get in here? Did Ben let you in?"

"You changed the locks! Is that what you said? No, no, no, you see that does not work for me. I want a key. Ben did not let me in. I don't even know where the little snot is. Don't you ever do that again, you bastard. Do you hear me?" Natalie shrilled.

"Shut up, Natalie. Just shut your trap. I'm sick and tired of your telling me what to do, how to do it, and when to do it. You packed up and left. Or did you forget that? You're not staying here. I can't afford you. I want you out of here right *now*. This very moment. Go!"

Natalie advanced into the kitchen until she was leaning across the table and right in Connor's face. "You must be suffering from deep, deep memory loss. You asked me to marry you so you could get custody of that little snot and all his money. You promised me the moon and the stars. You got the little snot, but I haven't seen the moon and stars yet. Not by a long shot. I can't live on twelve thousand dollars a month. I *won't* live on that. You need to make other arrangements. If you don't, I'm going to go to the kid's grandmother's lawyers and tell them what you did. You'll be living in a tent before you know it."

"And where do you think you'll be living, Natalie? Not in my tent, that's for sure. Do whatever the hell you want, just get out of my sight, and this time, take all of your crap with you. If you do not, I will donate every single bit of it to Goodwill or the Salvation Army. I'm sick of you, Natalie, and your phony everything. Do you hear me? I'm sick of you!" Connor roared so loud that Ben stuck his fingers in his ears to stifle the sound.

Ben felt his heart start to beat so fast he thought he was going to pass out when he saw Natalie sit down at the table. He watched as she picked up an egg roll and crunched down. "We both need to calm down here," she said, back-pedaling. "We need to talk this through. I'm prepared to be reasonable if you are."

"Define *reasonable*," Connor said coldly.

"All right, I admit I was a little over the top when I stormed out of here. I'm sorry about that. The problem is, Connor, you have not kept your promise to me. I trusted you to come through. I did what you asked, I married you so you could keep control of the kid. You even admitted to me that it was all about the money and that you weren't father material. I'm not mother material, either, and I admit it. I even told you that. I was honest and up front, but I went along with you. And yet here we are, with that snot-nosed kid neither of us wants. But the judge gave you custody and the kid's money because I, meaning me, pre-sented such a compelling argument about the family unit. I did that for you, Connor. For you, and don't you ever forget it. So think twice before you threaten to kick me out. Plus, sweetie, I have it all right here on my cell phone. Your ardent plea to me to help you, so we'd both be rich."

Ben almost reared back when he heard Connor bellow, "You recorded all that!"

"Well, yeah, sweetie. I kind of figured this day might come. Call it insurance."

"That's blackmail!" Connor roared.

"Like I said, sweetie, call it whatever you want. I call it insurance. Now, are we going to talk, or are we going to continue to fight with each other?"

"There's nothing to talk about," Connor grumbled. "This is the third month with no money for Ben's upkeep. We're operating on a shoestring. The utilities are going to be shut off. You racked up a couple of hundred thousand dollars in bills. I've just been paying the interest. When that infor-mation finds its way to Eleanor Lymen's lawyers, what do you think the outcome will be? Back to court, and I lose custody of Ben. You and I are out in the street or in that tent you mentioned earlier. Assuming that we avoid going to prison."

"We need to go talk to that judge or at the very least a lawyer. A court order is a court order."

"Sometimes you are so stupid, I can't stand talking to you, Natalie. The lawyers told us that Eleanor divested herself of all her assets. She sold the Circle and the Institute to Rita and Irene. There is nothing to gain by going to the lawyers. There is no money. We might have won in court, but Eleanor won in the money department. She left, and no one knows where she is. This was her plan all along. And she did it before the court order came down. The key word here, Natalie, is *before*. She outsmarted us. Don't you get it?"

"Actually, you jerk, I do get it," Natalie snarled. "You were the one who once told me, early on, that Rita and Irene named Diana and Ben as their only heirs. I assume that Eleanor transferred everything to Irene, Rita, or both. So that has to mean all of Eleanor's money is now theirs and will find its way to Ben since his mother died. We get a lawyer to freeze *their* assets. There has to be a paper trail somewhere, and did you forget those monster insurance policies Eleanor took out on Ben and his mother?"

"That's apples and oranges, Natalie."

"You really are stupid, you know that!" Natalie exploded. "Think, Connor! If the little snot has an accident, you collect his insurance. That money will tide us over until the *big* payoff. Then you become the only heir. It might take a while, but with that kind of money involved, the courts will do double time making sure it gets to you. The best news is that those three women will spend their remaining years in jail. How cool is that?"

Ben could hardly believe what he was hearing. He

started to shake and had to hug himself so tight, he could barely breathe. He started to pray, saying all the prayers his grandmother had taught him as tears trickled down his cheeks. He didn't want to die. Sometimes he thought he did, when things were going badly, so he could be with his mother. But right now, he did not want to die.

"No! No! He's just a kid. How could you even think such a thing? You're deranged, Natalie."

Natalie laughed, and Ben started to shake even more. He had to get out of here as soon as possible.

"And you're Mary Poppins's husband! You need to get real here. It's the only solution. If you're that squeamish, I'll do it myself."

"Jesus, Mary, and Joseph, no! I won't lift a finger to help you. I don't care if I go to jail or not."

"That can be arranged so easily, Connor. Or, you could wake up dead right next to your stepson. You made a promise to me, and I counted on it, and now you're backsliding. That doesn't work for me. I had great plans for all that money, and I was going to include you in those plans. Well, you can forget that now," Natalie said coldly. "I'm going to bed. You just sit here and think about this conversation and what you're going to do. We'll talk again in the morning, when Ben goes to the Institute. Good night, my sweet, obedient husband."

Ben gulped and swiped at his tears. He needed to think. He could outwit Natalie, he was sure of it. Well, almost sure of it. He knew in his gut that Connor would fall into line with Natalie's plan, no matter what he was saying right now.

Ben sat frozen in place, waiting to see what Connor would do. Within seconds, he heard the kitchen door open, then the pinging sound, and the robotic words, "Kitchen door open." Of course, Connor was going out to smoke a cigarette, since Natalie wouldn't let him smoke in the house.

She could smoke, but Connor was not allowed to because she said his cigarettes stunk more than hers did. Seven minutes. Ben had timed how long it took Connor to smoke a cigarette on more than one occasion, and it was always seven minutes.

Seven minutes for him to do . . . what? Ben's mind started to race as fast as his heartbeat. It was at times like this when he wished he had a watch. But he was pretty good at keeping track of the time. He opened the door to the laundry room all the way and was about to leave when he had an idea. He turned the dryer to ten minutes even though his clothes were dry, then ran to the family room, where he flopped down on the couch and pretended to be asleep. He started to count down the minutes. When he got to seven minutes, he hopped off the couch and made his way to the laundry room just as Connor opened the back door and stepped into the kitchen. Man and boy glared at one another. "What are you doing down here?"

"Getting my clothes out of the dryer. Connor, I need some new clothes. My jeans have holes in them, and my underwear is too tight. My big toe is sticking out of my socks. I need new sneakers and a winter jacket, too. It's starting to get cold out. Or should I tell them at the Institute? Maybe they'll get me what I need."

Connor did a quick calculation in his head. Two hundred fifty dollars at the most. The winter jacket would set him back the majority of it. He'd given the kid a hundred dollars earlier. That would leave him with about 125 dollars tops. That was every penny he had to his name. "I'll take care of it this week," he said gruffly. "It's almost bedtime, so get your clothes and head on upstairs." Ben sighed as the dryer gave off a keening sound. *Good move, Ben,* he congratulated himself.

Ben scooped his clothes out of the dryer and tossed them into a laundry basket instead of folding them the way his grandmother had taught him. So he would wear wrinkled clothes. Who cares?

Always polite because he had been taught to respect his elders, even those bent on killing him, Ben said good night and headed for the stairs, hoping he would not see Natalie as he made his way to his room. He lucked out—Natalie was nowhere in sight. Inside his room, he closed the door and started to fold his clothes, just to have something to do while his brain raced all over the place. First and foremost, he had to get out of here. Out of this house. *Like now. Immediately.*

Where to go? Yes, he could get into his grandmother's house, but that was the first place the police would go to look for him. Assuming Connor and Natalie would report him missing. They were both late sleepers. On Mondays, his day to go to the Institute, he was up and out and at the Institute before they even got up. They wouldn't even know he was missing until sometime tomorrow afternoon. He had to go tonight, but where could he go? Maybe Rita's or Irene's house. Maybe he could go in through one of the basement windows. If he could get in there, he could hide out until it was time to meet up with Izzy on Tuesday. Or maybe he could go to Izzy's office and hide out there. No, he'd be exposed. He needed to be indoors and safe. But then, how would he get in touch with Izzy about meeting her on Tuesday? He'd need a phone for that, and he didn't have one.

Ben's eyes popped wide. He had money to buy one now. One of those they called burner phones that couldn't be traced. The Rite Aid drugstore in the neighborhood was open twenty-four hours a day. When he left here, he could buy one. Problem solved.

Sort of. Kind of.

Ben looked around his room, trying to decide what to do. His computer said it was twenty after nine. Time to gather up what he would need, make sure he didn't leave anything incriminating behind, then wait another hour or so and leave.

But . . . how was he going to defeat the gizmo on the doors, the robotic voice that announced each opening and closing? He closed his eyes and brought up a mental picture of the front door and where the little square was positioned. Top or bottom? Middle of the door? The bottom! His fist shot high in the air. How many times had he stubbed his toe on it? All he had to do was peel it off. He'd seen Connor replace it many times when he'd knocked it loose. Good! Good! He knew the code to turn off the alarm. No problem there since it didn't make any noise, either, when turned on or off. The only thing that happened was that the red light would turn green, and vice versa. Escape was almost guaranteed.

Ben emptied out his backpack and stacked the books neatly on his desk. Since he had no plans to go to the Institute tomorrow, there was no sense in loading up his backpack. If he changed his mind about showing up, he could always use the Institute's books. His biggest worry was that they might call the house to see where he was, but he brightened almost immediately because Connor and Natalie never answered the phone because the only people who called were bill collectors. He decided he was safe on that score.

Ben removed the reports he'd paid for, rolled them up, and put them on the bottom of his backpack, along with clean underwear and two clean shirts and socks with holes in them. He could wear the same jeans for a few days, then buy some new ones. He ran into the bathroom for his toothbrush and toothpaste and threw them in the backpack.

Ben ran to the closet, removed his grandmother's credit

card, and put it in his shoe. The slim stack of hundred-dollar bills was wrapped around his ankle, with his sock pulled all the way up to his knee. He stopped for a moment to think. He still had the remaining twenty-dollar bills that had not been used to pay the pizza deliveryman in his pocket, so he could use them at Rite Aid.

Before he turned off his computer, Ben looked down at the corner of his computer to see the time. It was ten fifteen. He'd wait fifteen more minutes, then leave. He quietly opened the door and peeked out into the dim hallway. He looked down at the end of the hall, where the master suite was. He could see light shining under the door, and the door was closed. No sounds could be heard. No point in waiting. He backed up into his room, shrugged into his windbreaker, and slipped his backpack over his shoulders. His breathing sped up. He turned off the light, closed the door softly, and tiptoed down the hall to the steps.

In the foyer, he waited for his eyes to adjust to the dim light cast by the minilight on the baseboard before he bent over and pulled off the small electronic device on the bottom of the door. He dropped it into a vase on the little table under the alarm keypad. Ben sucked in his breath and punched in the numbers. He sighed in relief when he saw the red light turn to green. He was out the door in a nanosecond and running like his life depended on it, which, in a way, he supposed it did.

Ben half ran and half jogged to the Rite Aid. He was sure someone would question what a little kid like him was doing out at ten-thirty at night. But no one did. The young girl behind the counter was too busy reading a romance novel to pay attention to him. She simply rang up the phone, the mini Maglite, and a carton of milk, then bagged his purchases and handed Ben the receipt.

Ben flew out of the store and headed for the Circle. He

was getting tired now, so instead of running, he simply walked and tried to whistle, but the gap between his teeth wouldn't allow any sound to escape. By the time he reached the Circle, he was exhausted. It seemed to take him forever to find the key in his pocket that would unlock the main gate, but eventually he found it. His hand was shaking so badly, it took him three tries before he got it open.

The three sodium vapor lights cast a dim yellow illumination over the entire Circle. He walked as fast as he could to Rita's house, where he walked around the back until he saw the basement window. He knew it would be locked, and it was. No one other than maybe a midget or he could squeeze through the opening if the window were open. Straggly, overgrown bushes all but hid the window. With no other option available, Ben kicked the glass until it shattered. He carefully poked all the glass away, crawled through the opening, and dropped to the floor. He turned on the Maglite to see nothing but emptiness, which was good. He looked back at the window, wondering if anyone would see or even think to look at it. The bushes would bounce back into place and likely cover the broken window.

There was one more obstacle, and it hit Ben like a ton of bricks falling on top of him. What if Rita had locked the door in the kitchen that led to the basement? If she had, how was he going to get into the house? He climbed the steps, praying and crossing his fingers as he made his way to the top. He shined the Maglite on the doorknob and turned it. He almost fainted in relief when the door opened into the dark kitchen. Ben aimed his light at the floor as he moved around.

He knew this house, Rita Dolan's, as well as he knew his grandmother's.

The time on the grandfather clock on the landing of the stairs said it was twenty after eleven.

Ben headed straight down the hall to the guest bed-room. He shed his clothes, then opened one of the dresser drawers, the one that used to hold pajamas for when he slept over. They were too small now, but he didn't care. He pulled them on and crawled into bed.

"You did okay, you're safe now," he muttered to him-self, before he drifted off to sleep.

Chapter 6

Ben Ryan's eyes snapped open. He instantly knew that the time was 6:42. He knew this because he woke every day at the exact same time without the aid of an alarm clock. He also knew where he was, as well as all the events that had transpired before he crawled into the bed in the guest bedroom at Rita Dolan's house.

Ben bolted upright and reached for the burner phone he'd purchased the night before at Rite Aid. He was glad for the limited light on the phone to help him dial the numbers of the Institute. He pressed in the digits and waited. Dr. Montgomery usually had desk duty until eight-thirty, at which point all calls went to voice mail until lunchtime.

"This is Benjamin Ryan, Dr. Montgomery. I'm calling to ask you to inform Dr. Evans that I will not be in today. I either have a twenty-four-, forty-eight-, or seventy-two-hour stomach virus. I'm leaning toward the forty-eight-hour virus, which means there is a ninety-eight-percent certainty that I will not be in class tomorrow either to pick up my assignments. Possibly not even Wednesday. Please tell Dr. Evans I completed all my assignments and took the liberty of moving ahead on my own, which means I will not fall behind."

"Very well, Mr. Ryan. I will relay your message to Dr.

Evans," the brisk voice on the other end of the line said. A moment later, the connection was broken.

Ben turned off the phone and dived back under the covers. He was asleep within seconds and didn't wake up again until ten-thirty. What to do first, eat or take a shower? He looked down at the pajamas he was wearing, knowing they were two sizes too small and that he looked ridiculous. Not that he cared. He was hungry but not that hungry, so he opted for the shower. He soaped up and washed his hair. He liked the flowery scent of the shampoo Rita had, which reminded him of her. He felt sad for a moment, but it didn't last.

Ben dressed and combed his curly hair, which fell in wet ringlets all over his head. He really needed to get a haircut before people started to mistake him for a girl. He put it on his mental list of things to do.

The bed beckoned. He knew at some point the cops would search all the houses on the Circle, but not until Connor realized he'd gone missing. But that would not happen for a while yet. Good old Connor wouldn't notice his absence until about three or three-thirty. Natalie wouldn't notice his absence for a week, if then. He giggled at the thought. Then he made the bed. He stood back and tried to view it the way he thought a cop would. Neatly made, no creases anywhere, the sides hanging just the way they were before he went to sleep in it.

The cell phone went into his hip pocket. His backpack was zipped. There were no stray socks or underwear anywhere. The room was clear. As far as anyone could tell, no one had been here since Rita had left.

The bathroom was a different story. Wet towels. The shower stall was wet. The shower mat was wet. Well, that's why GE made dryers! First, he reached for clean towels and dried down the shower walls and the floor. It took three big towels to complete the job. Since he couldn't reach the showerhead, he swung one óf the towels up and across until he couldn't see a speck of water anywhere. He even dried off the bar of soap and the soap dish. He made sure the shampoo bottle cap was dry and tight.

Ben looked around, trying to view the huge bathroom with grown-up eyes that would be searching for clues as to whether anyone had been here or not. He gave himself a mental slap to the side of the head. The shower door. It was open when he first got here. He'd closed it, and it was *wet*. He ran to the linen closet and pulled out a clean towel and set to work. He even dried the bottom metal strip until it felt dry to the touch.

Now he was good to go. He settled his backpack more firmly on his back, bundled up all the wet towels, and carried them downstairs to the dryer. He plugged it in and set the time for thirty minutes.

Now he could eat. Ben headed straight for the pantry, where Rita stored all her canned goods and staples. The number of items he had to choose from was not particularly large. Some canned soup, canned tuna, canned pineapple, sugar, flour, and cracker meal in airtight jars. He almost jumped for joy when he saw a box of Raisin Bran, the kind that had two scoops of raisins, and a box of Frosted Flakes. He reached for the Raisin Bran. Then he remembered why Rita probably bought it in the first place. He didn't need *that* kind of problem while he was on the run. He settled for the Frosted Flakes and ate two big bowls, almost emptying the box. He finished what was left of the milk he'd bought by drinking it from the carton. He rinsed it thoroughly, then crushed the container and stuck it in his backpack. He emptied the rest of the cereal into the sink and ran the garbage disposal, ripped the box apart, and put the pieces in his backpack. Back in the kitchen, he unplugged the refrigerator.

"I think I would make a pretty good criminal," he muttered to himself as he washed and dried the bowl and spoon and returned them to their proper place. He then dried the sink with paper towels that he found under the sink and stuffed them in his backpack. *Leave no clues behind* was his thought.

Now it was time to call Izzy. It took him a good five minutes to find the business card she'd given him. Everything he needed was on the card: the name of her business, the address, the firm's telephone number, and, on the back, her private cell phone number, which she had told him he could call day or night. He punched in the numbers and was stunned when the call went directly to voice mail. He waited ten minutes and hit REDIAL. The call once again went to voice mail. A blossom of fear fluttered in his stomach. Maybe she was in a meeting and had turned off her phone. He decided to give it another few minutes before he called again. When his third call went to voice mail, he really started to panic.

Ben took a deep breath, then another, until he calmed down. He picked up the phone and called the main number of Isabelle's office. A cheerful voice offered a greeting.

"This is Ben Ryan, ma'am. I need to get in touch with Isabelle as soon as possible. She gave me her private cell phone number, and I called it three times, but it went to voice mail each time. Can you please get in touch with her and tell her it's urgent that we talk?"

"And are you a client?"

"Yes. No. I don't know. Isabelle is my friend. Just tell her to meet me at . . . at number three. She'll know what that means. I'm in danger. Tell her I didn't go to . . . to school today. Also, tell her I can't stay here long. Will you please do that?"

The voice on the other end of the phone turned hesitant. "Did you say school?"

"Yes. It's complicated, ma'am. Just tell her I'm in danger." Ben broke the connection before the voice could question him further.

Ben was about to sit down at the kitchen table when the dryer pinged. He ran into the laundry room. He pulled out the towels and folded them, then placed them in the yellow laundry basket at the side of the dryer. Then he pulled the plug on the dryer. He felt certain that towels in a laundry basket wouldn't send up any red flags.

Back at the table, Ben sat with his hands folded. He needed to fall back and regroup. How much time was he going to give Isabelle? It was noon now. At best, he had three, maybe four hours before Connor would realize he was missing. The big question was: What would Connor do about it? Would he call the police? Unlikely. Would he call the Institute? Unlikely. What would he do? He'd probably wait a little while longer. He'd notice that Ben's bike was still there. When it got dark around a quarter to five or so, and the streetlights came on, he might start to feel some concern. Maybe. Or he'd wait it out. But for how long? Would Connor even entertain the idea that he, Ben, might have run away? He had to admit he didn't know. Natalie would be all for letting him stay out as long as he wanted to, saying he'd come home when he was hungry, and that's when you beat the living hell out of the little snot. She'd tell Connor he was a weak, sniveling man, and she was going to take over. Ben shuddered at the thought.

Where are you, Izzy? I need you. I really need you. He wanted to cry so bad that his eyeballs burned.

Less than three miles away, Isabelle and Nikki were sitting in front of a man whose name was Peter Olsen.

"I guess you ladies are wondering about the spartan conditions here. Let me explain. My dad, Peter Senior, is in rehab because he had two hip replacements that went bad. His doctors are trying to decide their next course of action. I took a leave of absence to come here, wind things down, and help my dad. I'm a federal prosecutor. I know your husband, Jack, quite well, Ms. Quinn. We miss him very much. He's doing well, I hope."

"He is. I'll be sure to tell him I met you," Nikki said.

"What can I do for you ladies?"

Isabelle jumped right in just as her cell phone vibrated in her pocket. She was torn for a moment. Nothing was more important than what she was doing right now. She chose to ignore it and quickly explained the reason for their visit. "I understand about attorney-client privilege, but this is a little boy we're talking about. Will you at least call your father and ask him to have Eleanor Lymen call me. Ellie is a friend, and she has my number."

"This is about the custody case, right?" Both women nodded.

"I followed it, and, of course, talked to Dad about it daily. Maybe it would be better if you talked to him directly. He's at the Coastal Center, ten minutes away. We can walk it if you're interested in the exercise, or you can follow me. I just came in today to check the e-mails and phone messages. In three weeks, this firm is shutting down. The other lawyers in the practice have already joined other firms. It's killing my dad, but sometimes you just gotta do what you gotta do. He's looking at months of therapy, and there is no guarantee that it will work."

The sisters elected to follow Peter Jr. in their car.

On the way out of the building and across the parking lot, Peter Jr. chatted a mile a minute. "I have a son Ben's age. It would kill me to have him ripped away from me. It about killed my dad that he lost that case. Mrs. Lymen . . . well, she was inconsolable, as were her two friends, whose names I can't remember right this minute."

"Rita and Irene," Isabelle volunteered.

"Yes, yes, that's it. Dad thought he had it locked up, but

in the end, grandparents have no rights. That guy Connor had legally adopted Ben. And then he got married to seal the deal. From that point on, our side was dead in the water. Seriously, my dad went downhill after that.

"It was all he thought about, talked about. He used to play golf and poker with that judge. To this day, he has never spoken to him again, meaning the judge. The other golfers and poker players came down on the side of my dad, and that judge resigned from the bench about four months ago. Maybe you saw it in the papers."

"No," both women said in unison.

"The thing is, the judge was correct in his ruling. He went by the law, but sometimes you have to bend the law. At least that's how I see it, especially when a child is involved, and a special child like Ben to boot. My dad tried to console Eleanor, tried to get her fired up to take up the cause of grandparents. For whatever her reasons, it didn't happen."

When they reached their respective vehicles, Peter Jr. laughed as he pointed to his minivan. "Hey, it runs. It's great for taking nine Little Leaguers here and there and six hopeful ballerinas all over hell and creation."

"As long as it runs and gets you from point A to point B, that's all that matters," Isabelle said, opening the door of her Audi and climbing behind the wheel. "I know where the Coastal Center is, so if you lose us at a traffic light, we'll meet you there," Isabelle said as her phone vibrated in her pocket for the *third* time. Whoever was calling her was certainly persistent. She handed the phone to Nikki and asked her to check to see if she had any messages.

"No messages, and the number comes up as restricted. They'll call back, they always do. Whatever did we do before we had cell phones?"

"It was another way of life. So what do you think, Nik?"

"I think Peter Senior is going to help us. As much as he can. Will he break the law and betray that attorney-client privilege? I think so. It's just a gut feeling. You?"

"I think so, too. Peter Junior seems like a nice guy. He cares about his dad, so that says a lot about Peter Senior when his son cares for him. That's my opinion."

"I agree. Hey, your phone is vibrating. You want me to take the call?"

"Sure."

Nikki clicked on the phone and listened. "This is Nikki, Isabelle's friend. She's driving. She said to tell me whatever it is you're calling about." Nikki listened, her eyes popping wide. "Of course I'll tell her. Is he going to call back? Okay, okay, if he does, tell him to call Isabelle's number again. Someone will answer it this time."

"What? Did something happen to Abner, to the boys? What?"

"No, no. It's Ben. He's the one who called you. Then he called your office and said he ran away because he's in danger. He said he didn't go to school today. He said he's at number three, and you would know where that is. He also said he didn't know how long he could stay there. Where's number three, Isabelle?"

"That's it! That's it! What the hell is number three? Why didn't he leave a number? Oh, my God, that kid is on the loose, and if he thinks he's in danger, then he is. He's only eight years old, Nikki. Eight! Oh, God, what does it mean? I have no clue what number three is," Isabelle wailed.

Nikki was as agitated as Isabelle but had no answers. "We're here. We need to make this short and sweet. I'll do the talking and you *think*. If Ben thinks you know what number three means, then you do know. So start thinking. Okay?"

Isabelle nodded as she climbed out of the car to follow

Peter Jr. into the Coastal Center, her thoughts all over the map.

Meeting Peter Olsen Sr. for the first time sent shock waves through both women. He was in a world of pain, and it was evident to his son, also, who started to fuss over him. Senior waved him off. "I'm okay, Junior. They just gave me a shot, and it will kick in in a few minutes. Talk fast before I fall asleep."

Nikki went right into her spiel as Isabelle kneaded her hands and fidgeted in her seat. She heard everything everyone was saying, she even understood it, but her thoughts were with Ben and what "number three" meant.

"Sign this retainer. A dollar will cement the deal," Peter Junior said, pulling a single sheet of paper out of his briefcase. Both women signed the retainer and handed over two one-dollar bills.

Satisfied, Senior said, "Ellie checks in once a week, never the same day or the same time. I don't have a number for her. If I did, I'd gladly give it to you. She wanted it this way. She said it was for my own protection, so I wouldn't have to lie for her. I agreed. When I realized that we were fighting a lost cause, I put Ellie in touch with some . . . ah . . . financial people who helped her. Eleanor Lymen, at this point in time, is a pauper. Rita and Irene, her two best friends, more like sisters, actually, were wealthy in their own right and are now doubly wealthy. Young Ben is the beneficiary of all that wealth. Originally, Diana was the beneficiary, but when she was killed, we changed everything over to Ben.

"The firm at the time hired private detectives to watch over Ben. But after three months with no changes in the routine, we canceled them. I didn't see any sense in throwing good money after bad. Ellie was a little upset, but the agency didn't want to renew the contract we had with them. Young Ben is on his own, so to speak."

"Not really, Pop. Ben found Ms. Flanders, and they struck up a friendship. He asked her to help him find his grandmother. I think things have gone south in the Ryan household because the money stopped flowing. It's that simple. What's your plan, or haven't you developed one yet?"

Seeing Senior's eyes start to droop, Isabelle rushed to explain about the morning calls from Ben. "We're going to snatch him. Take him somewhere safe. You okay with that?" she asked, steel ringing in her voice.

"Hell, yes, missy," Senior barked. Junior nodded.

"First we have to figure out what 'number three' means," Nikki said.

Senior clucked his tongue. "Number three is Rita's house. It was the third one finished if you recall, Ms. Flanders."

"Oh, my God, you are so right! Eleanor had a champagne party that day, and we cracked a bottle over the light post at the end of the driveway. We have to leave right now," she said, jumping up, with Nikki right behind her. "Save that boy, ladies," Senior said, slurring his words. Junior just nodded.

Outside, in the brisk autumn air, the two sisters looked at each other. "That went better than I expected," Nikki said. "If the cops get around to talking to them, they won't give up anything. I'd bet my license on it."

"Me too," Isabelle said as she stared at her car. "This is going to be tricky, Nikki. The front of every house on the Circle can be seen clear as day from the front windows of the Institute by people who are on a break. Ben told me that people, mainly the instructors, like to stare out the windows at the Circle because it's so pretty. We need to be preemptive here. I can get us in the walk-through gate since I have a key. But when we leave, there will be three of us, not two. Someone is bound to see us.

"However, I could walk through the gate, go around,

and open the drive-through gate, and you can drive through on the ring road, we pick up Ben, and drive out. The problem with that is, our license plate will be visible to anyone watching. Any ideas?" Isabelle asked.

Nikki's eyes sparked at the challenge. "Is that a hoodie in the backseat?"

"Yes. I keep it in the car in case I'm on-site and it rains. Why?"

"Put it on, keep your head down, walk through the gate, open the drive-through gate, I pick you up, and we drive to Rita's house. Listen to this, I just had a brilliant idea. I know how to alter your license plate for the trip out."

"What? What?"

"Do you have any eyeliner with you?"

"Of course. Why do you ask?"

"Your license plate has three numerals on it. There's a one, a three, and another one. Or it might be an I, not sure. We make the ones into fours and the three into an eight. Am I a genius or what?"

Isabelle laughed. "Five more minutes, and we'll be there. I wonder how he got into the house. He told me he didn't have keys to those two houses, just his grandmother's key in the birdhouse.

"Best guess is he broke a cellar window and crawled in that way. He wouldn't risk the front door. There is probably an alarm of some kind, so he'd be afraid to set it off. Therefore, the only other option would be the cellar. Usually, those windows are pretty small, but a little kid could wiggle through. It's a thought, Isabelle, nothing more."

"Ben is a very resourceful kid. He might only be eight, but he seems more like eighty sometimes. He's a college student. And yet he's still a little boy. Okay, we're here. Let's do it!"

Isabelle parked a half block from the Circle. She got out and donned the hoodie while Nikki climbed behind the

wheel. "I'll walk the rest of the way. Give me five full minutes, and by the time you get there, just drive through like
a bat out of hell, the gate will close right behind you, so
don't let up on the gas. Go left, and Rita's is the first
house. I'll meet you there."

It all went just the way Isabelle said it would. Nikki
floored the gas, whizzed through the open gates, and made
the left turn on two wheels. She broke out in a cold sweat
the minute she brought the car to a full stop behind Rita
Dolan's house. She climbed out on shaky legs. Isabelle
hugged her. Nikki noticed that Isabelle was shaking as
badly as she was.

"Now what?" Nikki asked.

"It's a given we can't go around to the front. Let's try
the back door. We can bang on it, or if there's a doorbell,
ring it. We can't yell or shout, someone might hear us. If
that doesn't produce any results, we'll start thinking about
the cellar."

As plans went, it was the best they could do.

Inside Rita Dolan's house, Ben heard the sound of a car
engine. His heart kicked up several beats when he heard
the engine cut off. He ran to the pantry and climbed up on
a stool so he could see out the window. His fist shot high
in the air, and he was off the stool and running to the back
door. He was so excited he could hardly breathe. He blew
a kiss to Isabelle, who grinned from ear to ear.

"I can't go out through the doors," he yelled. "The alarm
is on. The alarm company records the times of entries and
exits. Did you hear me?" Isabelle nodded.

"I got in through the cellar. I'll have to leave that way.
Go around to the side and you'll see the window. It's up
high, so I don't know how I'm going to get out."

"Just go there now, we'll figure something out. Careful,
Ben."

"I'm always careful, Izzy. Thanks for coming. I was

starting to get scared, but I knew in my heart that you'd come."

Nikki squeezed Isabelle's arm to show she was feeling the same thing she was. A kid in need, and here they were to the rescue.

Nikki and Isabelle made their way around the house. They walked bent over to peer through the dense shrubbery that hugged the foundation. "There it is. I almost didn't see it," Isabelle squealed.

The sisters plowed through the prickly bushes until they reached the small window. She called out to Ben.

"I'm here," he replied. "I have to find something to put under the window. I tried jumping, but I can't jump that high."

"Everyone has a ladder of some kind. It might be hanging on a hook on the wall. Look around and tell me what you see."

Ben whipped his Maglite about. "I can't see anything because there isn't anything to see. This looks like a brand-new cellar would. Connor's basement is so full of junk, you have to step on top of stuff to get to the other side. Ooooh, wait, there is a ladder, but it's not big. Only four steps. Five if you count the top."

"Can you carry it, Ben?" Isabelle asked anxiously.

"No, but I can drag it. I can do it. No, that was wrong. I *will* do it. You always have to be positive."

The women listened as the little boy dragged the ladder across the concrete basement floor. It was an ear-grating sound. Ben was huffing and puffing, but he finally made it to the window with the ladder. He struggled to take deep breaths. Safety was just minutes away.

"Can you get the ladder upright or is it too heavy?" Isabelle called down.

"I think I can do it."

Isabelle and Nikki shouted encouragement as the little boy struggled with all his might to get the ladder in an upright position. "I did it! I did it!"

"Good. Now spread it open and climb up. Be careful. When you get to the top, we'll pull you through. Is the ladder shaky?"

"Yes, it is."

"Okay, then put both feet on each step. Hold on to the sides. We can barely see you. I'm going to lean down as far as I can, and Nikki will hold on to my belt, so I don't fall. When you see my hands, stretch yours out, and I'll pull you the rest of the way."

Ben swallowed hard as he climbed, doing exactly what Isabelle told him to do. When he saw her arms, he thought he was going to faint. He reached up. No touch had ever felt as good as those two hands gripping his wrists.

"Holy shit!" Ben said as he tumbled to the ground. "Oooh, I'm sorry. I didn't mean to say that. I'm not allowed to use those words. My grandmother used to put soap in my mouth when I forgot. I'm up to a whole bar by now. I won't say it again. I promise."

"It's okay. I felt like saying the same thing myself. I think your grandmother will understand when you 'fess up. You will 'fess up, right?" Isabelle teased.

"Absolutely. As long as I don't forget," Ben said, showing off his gap-toothed smile.

Climbing the ladder again, Ben steadied himself on the top step, then reached once again for Isabelle's outstretched arms. This time he managed not to fall, and Isabelle pulled him through the window onto the ground in back of Rita's house.

"Ben, this is Nikki Quinn; she's one of my best friends. She's going to help us find your grandmother."

"Pleased to meet you. Am I allowed to call you Nikki?

That's a nickname, right? Only friends call each other by their nicknames."

"Yes, you can call me Nikki. I hope you will consider me a friend," Nikki said.

"I do. I do. I just like to make sure so I don't make a mistake. Sometimes one can take liberties. I haven't been able to master the differences. You know, like when it's okay to tell a little white lie, so no one's feelings get hurt. That kind of thing."

He's only eight years old, Isabelle reminded herself.

"That's all for another day. We need to get out of here, and the sooner the better. But first Nikki and I have to do something to make sure our getaway is clean."

Ben watched as Nikki changed the numbers on Isabelle's license plate with the aid of her mascara brush. His jaw dropped, and his eyes popped wide. "I get it," he chortled. "You changed it so when you drive through the gate, anyone watching from the Institute will see the license plate and possibly write it down to give to the police when they come here looking for me. That is very clever, Nikki. I can't say I would ever have come up with that idea. It's pure genius."

Nikki laughed. "And here I am, just a plain old lawyer breaking the law. Doncha just love it?"

Ben laughed, showing that gap-toothed smile that rivaled the sun. "I don't think I ever had so much fun doing things I'm not supposed to do with people who are doing the same thing." He was still giggling when he climbed into the car and automatically dropped to the floor, without having to be told.

Safe and sound. He was finally safe and sound. Three of the best words in the English language. He said them again and again as he grinned from ear to ear. He'd outwitted Connor and Natalie. He'd actually done it, and now he was safe and sound.

Isabelle took one last look at the shrubbery to make sure the window was once again fully covered. It was impossible to see unless you stood right in front of it, and even then, it looked like a whole branch was growing right out of the window. Design was everything.

Their exit from the Circle was as flawless as their entry. Once they hit the highway, Isabelle told Ben he could get up and to buckle up.

"Where are we going?" Ben asked.

"First, we're going to my house to switch out vehicles. Then we're going to Pinewood, where the rest of my friends are waiting for us to bring you to them."

"Do you think there will be any food there?"

"Count on it. What would you like?"

"Well, if I have a choice, I'd pick spaghetti and meat-balls."

"Done!" Nikki said, sending off a text to Myra. She finished with, *Our ETA is 1 hour.*

Ben wanted to talk to explain the circumstances, but Isabelle told him to wait till they got to the farm, so everyone could hear at the same time. The rest of the conversation concerned Lady and her pups and how they loved kids.

When Isabelle pulled into the driveway, Ben hopped out. "Izzy, you live in a pickle factory!"

"Uh-huh. I'll show you around some other time. We just came here to switch out vehicles. We're going to take my husband's truck and park this one in its place."

"I never rode in a truck before. That sure does look big. Must have a lot of horsepower under that hood."

He's only eight, Isabelle reminded herself once again. "Yep. It just eats up the road. We'll be at Pinewood before you know it."

Ben climbed into the back, muttering about how cool it

was. When the garage door closed behind him, Isabelle heard him murmur, "A pickle factory. Who knew?" She smiled to herself, then she offered up a silent little prayer of thanks that things had gone as well as could be expected under the circumstances.

Chapter 7

It started to rain ten minutes into the drive out to Pinewood. The sisters and Ben made small talk about the long drive, the farm, and what Ben could expect once they arrived. Nikki told him about Myra's service dog, Lady, and her four pups, about Annie, who lived down the road on another farm, and how she herself lived across the field in still another farmhouse just a hop, skip, and a jump from Myra, who was her adopted mother. "In the winter, with snow on the ground, we use snowmobiles to visit Myra. In the summer, we use a dune buggy or a golf cart, providing the ground isn't too wet. Sometimes we even walk across the field just for the exercise."

All Ben needed to hear were the words "adopted mother" and he was full of questions. Nikki explained her situation and was stunned when Ben said, "You sure are one of the lucky ones." He then proceeded to tell them stories about his stepmother, Natalie, that horrified both women.

"Let's not talk about Natalie anymore, Ben. We're going to take care of Natalie, believe me, so don't give her another thought. By the way, I bought you some things. They're in the bag next to you on the backseat."

The two women listened to the rustle of the bag and the tissue paper, then the boy's exclamation of, "Holy cow! A real watch! A Mickey Mouse watch! I never had a watch before. I love it, Izzy. Thank you, thank you," he said, fastening the watch on his thin wrist. "It fits!" he bellowed. Isabelle laughed out loud.

"A real cell phone! I don't believe it! I bought a burner phone last night at Rite Aid. That's how I called you. What kind of phone is this?"

"I bought it before I knew you took it on the lam, Ben. I was going to give it to you tomorrow. See that star at the bottom? If you press the star, help will come to you right away no matter where you are. For God's sake, don't press it unless you're in danger. Read the manual so you understand how it works. I already programmed my number into the directory, along with all my friends' numbers. The people you're going to meet at the farm. You can ditch the burner phone or keep it in reserve, that's up to you."

"A whistle! I never had a whistle. What's it for?" He blew it, his head jerking back at the sound. Isabelle and Nikki almost jumped out of their skin at the high-pitched squeal of sound.

"Double help. If you think you're in trouble, you blow the whistle, then press the star on the phone. I told you, I gotcha covered, little guy."

"This is absolutely amazing!" Ben said, admiring the watch on his wrist. He hung the whistle around his neck but tucked it under his tee shirt.

Isabelle risked a glance in the rearview window to see her new best friend skimming through the phone booklet. "Okay, I got it! Perfect! Just perfect!" He chortled gleefully a few minutes later.

"Seriously, Ben? You just skimmed that booklet!"

"Izzy! Izzy! I think you're forgetting who you're talking to. Do you want me to recite, and I can, verbatim, how to use this phone called a Jitterbug?"

He's only eight years old. Not eight going on nine. He

just turned eight two weeks ago. "I'm just a mere mortal, Ben. Forgive me, sometimes I forget. No, no need to recite the instructions. I trust you."

"Okay then. I sure do like this watch. I think this is the best present I ever got."

Nikki poked Isabelle in the thigh. Isabelle looked over to see the moistness in Nikki's eyes. Her own eyes felt a little prickly.

"I think the rain is setting in for the rest of the day. It's coming down pretty heavy right now. I hope the road doesn't flood, but if it does, this truck sits up high, so we're good," Isabelle said, just to have something to say. She hoped her worry didn't show, especially to young Ben.

"How much farther is it?" Ben asked as he waved his arm every which way so he could admire his new watch.

"About ten more miles, but it's going to take us a while longer with this torrential rain and the heavy traffic."

"If you were at the Institute, how would you get home in this weather, Ben?" Nikki asked.

"Nice days, I take my bike. Other days, I walk. It's not that far. It takes me twenty minutes. But to answer your question, I'd probably wait it out."

"What about the days when it's raining early in the morning?" Nikki asked, an edge in her voice.

"I have a rain slicker and boots," Ben responded, still admiring the watch on his wrist from yet another angle.

"Doesn't your stepfather or Natalie ever drive you?"

"Are you kidding me! Natalie doesn't get up till lunchtime. Sometimes, if Connor doesn't have work, he sleeps till four."

Nikki's mouth stretched to an angry straight line. She made a mental note to be sure that when they meted out their particular brand of justice, this neglect would be at the top of the list of sins to be punished.

The rest of the trip to Pinewood was made in virtual silence, all the occupants busy with their own thoughts.

The rain continued to beat down in torrents as the windshield wipers fought the avalanche of water cascading down the windshield, making visibility almost nil.

Isabelle almost missed the turnoff to the farm. She saw the red caution reflectors on the signpost just in time. She put on her signal light and barreled ahead. Then she stopped once she was clear of traffic and on the road leading to the farmhouse. "That has to be the hairiest, scariest drive I've ever had in my whole entire life. I need a couple of minutes to calm down. I can make the rest of this drive with my eyes closed, but right now, I just need to . . . to take deep breaths. Thank God for this truck!"

Nikki appeared to be as shaken as Isabelle. Not so Ben in the backseat, who was oblivious to the weather conditions because he was still marveling over his new watch and phone. He jolted forward when Isabelle stopped the truck. "Are we at our destination?"

"In a manner of speaking. It's just a mile or so up the road. I thought I would stop for a few minutes to see if the rain lets up a bit. It's hard to see right now," Isabelle said in a shaky voice.

"It should let up in about eleven minutes," Ben said as he continued to wave his arm about in order to admire his brand-new watch.

Nikki turned around, and asked, "How do you know that, Ben?"

"It's complicated. I can go into detail, but I'm not sure if you want to listen to statistics. It started to rain normally approximately ninety minutes ago before it intensified. Trust me," he said, peering out the window. "Ten more minutes, Izzy, and you can start to drive to our destination."

In spite of herself, Nikki looked at her own watch to check the time. "Ah, that's okay, we'll take your word for it."

"You do realize that meteorologists are only accurate half the time, right? And did you know there is a weatherman in Florida whose real name is Al Sunshine? It's true. I realize that's trivia, but knowledge is power."

He's only eight years old, Isabelle thought for the umpteenth time.

"Truer words were never spoken," was the best Nikki could come up with. Her eyes were glued to her watch, as were Isabelle's. Time moved at a snail's space as the minutes ticked by, and the torrential rain continued to pound away on the truck's roof.

With one minute to go, Isabelle looked at Nikki, whose jaw was dropping. The thunder on the roof had lessened to a patter, then it was almost totally silent.

"Told you!" piped up a voice from the backseat. "Now you can drive, Izzy, visibility is very good. You better hurry, though, another trough will be coming through in approximately thirteen minutes. This is just a lull. If I were you, I would put the pedal to the metal and get us to where we're going or we might wash away in a flood."

Isabelle didn't bother to respond; she put the pedal to the metal as instructed and tore down the long, winding road. She cleared the gate at breakneck speed, thankful that Myra, with Lady's warning, had opened the gate. She parked, and yelled, "Run for it, here comes the rain."

The sisters were all clustered in the kitchen, holding out towels, while Lady and her pups barked a greeting and welcomed the newcomer, who was so overcome that he froze on the spot, his eyes full of panic.

"Easy, little guy, everyone is a friend here. The dogs are welcoming you. Relax. Slow, easy breaths, Ben. You're safe and sound here. Trust us, okay?"

Ben nodded.

"First things first. Dry clothes for everyone. We'll dry Ben's clothes while you all run upstairs and change. Nikki, find a shirt or something of Jack's that he keeps here for times he has to stay over for Ben until his things are dry."

Nikki ushered Ben toward the back kitchen staircase, the dogs bounding ahead of them. Ten minutes later, they were all back in the kitchen, where everyone seemed to be doing something.

Braver now that he hadn't been eaten alive by the dogs, Ben said, "It smells really good in here."

"Spaghetti," Annie said. "Isabelle said that's what you requested. So that's what you're going to get. We'll eat in the dining room since there are too many of us to fit around the kitchen table."

"Two large blossoms of chopped basil, seven cloves of minced garlic, one medium onion diced, one full cup of grated Parmesan cheese, and a fistful of parsley added to the sauce. Did I get it right?" Ben asked anxiously as he continued to sniff at the delectable aromas in the kitchen.

The sisters stopped and gaped at the little boy. "How . . . how do you know that?" Kathryn asked.

"I watch *Iron Chef* and the other cooking shows. That's supposed to be the perfect spaghetti recipe. Was I right?" He twinkled, showing his gap-toothed smile.

"Spot on!" Annie laughed.

Braver still, Ben asked if they used two full cups of grated cheese in the meatballs with another four cloves of minced garlic. "Ground chuck is the best and most flavorful of all the ground meats, but you probably already know that. I can't wait to taste it."

"Spot on again," Annie said. She had no idea if the boy was right or not since she had ordered the spaghetti from Angelo's Italian Ristorante.

"I think it's time for introductions now," Isabelle said, as Ben manfully held out his hand for a handshake.

"We don't shake hands here, we hug," Alexis said as she wrapped her arms around the skinny little boy. The sisters took turns hugging the happy little boy, with the dogs yipping and yapping the whole time.

"Time to eat!" Maggie said as she busied herself at the stove. "Yoko and I will bring it in. Kathryn, you handle the garlic bread."

"Ben, what would you like to drink?" Myra asked.

"Milk if you have it, ma'am," he responded.

Myra held up her hands, palms outward. "Stop right there! My name is Myra. None of us want to be called 'ma'am.' We're informal here. We're a family, and that means we're all equal. Okay?"

"Yes, I am personally okay with that information. I like informal situations. I was just speaking the way my grandmother taught me. Adults, she said, were either ma'am or sir. I didn't want to make a mistake and have you think I had no manners."

Maggie carried the oversize tureen full to the brim with spaghetti and meatballs. Two long-handled forks were stuck in the middle. Behind her, Kathryn carried a platter filled high with fragrant garlic bread. Ben literally swooned at what he was seeing and smelling.

Thirty minutes later, there was very little spaghetti left in the bottom of the tureen. All the garlic bread was gone.

"Sorry, there's no dessert today. We didn't have the time to prepare anything," Annie said by way of apology.

"I couldn't eat it if there was," Ben said. "I think that was the best spaghetti I've ever eaten in my whole life. You should market your recipe, Annie."

Annie laughed. She looked across at Ben and said, "I cheated. We didn't have time to cook spaghetti sauce, so we ordered it and doctored it up a little, so none of us can take credit for it."

Ben laughed, a deep belly laugh that made the others laugh right along with him. At that moment in time, every woman in the room fell totally in love with the curly-haired little boy.

"Cleanup time!" Nikki said. "No, not you, Ben. You're our guest."

Thirteen minutes later, the kitchen was cleaned and everything in its place. The only sign that they'd eaten spaghetti was the aroma lingering in the air.

There was a small amount of confusion as everyone headed for the dining room, where the sisters took their seats. Isabelle pulled out a chair next to her for Ben. He scooted up and sat up straight, his backpack on the floor at his feet. He looked around and waited. He felt tense until he felt Isabelle's hand on his arm. He looked over at her and smiled. He was in good hands, he was sure of it.

Myra called the impromptu meeting to order. "Isabelle told us what she knows, which isn't all that much. We know nothing about what transpired in your young life from the time she saw you last, and that was three days ago. We need you to bring us up to date. Can you do that?"

Ben nodded. "Yes. Are you the leader of this club?"

Myra smiled. "No, Ben, I'm not the leader. We don't have a leader. We're all equal here. What that means is, we vote on everything. No one has more authority than any-one else in this group. I'm not sure we're a club. We prefer to think of ourselves as fixers. We try to fix things for peo-ple who have been wronged. If you have any questions, this would be a good time for you to ask them."

"Do any of you ladies," he asked, looking around, "know my grandmother?"

"No, Ben, none of us, with the exception of Isabelle,

knows your grandmother or her friends Rita and Irene. We didn't know your mother, either. We are strangers to everyone involved in this situation. You have to tell us everything, so we can help you. Unless you decide to change your mind," Annie said.

"Do you think you can find my grandmother?"

Maggie leaned forward. "We think so, Ben. We need you to tell us everything you know, even if you think it isn't important. You never know what will tip the scales in that direction."

"Ben, think of our minds as a blank slate, and we're waiting to chalk-mark our first entry. What that is has to come from you," Isabelle said quietly.

"I don't remember my mother. I don't know who my father is. My grandmother said when I was older, she would talk to me about . . . about all of that. After I was born, I lived with my grandmother until my mother married Connor Ryan because, until that happened, my mother didn't or couldn't take care of me. Grandma said motherhood wasn't in her DNA. I have a lot of pictures of her. She was very pretty. I think I know what my grandmother meant when she said motherhood wasn't in her DNA. Grandma has a painting of her hanging over the mantel. Artists say the eyes are the mirrors of the soul. The person who painted the picture either didn't capture that or what he painted was all there was to see. My mother's eyes were blank; they didn't register anything. I spent a lot of time standing on a stool so I could look up at the picture.

"One time, I heard Rita talking to Irene about my mother's being *challenged*. I know what that means. But no one would talk to me about it, so I had to figure it out myself. Then, when I was four and went to live with Connor and Natalie, I would hear *them* talking about my mother. Natalie said my mother was so smart that she was stupid. Then Connor would say things, gross things that made me want to cry. The only reason Connor adopted me was so my mother would marry him, and he would get her money. I guess she had lots of money, but I don't know that for sure."

"Do you know where and how your mother met Connor?" Nikki asked.

"I asked Connor once, and he said he met my mother at a show he was giving to attract new business. She asked him to make her a unicorn. He did, and he said she loved it. I never saw it. Then he said she pursued him, and eventually, they got married. That's all I know."

"So what happened after I saw you on Friday, Ben?" Isabelle asked.

"I went back to my grandmother's house and let myself in. The first time I went, months ago, I wanted to see if my grandmother had left me a clue or a sign that she would know I would understand. I started to cry, so I left. I never went back until Saturday. I made up my mind that I was going to stay till I found something. And I did find something, in Freddie. I feel really stupid that I didn't find it the first time. Freddie is a big teddy bear with an opening in the back to keep your pajamas in. I picked it off the shelf and knew right away that's where Grandma put whatever she wanted me to find. I took everything out and stuck it in my pants and went home to look at it. She . . . she . . . wrote me a letter," Ben said in a choked voice. He bent down and fished around inside his backpack and pulled out the letter. He handed it to Isabelle, who read it, then passed it around the table until Myra read it and handed it back to Ben.

"I felt so bad that I didn't find it the first time. I knew that Grandma wouldn't leave me at the mercy of Connor if she thought I wasn't going to be safe." He carefully folded the letter and returned it to his backpack. His eyes were bright with unshed tears.

"What else was in the bear?" Kathryn asked.

"A lot of credit cards. Money. Deeds. Stuff. I kept one credit card and four of the hundred-dollar bills. I hid them in my shoe in the closet. No one ever goes in my room. At least that I know of. But I got nervous, so I took everything but the four hundred dollars and the card back and put them all back in Freddie."

"Isabelle took us all there yesterday, and we found it. The contents are safe with us now," Annie said gently. "You don't have to worry about it from here on in." The relief on the little boy's face was so palpable, Annie wanted to get up and hug him. She smiled when she saw Isabelle put her arm around his bony shoulders.

"Then what happened?" Yoko asked.

"Then Natalie and Connor had a big fight, and Natalie packed up and left. I was *soooo* happy! I think Connor was happy, too, because he changed the locks on the doors. On Sunday, Connor went out in the afternoon. He never goes anywhere on a Sunday afternoon. With both of them out of the house, I took a chance and did everything I was not supposed to do. I knew the minute I saw Natalie's hair on the dresser that she was coming back."

"I think you need to explain that, Ben," Maggie said.

"Her hair! She left it behind in her room. It was right there on the dresser. Six long pieces of hair. Connor said there was nothing real about her. Phony hair, contact lenses, nose job, lip injections, boob job, acrylic fingernails and toenails. He was always taunting her about it, especially when she wanted money. They might be married legally, but it's a sham marriage. It's like one of those marriages where a rich foreigner wants to become a US citizen and he marries an American. They have a business arrangement in order to get my mother's money."

"How do you know all this?" Alexis asked.

"It's not like I eavesdrop. All the two of them do is

scream and yell at each other. I can't help but overhear, and they didn't seem to care if I heard or not."

"Then what happened?" Isabelle asked.

"When Connor left, like I said, I started to look everywhere that was off-limits to me. I wasn't allowed in the study, so I went there after I checked out the master bedroom. As far as I can tell, the master bedroom is really her bedroom. Connor sleeps in the guest bedroom. Natalie must have six hundred pairs of shoes. For sure she'd never leave those behind. Or her hair. I didn't find anything else in the room. There were none of Connor's clothes.

"I went to the study because I wanted to see if I could find out how much money the lawyers paid Connor every month as child support. Connor told Natalie the money stopped coming three months ago, and they were broke. I found the records. He got twelve thousand dollars a month for me. All of the utilities are about to be turned off for nonpayment. There were bills that totaled close to two hundred thousand dollars that were overdue.

"Oh, and prior to that I asked Connor for money, and he gave me a hundred dollars. When he returned later, I told him I needed new clothes, and if he didn't come through, I was going to tell them at the Institute. Then I ordered a pizza, an antipasto, which is still in the refrigerator, and some soda pop. When it came, I forgot to lock the front door because my hands were full. That was before I went where I wasn't supposed to go.

"I was just getting ready to leave the study when the front door opened, and I heard Natalie call Connor's name. When you open any of the doors in the house, this thing on the door says, 'Front door opening' or 'Kitchen door opening.' She's not very observant, or she would have noticed that Connor's car was gone. Actually, the car is my mother's car. Anyway, I could hear her getting madder by the minute. I hid behind the sofa and prayed she wouldn't find me. She didn't. The minute she went upstairs, I ran to the laundry room, where I was drying the clothes that I had washed. I figured if she found me there, it would be okay."

"You do your own laundry?" Nikki asked.

"I'm quite good at it. I usually separate the whites from the colors, but yesterday I just threw it all in together. I was nervous.

"Then Connor came back, and the two of them went at it all over again. It was all about the money. That's when Natalie said they had to take drastic measures. She said Connor promised her the moon and the stars if she would marry him so he could get full custody of me and all of my mother's money. It was a business arrangement. Connor kept saying there was nothing he could do, that my grandmother had gotten rid of all of her money. And that's when Natalie said they needed to get rid of me. Connor balked, but she said he was a *wuss* and she'd do it herself. They were planning on killing me. I didn't know what to do, so I stayed in the laundry room until Natalie went back upstairs. I came out of the laundry room just as Connor walked into the kitchen. I think I gave a stellar performance. I pointed to the dryer and said I was waiting for it to go off. He had Chinese food. I think he believed me and didn't think I heard them. Thinking that the best defense is a good offense, that's when I told Connor that I needed new clothes."

Myra gasped. "What did you do after that?"

"I went upstairs and sat down to think. I knew I had to leave. I figured I'd wait till it was really dark and go to the Circle. I picked Rita's house. But first I went to Rite Aid and bought a burner phone, a Maglite, and a quart of milk. I left around ten-thirty. I had to take the gizmo off the door, so it wouldn't talk when I opened it. I know how to turn off the alarm. I only took a few clothes, the credit card, the money, and the reports. I went right to Rita's house, broke the window in the cellar, and climbed through. I stayed there all night until this morning, when I tried calling Isabelle."

"Whoa, whoa, whoa, what reports?" Maggie asked.

Ben giggled. "I went online and found one of those search and find out anything about anyone Web sites for twenty-nine ninety-five. I could have signed up for the deluxe package for fifty-nine ninety-five, but I didn't. I have them right here. One for Natalie, one for Connor, and one for Isabelle."

Isabelle's jaw dropped. "You little stinker! You actually ran a check on me?"

Ben turned in his chair and looked Isabelle in the eye. "If you were in my shoes, you would have done the same thing. We did meet strangely. For all I know, you could have been cultivating me. Besides, you know what President Reagan said, don't you?"

"No, what did President Reagan say?" Isabelle snapped.

Ben smiled. "He said, 'Trust but verify.' "

The sisters hooted with laughter. "Okay, you got me on that one," Isabelle said. "How'd I come out?"

"Double vanilla. Connor was plain vanilla. Natalie was rocky road. Here," he said, rummaging again in his backpack for the reports. "There's not all that much there. Maybe I should have gone for the deluxe fifty-nine ninety-five package. The reports are not up to date, either, so I probably made the right choice."

The sisters perused the reports but made no comments. Annie took the lead. "Then what happened?"

"I tried calling Isabelle, but it kept going to voice mail. Then I called her office, and finally, we connected. I told her where I was and we made a plan to get me here and here I am. Oh, I called the Institute before seven this morning to tell them I had either a twenty-four-, forty-eight-, or seventy-two-hour virus and wouldn't be in today to collect my new assignments and most likely not tomorrow, either. I figured we would need that much time to make a plan."

All the sisters leaned forward. Kathryn took the lead. "But, Ben, what happens when you don't return from school today?"

"I don't know for sure. They won't realize I'm gone till it starts to get dark. Or they might just assume I'm up in my room. I think they might panic at first, then Natalie will come up with something that will calm Connor down. By the way, she recorded and played a recording she made on her phone of the deal she made with Connor to get control of me and my mother's money. I heard it all. Connor was livid. But in the end, he always does what she tells him to do."

"Will they go to the police?" Kathryn persisted.

"I don't think so. They will probably call the Institute, then the cat is out of the bag. They will see that my bike is still there, so they will know that I couldn't have gone far. They will assume, and this is just my opinion, that I went to the Circle, so they'll go to the Circle and break into the three houses to see if I'm in one of them. They won't want to call attention to the fact that I've gone missing. Natalie had a plan to go to their lawyers and demand money, either today or tomorrow."

"I think we've got it down pat," Annie said. "I have an idea, so why don't you go into the family room with the dogs and get acquainted with them. They love to play, and they really love to have their bellies rubbed. There's a nice fire going, and they like to nap there. Can you see yourself doing that, Ben?"

"Oh yes, ma—Annie, I can." He was off his chair and headed for the door, Lady and her pups yipping and yapping as they shooed him ahead.

"He's only eight years old," Isabelle whispered loud enough so the others could hear.

"I know, dear. But he's safe now. That's all that matters at this moment in time," Myra said.

"We forgot to ask him if he had any idea where his grandmother and her friends might have gone," Yoko said fretfully.

"I think I know," Annie said quietly, so quietly the others had to lean forward to hear what she had to say. "The letter she wrote to Ben. Think about it. She said she did something terrible, and she had to make it right, and she was the only one who could do that. I think, and it's just my opinion, that she had something to do with her daughter's friend, Ben's father, leaving before Ben was born. I've been sitting here thinking and thinking, and nothing else makes sense to me. Eleanor Lymen and her friends are looking for Ben's biological father. I would also bet my tiara that whoever he is, he has no idea that he has a son."

The sisters looked at Annie with wide eyes as they processed all that she had just said about why Eleanor had left.

"Speaking strictly for myself, I think you are dead right, Annie," Myra said.

"How are we going to help? We don't even know his name," Yoko said.

"Someone has to know his name. Maybe someone at the Institute knows."

"But Diana didn't want to have anything to do with the Institute. How likely is it that someone there would know?" Kathryn asked.

"Maybe we should call Avery Snowden to help us out, or has he been commissioned by the boys? Does anyone know?"

No one knew.

"It's a place to start, so let's call him," Myra said.

Chapter 8

It was a diner just like any other diner the world over. A huge, colorful sign high above the eatery proclaimed in bright neon that it was DAVE'S DINER. Underneath the owner's name in smaller letters it read, BEST EATS IN THE STATE OF MISSISSIPPI.

The interior was also just like every other diner. There were bright red vinyl booths patched up with gray duct tape. And there were condiments on Formica tabletops that were chipped and cracked and full of stains that were impossible to remove.

Dave's Diner was always full to capacity, with a waiting line that stretched outside.

More than one regular, trucker or someone just passing through, said you got a lot of bang for your buck, and the food was homemade and *good*. Plus, Dave only charged for the first cup of coffee; refills were free. Even a refill to take on the road.

Eleanor Lymen and her two best friends, Irene and Rita, waited their turn for a booth. All three women looked tired and weary and badly in need of their first cup of coffee of the day.

A waitress who looked as tired as the three women approached and led them to a booth in the back. She smiled.

"I'm going to turn you over to my replacement because my shift just ended. Enjoy your breakfast, ladies."

Eleanor handed a twenty-dollar bill to the woman. Waitressing was hard work, and the smile she received in exchange for the bill was worth the twenty dollars so early in the morning. To the waitress and to Eleanor.

All three women guzzled their first cup and waited for Irene to refill their cups from the decanter on the table. "Now we can talk," she said.

"Talk now before we eat or after?" Eleanor asked. "Also, today is the day I have to call Peter Olsen. I say we eat first."

"Works for me," Irene and Rita replied agreeably.

Forty-five minutes later, their plates clean of the waffles, sausage, and brown gravy Dave's Diner was known for, the women settled back with fresh cups of coffee while Eleanor called her longtime lawyer for her weekly report on young Ben.

Both women leaned forward to listen more closely. The only problem was that Eleanor was listening and not talking. The look of pure panic on their friend's face told them something troubling had happened.

The call lasted a full ten minutes, with Eleanor jotting down a phone number on a clean paper napkin.

"I . . . I didn't expect . . . I should have . . . I must have been out of my mind to start on this venture, which has gotten us nowhere in close to six months. Peter Senior is still in rehab because his body rejected his second hip replacement. He never told me. Peter Junior answered the phone."

"Will you please get to the point, Ellie," Irene said.

"Ben ran away from home. Isabelle Flanders, the architect who designed our houses, as well as the Circle and the Institute, went to see Peter yesterday. It seems she and Ben struck up an acquaintance, and she has been trying to help him. What Peter Junior told me was that on good-weather days, Isabelle goes to the little park across from the Circle at lunchtime. Ben would ride through the park on his bike, and at first, he would wave, then it was 'hi,' then they started having conversations. Ben was comfortable with her, especially after he found out she knew me, and you two also.

"Mostly they met up on a Tuesday. Ben, as you know, goes to the Institute on Mondays. Anyway, their meetings finally progressed to lunch that Isabelle provided, and Ben opened up to her. Ben asked her if she could help find me. She told him she had friends who were experts in finding people. They were supposed to meet up today."

"Are those . . . those miserable people mistreating Ben?" Rita asked, a catch in her voice.

"Isabelle didn't think so. She told Peter Junior and Senior that she never saw a mark or bruise on him, and he was usually cheerful. But on Sunday, Ben packed up and ran away. Peter Junior didn't find out that part until yesterday. It seems Ben left late at night, bought a burner phone, a flashlight, and a quart of milk at the Rite Aid near his house. I know he stayed the night in one of our houses. He had the foresight to buy milk. We all left staples in our pantries when we left, so he probably thought he could eat cereal. He would feel safe at the Circle. He would consider it a safe haven.

"Flash forward. Yesterday, he finally managed to get hold of Isabelle. Isabelle and her friend Nikki went to the Circle, looking for him. He was staying in your house, Rita. The boy is safe and sound. Right now, that's all that matters. Ben is safe and in Isabelle's care."

Irene looked at Eleanor, who had tears in her eyes. "Don't cry, Ellie, the boy is safe and sound, you just said so. What made him run away in the middle of the night? Did Peter Junior say?"

Ellie tried to clear her throat several times before she could get the words out. "Ben overheard Connor's wife telling Connor that the only way they were going to get Ben's money was to do away with him. Those words mean to me they were planning on killing Ben. That little boy heard that. Because he is as smart as he is, Ben understood what they were saying. Another child his age might not have put two and two together. Can you imagine what Ben must have thought or felt? I will say, he acted quickly."

"Insurance money would go straight to Connor. Diana's money in trust would go to Connor if something happened to Ben. Am I right on that?" Rita asked.

"Right as rain. Connor legally adopted Ben, so he would inherit. Right now, the two of them must seriously be hurting for money since all payments stopped three months ago. After Isabelle and her friends found Ben, Isabelle's friend Nikki called Peter Junior to bring him up to date. She told him that Ben called the Institute first thing yesterday morning to tell them he had either a twenty-four-, forty-eight-, or seventy-two-hour virus and wouldn't be in but that he had completed all of his assigned work and was advancing on his own. That tells me he needed the time to reach Isabelle and get to safety. The Ryans must be pretty lax as to his comings and goings not to notice he was gone," Ellie said, doing her best not to cry.

"We need to pack up and go home," Irene said. And Rita agreed.

Ellie stared at her two best friends in the whole world and nodded.

Irene poured more coffee.

"Isabelle wants me to call her. I think I should. You both know what a lovely person she is, and Ben is in good hands if he's with her. I'm sure she has him somewhere safe. Peter Junior agreed, but he also said I need to get home."

"Call her," Rita and Irene said in unison.

Ellie placed the call, and the moment Isabelle clicked on, her first words were, "Is my grandson okay?"

"Yes, Ellie, he is," Isabelle answered, knowing instantly whom she was speaking with. "He's with friends of mine. Where are you? Why did you leave without telling Ben? He thought you had abandoned him."

"I know, I know. I . . . I left him a letter," Ellie said, her voice tormented.

"I know, but he didn't find it until the other day. When he sneaked into your house right after you left, he said he was crying so hard he left and didn't go to his room. Something like that. He just found the letter on Saturday. Anyway, he has your letter now, and we have the contents of Freddie the bear. Where are you?"

"Outskirts of some place in Mississippi. It's rural. My friends and I have been searching for Ben's father. I have to find him, Isabelle. He doesn't even know about Ben. That's on me, and I've regretted sending him away every hour of the day since I did it. It's a long and complicated story for another time. He's here somewhere in Mississippi, and we're trying to find him. He's a doctor. He travels around in two big buses loaded with medicine, food, water, and blankets and ministers to those in need. And I thought he wasn't good enough for my daughter! What a stupid, foolish old woman I am. I can't go home till I find him. If you assure me Ben is safe, then I need to do this, more for Ben than me. I think we're close to finding him."

"Ben is fine, Ellie. He's in a very good environment for now. Don't wait too long. I'll tell him I spoke to you, but you can call him yourself. I bought him a phone, you know the one that has the 5* to call for help. And a whistle. That was before we found out the Ryans were planning to . . . to . . . harm him." Isabelle rattled off the number of the cell phone, and Ellie scribbled it on the same napkin on which she'd scribbled Isabelle's number.

"Ellie, how do you know where Ben's father is and what he does?"

"Social media. Where else? He has a website, a blog, and a few other things. People get in touch if they need help. He doesn't charge for his services. And we've talked to people whom he has helped, but he's always been one step ahead of us. This is the closest we've come to finding him after six long months of searching."

"Then you need to stay and complete your mission. We'll take care of Ben. Once you call him and talk to him, I think you'll realize he's in good hands."

"But will the boy forgive me for what I've done?"

Isabelle struggled for the right words. "I don't know the answer to that, Ellie. What I do know is, he loves you with all his heart. And he loves Rita and Irene, too. I will tell you this—when he read the letter you left for him, he said that when you do something wrong, and if you make it right, that's all that matters. He said you taught him that."

Ellie started to cry. Irene reached for the phone, identified herself, and gave her Ellie's phone number. "We're going to leave now, we have a seven-hour drive to where we think Ben's father is going next."

"What's his name?" Isabelle asked.

"Jonathan Philbran."

"The Philbrans of Boston?" Isabelle asked, awe ringing in her voice.

"Yes. Of course, when he was in Diana's life, we didn't know that. We assumed, and wrongly so, that he was a grifter preying on Diana. Like Ellie said, it's complicated."

"Uh-huh. Well, I won't say anything about his father to Ben. That's Ellie's job. Good luck."

Irene ended the call and handed the phone back to Ellie, who stuck it in her pocket.

"We should leave right now. We've occupied this table long enough, and the line is still pretty long. Be sure to leave a *big* tip," Rita said.

The kitchen at Pinewood was bustling with activity as breakfast got under way. Ben was loving every minute of it. Rather than stay and get in the way, he volunteered to take the dogs out for a good long run. "I just love these dogs!" He laughed excitedly. "They all slept on my bed last night. They were so warm and cozy. It's a good thing the bed was big. I only had a twin bed at Connor's house," he babbled as he tried tickling each dog behind the ears.

"It's not Connor's house, Ben. It's yours," Isabelle gently corrected him. "The court just allowed him to live there with you till you come of age."

"That is true. Sometimes I forget stuff like that. Thank you for bringing me up short," he said solemnly. Ben turned around and opened the door where the dogs were lined up and waiting patiently. The sisters all ran to the kitchen window when they heard all the whooping, hollering, and barking coming from the backyard.

Annie swallowed hard. "I love seeing what we're seeing. At heart, he is still a little boy. I don't care if he's already in college or that he's some kind of genius. Right now, he's just a little boy doing what little boys do, having fun."

"Amen," the sisters said in unison.

The sisters continued with the preparations for breakfast, which consisted of scrambled eggs, bacon, sausage, and warm biscuits out of a can that only had to be warmed up.

Three different conversations were taking place. Annie explained that Avery Snowden could only offer two days' worth of work because he had to go across the pond to take care of some top-secret work for, as he put it, "you know who."

"Two days is better than nothing, I guess, so I told him

to dig into finding Ben's biological father. I have to call him back now that we have a name. It will make his job a lot easier. I also told him to run a check on Connor's wife. Anything else I think we can handle on our own. And don't forget, we have Ben's twenty-nine ninety-five background checks on Natalie and Connor," Annie quipped.

"Do you want to know something else?" Annie asked, her dander rising. "If someone called me a freak-snot-nosed kid, I'd scratch their eyes out on the spot or shoot them between the eyes. Or maybe I'd peel the skin right off their face."

Nikki grinned. "Why don't you tell us how you *really* feel, Annie?"

Alexis, who was in charge of the scrambled eggs, shifted them onto a platter. Isabelle piled crisp, crunchy bacon on another platter, while Yoko transferred the sausage patties onto a third platter. Myra slid the biscuits into a cloth-lined bread basket.

Kathryn opened the door and let loose with a shrill whistle. One little boy and five dogs raced to the door. "Treats first, then wash your hands and head for the dining room. Ben, do you want milk or orange juice?"

"Milk, please. I sure am hungry. I love bacon," he said, as he handed out treats to the dogs before heading off to the powder room off the kitchen. He stared at himself in the mirror, especially at his unruly hair, which was beginning to look like Maggie's curly locks. His cheeks were bright pink. He smiled at himself. "Someday, you are going to be one handsome dude." He giggled at the thought that someday, girls would be interested in him, and not for his money.

Ben raced to the dining room and sat down next to Isabelle. Annie said grace. He dutifully bowed his head the way his grandmother had taught him.

And then it was time to eat, and eat he did, occasionally

slipping pieces of sausage and bacon to the dogs, who were clustered at his feet.

Breakfast over, the table cleared, the kitchen sparkling, Myra got down to business. "Ben, Isabelle talked to your grandmother this morning. She's going to be calling you sometime today. Isabelle, you spoke to Mrs. Lymen, so you should explain."

Ben bolted upright. "Did you really talk to her, Izzy? What did she say? Where is she? When is she coming home? Are Rita and Irene with her?" he asked, peppering her with questions, his excitement rising with each question.

"Yes, Ben, your grandmother called me this morning. Yesterday, Nikki and I went to see your grandmother's attorney, and he said when your grandmother called in, which she has been doing on a weekly basis, he would give her my number to call me. We lucked out because today was the day she happened to call in."

"What did she say? Did you tell her I just found the letter she left for me? She isn't upset with me, is she?"

"Not one little bit. I think, though, she was relieved that you finally found the letter. She said she thinks about you every hour of the day. She said she knows all of us here in this room will take care of you, but she needs just a bit more time to do what she started out to do. This is just a guess on my part, but I think you'll be seeing your grandmother in a few more days."

"Where is she, and what is she doing that takes six months to do?" Ben asked fretfully.

"Right now, she's in Mississippi. I don't know what she's doing there. I would assume taking care of whatever business needed to be attended to. I'm sure she will tell you when she gets back. That's all I know, Ben."

The sisters watched every emotion there was wash over the little boy's face. Then he grinned from ear to ear. "I think that's the best news I have ever heard. My grand-mother never says anything she doesn't mean. I can wait. I assume you all want to talk and discuss this latest devel-opment without me present, so can I go to the family room with the dogs?"

He's only eight years old, Isabelle told herself for the hundredth time. She nodded. Ben tried to whistle but just made a funny sound until he pulled out the whistle Isabelle had given him. He blew gently; just enough sound came through to alert the dogs. All five got up and followed him out of the room.

"That has to be the most endearing child I've ever met. I just want to hug and squeeze him," Kathryn said. The others agreed that they were having the same feeling.

"I had the early news on this morning to see if the Ryans had reported Ben missing. So far nothing," Myra said. "No word of any Amber alerts, no search parties forming. *Nada.*"

"They have to know by now that Ben is gone. Surely, someone checked on him yesterday. Or last night or even this morning. It's already eleven-thirty. Ben is home on Tuesdays," Maggie said.

"I think they're winging it right now because they don't know what to do. They're smart enough to know if they go to the police, the cat is out of the bag, and the courts might place Ben in foster care. They don't want that. They know he can take care of himself, so they aren't worried about his well-being. Not that his well-being has ever been one of their concerns. What they're worried about is who is helping him or where he'll go and to whom he will tell his tale," Nikki said.

"I think Nikki is right," Annie said.

"So what do we do now?" Isabelle asked.

"Speaking for myself, I was sort of, kind of, thinking I'd give Ben a haircut if he's agreeable," Alexis said. "We don't want him looking like a little girl, now, do we?" The sisters shook their heads from side to side.

"I was thinking about heading to the village to buy him some clothes. It's cold out right now, and it will get colder as the days go on. His clothes are skimpy at best," Maggie said.

"I'm thinking of calling Peter Olsen Junior again and letting him know how things are going. He asked us to keep him informed, so he could keep his dad up to date," Nikki said.

"How about if Yoko and I go to the Institute and see what, if anything, we can find out?" Kathryn asked.

"That leaves Annie and me," Myra said unhappily. "How about if Annie and I go to the Circle and poke around. We know where the key is to the Lymen house, so we could start there. If Connor and his wife somehow got in, I'm thinking they wouldn't be too careful about disturbing things the way we were when we did our search."

"I think it all sounds doable. I'll stay here with Ben and give him his haircut and keep an eye on things. If I get even a sniff of trouble, we'll head downstairs to the war room," Alexis said.

"Sounds good," Annie said. "Let's do it, ladies!"

Kathryn and Yoko were the first to leave. Yoko drove, with Annie and Myra behind them on their way to the Circle and Eleanor Lymen's house.

"Do we have a plan, Yoko, once we get there? I know you can handle any questions they pose and ask the pertinent ones because you have a child. I know nothing about children, sad to say," Kathryn said.

Yoko grinned. "I thought we'd just sort of wing it. From what I've read, the people who run the Institute are a bit different from your run-of-the-mill educators. Let's just see how it plays out. I like that little boy, I really do. What I don't like is that he has not had a normal childhood. Yes, I'm all for education, but how sad is it that he has no friends and has probably never climbed a tree or played in a muddy ditch the way most kids have."

"I hear you. Maybe we can change all that for him. I simply cannot wrap my head around the fact that if he continues his studies, he will graduate from college in December. Then what does the kid do? Go for his MBA, then his PhD? That just tells me he has no life. I sure hope his grandmother gets back here and takes control."

Annie, by now driving her car in front of them, turned on her signal light, gave a soft tap to her horn, and peeled left, while Yoko tapped her horn and kept going straight to visitor parking at the Institute.

"The lot is empty," Kathryn said.

Yoko grimaced. "It probably means they discourage visitors. Well, we'll see about that!"

"I think you should take the lead since you know more about kids than I do," Kathryn said as she climbed from the car to follow Yoko, who looked like a mother with a grim mission in mind.

"Here goes nothing," Yoko mumbled as she pressed the button on the outdoor intercom. When nothing happened, she pressed it again. When she pressed it a third time, a voice asked what they wanted. The voice went on to say admittance was by appointment only.

"Now you see, that doesn't work for me," Yoko said. "Eleanor Lymen personally told me to come here, and I would be admitted. She said, and this is verbatim, 'If they give you any crap, tell them they will be on the unemployment line tomorrow morning.' End of quote. Now, what's it going to be?"

"This is highly irregular. I have to check with Dr. Phillips. I'll just be a minute."

The voice was as good as her word. A minute later, the

door opened, and a tall, shaggy-haired man towered over them. Kathryn glared at him but said nothing.

"My colleague informed me that Mrs. Lymen said you were to be granted admittance. I wasn't notified, so that's where the confusion comes in. My apologies. Please come in and tell me what I can do for you. I'm Dr. Evan Phillips. I'm in charge of the Institute. And you are?"

"Kathryn Lucas, and this is Yoko Wong. We'd like a tour of the facility. Yoko's daughter knows Ben Ryan. Is he here today? We'd like to say hello and see him in his academic environment."

Ah . . . Mr. Ryan is out with a stomach virus that attacked him yesterday, I believe. I think he'll return tomorrow if his prediction is right that he had a forty-eight-hour bug of sorts. Sterling young man. We are so proud of him here at the Institute. It's hard to believe that he began this semester as a college freshman and will be a college graduate in December if he continues the way he has been going."

"It is amazing. Eleanor . . . Mrs. Lymen told me you would give me the indoctrination packet for my daughter Lily. She said she will speak with you directly on her return, which should be in the next few days."

Dr. Phillips massaged his sparse beard, his eyes suddenly flinty. "Mr. Connor Ryan called a short while ago and left a message. A long, detailed message, which in and of itself is unusual. At the end of the message, he asked if his mother-in-law had been in touch. He said young Ben worries about her. We don't take calls but let them go to voice mail until the noon hour, when we return all calls."

"I would imagine he's worried about his stepson," Yoko said.

"As a matter of fact, he said he was taking young Ben to the doctor's this afternoon to rule out appendicitis. Feel free to walk around, ladies, but please do not enter any of the rooms. You can observe students through the windows. I'll get your packet." And before either Kathryn or Yoko could blink, he was gone, his shiny wingtips slapping hard on the tile floor.

The moment Dr. Phillips was out of sight and earshot, Kathryn hissed, "That all tells me Ben's stepfather knows he's gone missing and is looking for information. He's got to be running scared. Walk faster, Isabelle, so we can get out of this place."

Yoko quickened her step, muttering as they peered into window after window. "This place is too sterile, too antiseptic for my liking. Lily wouldn't last a day here. There is not one smidgen of color anywhere. I wonder why Isabelle designed this to look more like a prison despite the beautiful interior features. I guess she must have had specific instructions, or else she made things bright and colorful, and things changed over the years since."

"Okay, I've seen enough. Let's go," Kathryn said as she stomped forward to arrive back at the entrance foyer just as Dr. Phillips arrived with a dull brown accordion-pleated folder that he handed over with a flourish. Yoko snatched it out of his hand and headed for the door, calling out her thanks over her shoulder. Kathryn remained mute.

Outside, in the brisk October air, the two sisters headed for Yoko's car, Kathryn hitting her speed dial for Myra's number. Myra sounded agitated to Kathryn's ears.

"We're leaving here now. Do you want us to join you or should we head back to the farm?"

"We're about to leave, too. This place looks like a tsunami hit it. Guess the Ryans were here, probably sometime last night. The good news is they didn't find the safe in the linen closet that Isabelle told us about, even though they tossed the house, including the closet, pretty good. Freddie the bear was on the bed with the zipper pulled down, so they know about sleep bears. They broke the kitchen door to get in. I don't know if the alarm was on or not. We need to ask Ben when we get back to the farm. Both Rita's and Irene's houses were tossed also. Ben was very specific about the alarm at Rita's house. I imagine the alarm company has been here at some point, along with the police. They probably chalked it up to random burglary."

"Well, then, Connor and his unholy bride came up empty. I'm certain they thought he would go to one of the three houses. No telling what they'll do now. But we aren't going to solve this yakking like magpies. We can do that when we meet up. Okay, we'll see you back at the farm," Kathryn said.

"Drive carefully, ladies," Myra said.

"You, too, Mom," Yoko drawled.

Chapter 9

Ben Ryan watched Alexis in the bathroom mirror as she snipped at his curly hair. He watched it fall to the floor, his eyes wide in shock. "I didn't think my hair had gotten so long. I guess I should have realized how fast it grows over the summer months."

"If it's okay with you, Ben, I'm going to send all this hair to a friend of mine who makes wigs for cancer patients."

"Oh, absolutely, that is okay. I wonder why I never thought of that. Probably because . . . because I never . . . that's sad," he finished up, just as his cell phone gave off a zippy little ditty. "Someone is calling me! My first phone call on my new phone! Do you believe that?" Ben asked as he rummaged in his pocket for the phone Isabelle had bought him. Thinking it was Isabelle, Ben grinned, and playfully said, "How's it hanging, Izzy?"

A second later Alexis heard the happiest squeal she'd ever heard in her life. She laid down the shears when she heard, "Granny! Is it really you? Are you okay? I'm okay! I'm getting a haircut, and we're going to donate my hair to someone Alexis knows who makes wigs for cancer patients. Where are you? When will I see you? Can I live with you again? It's really you! I'm sorry I didn't catch on sooner. These ladies are all nice, and there are five dogs here! Five, Granny, and they like me. They sleep with me, and boy, are they warm and cozy. The food is so good, and there's lots of it. I'm not one little bit hungry. Maggie is buying me some new clothes. When you come back, you will have to pay her back. My underwear was too tight," Ben babbled, breathlessly but happily.

Alexis walked to the kitchen door, the dogs in tow, just as Myra, Annie, Kathryn, and Yoko drove into the courtyard. She quickly explained that Eleanor Lymen was on the phone with her grandson. "I wanted him to feel free to be who he is with her," Alexis said as she crossed her arms over her chest to ward off the brisk wind. "You should have heard him. He was just like a normal little boy, all excited about talking to his granny. He sure does love her," Alexis said as she remembered her own granny and the special bond she had growing up on the farm where she was raised.

The women all nodded as they remembered their own grannies. "The houses on the Circle were trashed, especially Mrs. Lymen's. Obviously, the boy wasn't there, so they, the intruders, were also looking for something besides the boy. They didn't find the safe in the linen closet, however. All three doors to all three houses were broken, so we need to see about their getting repaired as soon as possible," Myra said. "So, to sum it all up, we have to assume the Ryans know Ben is gone, and they thought, correctly, as it turned out, that he would head to the only place he thought he would be safe. But they arrived much too late to find him still there. So, by now, they have to be in full panic mode." Myra looked at Kathryn and Yoko and asked how they had made out at the Institute.

Kathryn bristled as she reported on their findings. "The professor we met, apparently the guy who runs the Institute, had, in my most humble opinion, a very high, as in *very high*, snoot factor. It was like he thought he was talking to two idiot women, meaning Yoko and me. An elitist for sure. There was no way we would have gotten in without bandying about Eleanor Lymen's name. That was key. He told us that Ben was absent with a bug of some sort. Then they said that Mr. Connor Ryan had called and said he was taking Ben to the doctor to rule out appendicitis. I guess that was Ryan's way of finding out if Ben was there. Stupid is as stupid does," she announced, glaring at the three women next to her.

"I hated that place!" Yoko cried passionately. "There wasn't one ounce, one smidgen of color anywhere. It was a sterile, gray, antiseptic environment. Extremely depressing. Lily wouldn't last a day in such a place. You couldn't hear a sound anywhere. When we looked in the various room windows on our quick tour, none of the kids even looked up. They all looked like robots to me."

"Where are Nikki and Isabelle?" Annie asked.

"Isabelle was on the phone with a client and about to tell him or her to take a long walk off a short pier when we came out here. From what I heard, the client was disgruntled that she wouldn't drop everything to have a meeting with him. I think she cut him loose, because the last thing I heard was her saying she thought he would be happier with another architect and to stop by, and his deposit would be refunded. I assume she's in there lurking somewhere so she can overhear Ben," Alexis said.

"And Nikki?" Myra queried.

"Nikki was on hold with Mrs. Lymen's lawyer, so I would assume by now she is doing the same thing Isabelle is doing, listening," Alexis said.

"How long are we going to stand out here?" Kathryn asked.

"Until Ben gets off the phone," Alexis shot back. "He needs as much time as he can get with his grandmother. I never saw a kid so happy as Ben when he realized it was his grandmother who was calling him. If he had wings for arms, he would be soaring overhead, that's how happy he was."

"Why don't we walk around to the front of the house and go in the front door?" Yoko asked as she, too, crossed her arms over her chest to ward off the cold air.

"Excellent idea," Myra said, fishing the keys out of her handbag and leading the parade to the front door. The warm air welcomed them, along with all five dogs, who looked mightily perplexed since no one ever used the front door.

The small group immediately headed down the hall to the door to the dining room, through which room they could enter the kitchen. They clustered in a tight little group, their ears pressed to the door to the powder room, in time to hear Ben say, "Yes, Granny, I know, be still like a mountain and flow like a river. Yes, I remember who said it, Lao Tzu. I didn't forget. When you get back, can we sit in the kitchen and drink hot chocolate with those little marshmallows and *talk*? Okay, Granny, I know you have to go. I love you just as much. Tell Irene and Rita I miss them, too, and I love them. Hurry home, Granny. I'll count the hours on my new watch."

Nikki, who had finished speaking to Peter Jr., joined the group by the door and was standing next to Isabelle, who had also finished her phone call, felt her eyes burn at the happiness in the little boy's voice. She could see that Isabelle was in the same place mentally that she was after hearing Ben describe life in the Ryan household, with Natalie calling the shots.

"I can't wait to get my hands on that witch," Nikki hissed.

"You might have to fight me for that honor, Nikki," Isabelle hissed in return, joining the others, who had backed away from the door to the powder room in anticipation of Ben's exiting any moment.

The door to the powder room burst open, and Ben emerged, whooping and hollering as he ran across the kitchen to where Nikki and Isabelle were standing. The dogs chose that very moment to barrel into the kitchen from the dining room and cluster around Ben, who was telling the sisters, "That was my grandmother on the phone! Did you fire your client, Izzy?"

"Huh?"

"I heard you on the phone. You did that so you could stay here with me, right?"

Isabelle threw her hands in the air. "How could you hear me all the way across the room and still talk to your grandmother?"

"I can multitask. I'm a genius, remember?" Ben cackled with glee at the look on Isabelle's face. "So, did you terminate your client?"

Isabelle sighed. "As a matter of fact, I did. He was a real thorn in my side, so it's no great loss to the firm."

"Okay, kiddo, let's finish your haircut. You can all gab later," Alexis said, and she herded Ben toward the powder room off the kitchen. "We'll just be another twenty minutes or so," she called over her shoulder.

"Guess it's time for coffee then," Myra said as she reached for the coffee can. "Annie, check with Avery to see if he's come up with anything in regard to Ben's biological father. He should have something by now."

Maggie took that moment to walk through the door, two bulging shopping bags in her hands. "No, I didn't buy out the store. I left a few things," she said, laughing. "They make such cute kids' clothes these days. I even bought Ben a baseball cap. I hope he likes the Atlanta Braves. It was the only one they had left. And then I spotted a pet store and bought a few things for Hero. Here I am. Boy, I sure could use a good cup of coffee. Oh, I almost forgot, I stopped at Krispy Kreme and bought two dozen donuts. So, ladies, let's dig in here, because I am starving."

Fifteen minutes later, Ben appeared in the doorway and stood still until they noticed him. All the sisters *oooh*ed and *aaah*ed and said how handsome he was. They made room for him at the table. He eyed the donuts Annie had piled on a colorful autumn-leaf-patterned platter. Myra poured Ben a large glass of milk. He dug in and ate just as much as Maggie, to her absolute delight. Between bites of the donuts, she told him what was in the shopping bags and that he needed to go upstairs and try everything on to make sure she had bought the right sizes.

Ben bounced off the chair like he was spring-loaded. He dragged the shopping bags to the back staircase, with Lady helping by pushing him along.

"Now, that's a happy kid!" Alexis said. "It's like he won the lottery today. He talked for half an hour with his beloved granny, he got new clothes, and he had four do-nuts. Who could top that? Plus, he is allowing me to do-nate his hair to one of my pet charities."

"That's all well and good, but we're still at a standstill. What are we going to do about the Ryans? We need a plan!" Whatever else Annie was about to say stopped when her cell phone chirped. "Avery," she mouthed. The room went silent. The sisters listened, but Annie was mute and not saying anything. Avery, it appeared, was doing all the talking.

Ten minutes later, the sisters sighed when they saw Annie smile, say thank you, then end the call. "What?" they chorused as one.

"He's faxing us the documents he found about Ben's bi-ological father. He can't help us anymore because he was getting ready to board a flight for some, I guess, secret mission on the other side of the Atlantic. I guess 'you know who' must have something urgent that he has to attend to. Oh, well. We can't get upset over his failure to give us additional help because, as he put it, he contracted for this particular mission he's about to embark on weeks ago. He also volunteered that he had to turn down Charles's last request for help."

"I think we can navigate this on our own. We've done it before, so there's no reason to think we can't do it again. With Pearl's help, of course. We might have to put her on the payroll one of these days," Yoko said.

"Why?" Kathryn snapped. Everyone in the room knew and understood Kathryn and Pearl's fraught relationship, despite the fact that the former Supreme Court justice had proven herself an invaluable ally via her underground network used to funnel abused women and children to safety. "If she balks, we simply blackmail her. It won't come to that, as we all know. When it's time for the exfil, I'll call her. No worries there."

"I'll go to the war room and wait for Avery's fax," Nikki said. "I assume we're keeping this on the down low where Ben is concerned, right?" All the sisters nodded.

Nikki left the room just as Ben bounded down the steps, the dogs yipping and yapping at the speed with which he moved. In the kitchen, he did a whirly twirl, showing off his new jeans and a bright red striped rugby shirt. Perched on top of his curls was the Atlanta Braves baseball cap. He was grinning from ear to ear. "I really like the underwear, Maggie. Who is Ralph Lauren? I'd like to write him a thank-you note for making such comfortable underwear."

Isabelle smiled. She reveled at the moment that he was suddenly all little boy and not the Institute's star genius and a soon-to-be college graduate at the age of eight.

"Should I go off with the dogs, so you ladies can talk in private? I can take the dogs out for a run. They love it when I throw a stick, and they all chase after it."

Annie pondered the boy's question for a moment. "We're going to try and decide what our next move should be in regard to . . . to your . . . to Connor and Natalie. So, yes, taking the dogs for a nice run would work for us."

"Grandma always told me that action without thought is impulsiveness, and thought without action is procrastination. I think that makes sense."

Isabelle looked around at the others, who seemed to be having the same thought she was. "Go!" Ben didn't need to be told twice. He beelined for the door, the dogs crowding him so they could all squeeze through at the same time. The little boy's rich laughter was contagious.

"Let's do the dining-room table," Myra said.

"I'll bring the coffee," Yoko said.

"Where is Nikki? What's taking her so long?" Annie grumbled.

"Where is your patience today, Annie?" Myra asked. "I would imagine she is making copies of Avery's report, so we can all follow along at the same time. In the meantime, we need to come up with some kind of plan in regard to the Ryans. Let's all put our heads together and see what we can come up with."

"I think we need to give some serious thought to the possibility that the Ryans will pack up and leave," Maggie said. "That would mean time is of the essence."

"I don't see that happening," Annie said. "If everything Ben told us is true, and there is no reason to believe it isn't, Natalie Ryan is not going to give up all that money as long as she thinks there is some way she can finagle to keep it. Remember, Connor Ryan legally adopted the boy."

"That's right up there with the courts going with the letter of the law. If the biological father claims Ben, that means there will be a lengthy court fight. We've all seen stories about children being ripped away from one family to be given to another family. The biological father may claim he didn't know about Ben. That's a whole other can of worms. Who is to say if that's true or not," Alexis said, the lawyer in her coming out full force. "In the end, DNA will be the deciding factor. But, having said that, I've seen and heard of many judges ignoring that little fact and allowing the child to stay with the adoptive parents instead of disrupting his life."

"Ben will have a voice this time. That little boy is not your normal eight-year-old. He's about to become a college graduate. This time, the judge will have to listen and not be swayed by Natalie's honeyed drivel. We have to find a way to get her cell phone. Ben said she recorded Ryan asking her to participate in his scam. And we have to get those bills Ben said are in Ryan's desk, the ones that show how much of Ben's money they spent on themselves. The only way we can do that is to get into the house," Myra said.

"Okay, ladies, read it and weep," Nikki said from the doorway as she slapped down a stack of stapled papers in the middle of the table.

"Are we going to like this?" Annie asked.

"Oh, yeah," Nikki drawled. "Avery earned his money this time around for sure."

"Okay, everyone, get your copy, and I'll read aloud. Not much here, Nikki," she muttered.

"Might not be a lot, but it tells us all we want to know. Have at it, Annie." Nikki smiled as she slipped her reading glasses on.

Annie perched her own reading glasses on the bridge of her nose, cleared her throat, and started to read.

"Jonathan Philbran of the Boston Philbrans. That means he is a pureblood. Very wealthy family who made their fortunes back in the days of whalers. Basically fish to all of us.

"Avery has noted here that their fortune is more than robust. Jonathan's parents, and even as far back as his grandparents, are what Avery calls 'do-gooders.' Jonathan's parents travel the world preaching the gospel.

"Jonathan is an only child with what Avery describes as unlimited money in a trust set up for him at his birth. He was born in Boston, attended an ultra-elite academy, went on to Harvard, graduated, then decided he wanted to be a doctor. He is a full medical doctor and considered a general practitioner. He didn't specialize in any particular part of the body. He's thirty-seven years old.

"When he finished medical school, he took off a year to decide if that was really what he wanted to do. His degree from Harvard, by the way, is in astrophysics. A bit of a brainiac himself.

"Jonathan met Diana Lymen at a political rally. Avery's source, a close personal friend of Jonathan's from his days at Harvard, who Avery refused to name in this report, is impeccable.

"Here's where it gets interesting. Jonathan never legally changed his last name, but he would introduce himself as Jonathan Holland. He did this so people wouldn't know he came from money and would accept him for who he was, not for the name he carried.

"Diana Lymen, as well as her mother, never knew his real last name. Avery indicates that his source told him Diana and Eleanor Lymen did not even know he was a doctor. It seems that after the breakup, Jonathan went to Boston and stayed with Avery's source to lick his wounds."

Annie raised her head and looked around the table at the sisters, who were paying rapt attention. She continued. "Now it gets even dicier. Eleanor Lymen went to see him wherever he was living at the time he and Diana were in a relationship, and told him to get out of her daughter's life and gave him a check for a million dollars to do just that. According to the source, Jonathan never cashed the check and still has it as proof of her meddling. And it was made out to Jonathan Holland, not Jonathan Philbran. Jonathan has way more money than Eleanor Lymen, but she never knew that when she sent him away.

"Moving right along here, the source told Avery that Jonathan, because of his medical background, was ready to break off whatever kind of relationship he had with Diana. Jonathan told him that Diana lived in a world of unicorns, pixie dust, and fairies. In other words, she was mentally challenged, something Eleanor absolutely refused to believe.

"Avery's source confirmed that Jonathan confided in him that the turning point arrived when he asked Diana to marry him, and she said to him, 'Who are you again?' He said she would go in and out like that, as if the two of them were meeting each other for the first time. He said that up to then, Jonathan, like Eleanor, was in serious denial about Diana's mental health. The source said Jonathan loved Diana, truly loved her. They had a sexual relationship that Jonathan described as fantastic. Jonathan, as far as our source knows, does not know he has a son. He never married or had children of his own. The source said that Jonathan didn't find out about Diana's death until six months after it happened. The source didn't know how he found out, but after he learned about it, he ended up back with the source to recover after another meltdown. Apparently however he learned about Diana's death, he did not learn that she had a son. And even if he did, there is no particular reason to think he would have cottoned on to the fact that he was the boy's father.

"With the source's help, Jonathan recovered his equilibrium and started this medical unit to make use of his degree. He bought two big yellow buses and a camper. He outfitted them as clinics. He keeps them both stocked with water, medicine, food, blankets, and clothing. He has his own lab in the second bus and a technician. He had a

Facebook page, where he had one post saying what he was doing. It went viral, and people were waiting for him to arrive at a location from the route he posted. He's known as the traveling doctor. He drives around the country to poor and rural areas and ministers to the sick. If he comes across patients whose needs are beyond his capabilities, he makes sure they get what they need, and he pays for everything. When they arrive at a destination, they set up a tent and stay usually three days before they move on. Almost like Doctors Without Borders."

"What a wonderful thing for that man to do," Myra said, tears in her eyes. The sisters sniffed and swiped at their eyes in agreement. "But how did Avery even find out Jonathan's real name, much less about Harvard University?"

"Right now, as I read this, Dr. Jonathan Philbran, and he is using his birth name, is somewhere in Mississippi. Town and county were unknown to Avery's source. And that's it, ladies."

"Can you just try to picture his face when he finds out he has a son," Nikki said quietly.

"For whatever it's worth, Avery did not tell his source anything and definitely did not mention Ben. Avery told his source that he had a client who wanted to donate some kind of new X-ray machine and needed to know how to reach Jonathan for delivery. We are on the hook for that, my dears, which is immaterial at this point, but we will donate it at the proper time. Avery spoke for us, so we will honor that promise," Annie said. "But to answer your question, Myra, read the note at the bottom of the report, where he says one of the professors at the Institute went to school with him at Harvard and recognized him when he was in a relationship with Diana. Jonathan swore him to secrecy, and college brothers that they are, he agreed."

"I am so happy for that little boy. He's going to have a

real dad now. Well, maybe not right this second, but as soon as we take care of Natalie and Connor, he will," Isabelle said.

"So that's why Eleanor and her friends left, to find Jonathan and for her to make it right for Ben. I wonder how she found out and when she found out about Jonathan's alias. I have to wonder, if she'd won custody of Ben, would she have ever told that child about his father?" Alexis said.

"No!" was the explosive response from Isabelle. "I know her; she would have taken that secret to her grave. Like Alexis, I have to wonder how she found out who he was and what he does. In the end, though, we have to give her credit for what she's doing, which is to make the right decisions for Ben. Ben is all she has left of what was once her family. I also have to wonder how generous Jonathan will be in regard to Ben. The boy does love his grandmother, that's for sure."

"She probably hired a private detective to search him out. There are smart investigators out there other than Avery Snowden, even though he has an extensive staff." Myra sniffed.

"What's our next move?" Kathryn asked.

"I think we need to find a way to get into the Ryans' house—excuse me, Ben's house. According to Ben, they don't go out much at night. Usually just dinner. Connor doesn't work every single day of the week, sometimes only two or three days, which means we can't count on the house being empty during the daylight hours. Natalie, Ben said, goes shopping and lunches out just about every day; plus she has her beautification appointments," Yoko said. "I can't wait to get my hands on that witch!"

"I think we'll have to take turns staking out the house to get a feel for what they do during the day, then make a plan for the dark hours. We could probably come up with some gift idea, say they won some kind of prize or something. Maggie, dear, you are so good at stuff like that. You could say you're doing an article, or want to do one on Ben because he will get his college degree in December. And in appreciation for their talking to you, their reward is a night on the town, hotel, the whole nine yards. I think they'll snap it up in a heartbeat," Myra said.

Maggie laughed. "Okay, then. Consider it done."

Chapter 10

The two big yellow buses, a camper, and two SUVs rolled along into the small town of Sycamore, Mississippi, population 1,481, over a rough country road full of potholes, with scrub weeds growing out of the holes. Trees were sparse and already shedding their leaves. Dr. Jonathan Philbran knew they were in the right place when he saw the people lined up on the side of the road. He looked at his watch. He was only forty-five minutes behind schedule.

It only took Jonathan and his aides thirty minutes to set up their makeshift clinic. He put on his pristine white medical coat, reached for his stethoscope, and looped it around his neck. The Dr. Jonathan Philbran Clinic was open for business.

What Dr. Jonathan Philbran didn't know when he checked in his first patient was that, in a matter of hours, that day would change his life forever.

The time was ten minutes past the noon hour. Twenty-five miles away, Eleanor Lymen and her two friends stopped at a rural café that the women later claimed made the best fried chicken they had ever eaten.

Ninety minutes later, stuffed to the gills with all the delicious homemade food, Rita ordered three coffees to go.

Irene paid the bill, and the three women left the café with instructions on how to find the traveling doctor.

The three women were giddy yet apprehensive about the upcoming meeting.

Eleanor was too nervous and jittery to drive, so Rita took the wheel of the big Range Rover. Eleanor sat in the back, kneading her hands as she stared out at the countryside, her thoughts everywhere. What if Jonathan refused to talk to her? What if he didn't believe her? So many what-ifs. How could she have been so wrong about a person? Why had she been in such denial about her own daughter? How? As much as she hated to admit it, this was all on her, and she knew it. Irene and Rita knew it, too, but good friends that they were, they had never said a word of reproach. "There's no fool like an old fool," Eleanor muttered.

"Ellie, put a cork in it already. You can't undo the past, so accept it. What you *can* do now is make it right. Some people never get the chance to right a wrong. Consider yourself one of the lucky ones," Rita said.

"You're right, of course. I can see that group of people from here, near the blue tent. I guess we park and go to the end of the line. I don't want to interrupt Jonathan's caring for his patients. I'll stand in line. If you two want to stay in the car, that's okay."

"We've come this far together, and we aren't going to sit out the moment you confess all your sins and beg forgiveness," Irene said, a gentle smile on her face. "We love Ben as much as you do, and we are here to provide support. That's the bottom line."

"Then let's get to it." Eleanor squared her shoulders, took a deep breath, and stepped out of the Range Rover. Together, in single file, the three women headed to the end of the line of waiting patients.

"I count twenty-two people," Rita said. "That has to mean a couple of hours, maybe more."

"And your point is?" Ellie snapped.

"I have no point. I was merely making conversation," Rita replied testily.

"From what I can see, it's like an assembly line. There are two people in the tent with the doctor, and one person who is filling out patient information forms. Looks to me like this guy has it going on. No one appears to be wasting time or energy," Irene observed.

Finally, the last person in front of Ellie broke off and entered the tent. A young man approached with a clipboard and forms. He introduced himself as Dr. Edwin Lancaster. He reached for his pen and was about to ask Ellie her name when she said, "We're not patients. We just need to speak with the doctor on a personal matter. That's why we were at the end of the line. We didn't want to take time away from any of the patients."

The young doctor stared at the three women, not sure what he should do. "Do you know Dr. Jon? That's what we all call him around here."

"Yes, the three of us know Jonathan," Ellie said. "We've been trying to find him for months, but somehow we were always a day or two too late. Now that we have finally found him, we do need to speak with him, in person, about a very serious matter. You might say that the matter we need to speak to him about could change his life forever."

"Well, it looks like you are about to get that chance. His last patient just went to the lab to have blood drawn. Follow me." The three women followed the young doctor like ducklings trailing their mother.

"Jon, there's someone here to see you." The young doctor turned and walked off, leaving Jonathan and the three women alone.

Jonathan's jaw dropped, and his eyes popped so wide, Ellie thought they might fly right out of his head. "I imagine I'm the last person you ever expected to see, Jonathan. And I'm sorry about that. I'm not here to cause trouble. I'm here to . . . to . . . right some wrongs. Can we sit down and talk, or do you have things you still have to do?"

Stunned, Jonathan motioned to a bench, then he pulled up a stool and sat down because he didn't think his legs would hold him upright a moment longer. "To what do I owe the . . . pleasure of this visit? I have to be honest, I never thought I would see you again in my lifetime. You made the need for my . . . um . . . departure pretty clear to me that last day."

Eleanor closed her eyes and prayed for guidance. She nodded. "I don't have the words to tell you how sorry I am about all that. If I could turn back the clock, I would. It wasn't easy to track you down, *Mister Holland*. But I was determined to find you. The three of us have been on the road for six months searching for you. A couple of times we came close, but when we got to where you were supposed to be, you had already left."

"Why?" The question was a bark of surly sound.

"To . . . apologize to you. I made a mistake, and I need to make things right. And I wanted to do it face-to-face. I was wrong about you, so very wrong, and for that I am sincerely sorry. I had no right to send you off. *Buy* you off is more accurate. You never cashed the check, did you?"

Jonathan stared at Eleanor as he tried to think how to respond while he groped in his back pocket for his battered and tattered wallet. He withdrew a folded slip of paper. "This is your check. Even if you had made it out to Jonathan Philbran instead of Jonathan Holland, I still wouldn't have cashed it. I'm not even sure why I kept it, I just did. Sometimes over the years, I pulled it out and looked at it."

"Why not?" Irene asked. "A million dollars is a fortune."

"As you must know by now because you were able to find me, I certainly did not need the money. But more important was that I was already planning on leaving when you bribed me to leave. The day before you came to me, I had asked Diana to marry me, and her response was, 'Who are you again?' Until that moment, I was in such denial where Diana was concerned, just as you were, Mrs. Lymen. I couldn't and wouldn't accept that Diana was mentally challenged. I finally had to look the unicorns, the pixie dust, and the fairies in the eye and make a decision. And I had finally come to my senses when you approached me. I just let it all play out because I sensed you needed me gone. Like I said, I was going to leave anyway. I headed back to Boston to lick my wounds and grieve for what I had just lost. I want you to know that I loved your daughter with every breath in my body. There was nothing I wouldn't have done for her. I imagine that's how you felt about her, too, since you were her mother.

"I didn't know she had passed away until six months afterward. I had a complete meltdown not unlike the one after I left her. It took me a long time to . . . to come to terms with it all."

"I'm truly sorry, Jonathan, for all your suffering. I'm asking for forgiveness, but if you can't see yourself giving me that, I will understand. But that's only a very small part of the reason I wanted to find you. I have something to tell you. Maybe I should just show you instead."

Eleanor reached into her purse and withdrew a five-by-seven color photograph of Ben that had been taken at the Institute. She handed it over. "That's your son, Ben. He's seven years old in that picture. Now, he's eight, and he will be graduating from college in December. He is, to put it mildly, a child genius. He attends the Institute. He looks just like you. But your being a doctor, I'm sure you would want to do a DNA test."

Jonathan Philbran's face turned white. He reached out to grab hold of the folding table so he wouldn't fall off the stool he was sitting on. "You kept this from me for all these years? Why would you do that? My God, why?"

Eleanor bit down on her lip. *This,* she told herself, *is where the rubber meets the road.* "Because I'm a stupid old woman, and I wanted Ben all to myself. I didn't know anything about you other than, as it turned out, the alias you used, and I didn't think you would want to be burdened with a baby. At least that is what I told myself. But that is no excuse. And, of course, I knew nothing about you or where to find you. Diana simply wasn't capable of taking care of him. She thought of him as some doll she would play with, then walk away and forget about him, so Rita, Irene, and I raised him at first."

Jonathan's eyes were glued to the picture in his hands. "This is really my son?" he asked, awe ringing in his voice.

"Yes," the three women said in unison.

"Why now? Did something happen? Why did you wait eight years to seek me out? Is this some more of your game playing? Is your conscience bothering you after all these years?" Jonathan asked, bitterness ringing in his voice.

Ellie tried to stem the tears that were pricking at her eyelids. "No game playing. I told you that I wanted to keep him to myself, so yes, I have a guilty conscience. This is as real as it gets, Jonathan.

"Ben is a wonderful little boy. As I said earlier, he is a child genius. He lived with me up until Diana found this man at some wild concert and married him. Seven months after Ben was born, she just showed up at my door one day, introduced her new husband, and took Ben away, kicking and screaming. I think her husband, Connor Ryan, married her for her money. He adopted Ben lickety-split.

After Diana died, he left Ben with me for a couple of years until I went to court to get permanent custody. There was a court battle, and when Ben was four years old, I lost my battle. And let me tell you, I had a shark for a lawyer. Unfortunately, it turns out that grandparents have no rights, so I was unable to gain custody. I do not even have visitation rights, and Ben's stepfather hates my guts and will not allow me to see Ben. After I sued to obtain custody, Connor Ryan married some two-bit floozy, and the two of them presented themselves to the court as a loving family. Which they most definitely are not, not by a long shot. I filed every appeal there was, but to no avail. Ben's living conditions are not what either you or I would want for him.

"When my lawyer told me which way the wind was blowing, I divested myself of all my holdings so that they couldn't get Diana's or Ben's money. Right now, for all intents and purposes, I am a pauper dependent on my two friends here. I guess I should tell you that they now own all my former assets, which are all earmarked for Ben, along with their own assets.

"Ben rides his bike in the park off the Circle and happened to come in contact with a friend of mine, the architect who designed the Circle and the Institute, who became his friend over a period of a few months. When Ben became comfortable with her, and she told him she knew me well, he asked her if she could help find me. She said she had friends who would do that. I just found all this out a day or so ago. And here we are."

"Are his adoptive parents abusing the boy?" Jonathan barked.

"Physical abuse, no. He pretty much takes care of himself. He ran away over the weekend and went to Rita's house by climbing in the cellar window. He's a very resourceful little boy. Right now, he is safe and sound, and no one knows where he is except the three of us and the people who are watching over him. I assume that the Ryans are looking for him, but as far as anyone knows, they have not contacted the authorities. Believe me when I tell you he is safe with friends. I also need to tell you we could all go to jail for this. Also, you need to know that your son will graduate from college in December. Imagine that, a college graduate at the age of eight."

Jonathan, his eyes glazed, got up and walked around the tent in circles. He had a son. A son who was a child genius from the woman he had loved with all his heart. "What do you want me to do?"

"Come back with us as soon as you can make arrangements to do so. File for custody of the boy. You are his biological father. I don't know how much of a fight the Ryans will put up, since they were spending Diana and Ben's money like it was Monopoly money. That money has run out, and they're now desperate for funds. From their point of view, this is all about money and not about Ben at all. He is nothing more than a meal ticket to them. You need to understand that.

"The only thing I ask of you is that you let me and my friends see Ben from time to time. And I know I have no right to ask that of you, but I'm asking anyway."

Jonathan thought about Eleanor's words and the fact that he had just learned that he was the father of a child he'd never seen and didn't know about until ten minutes ago. He felt shell-shocked. "I would never deny a grandmother the right to see her grandson. Do you have any arrows in your quiver, Mrs. Lymen?"

"Only you and my friend who is taking care of Ben," she said softly.

Jonathan's mind raced as he contemplated his situation. He wanted to know more. He *needed* to know more. He needed to know every single little thing from the moment his son had exited Diana's womb. He wanted to know about every burp, how many bottles he had taken, how he slept, did he get all his shots, when his first tooth came in, when he said his first words, when he took his first step. He knew the only person who could tell him that was the woman staring at him with tears rolling down her cheeks.

Jonathan realized he didn't hate Eleanor Lymen; how could he, she was Diana's mother and his newfound son's grandmother. But right now he didn't like her very much. He stared at the three women, who reminded him at the moment of three precocious squirrels. They were waiting to hear something positive and forgiving from his lips.

Jonathan cleared his throat. "Obviously, we need to talk further. I have things to do here before we close up shop for the night. There's a little hole-in-the-wall café about ten miles down the road. There is nothing gourmet about it, nor does it sell alcohol. I can meet you there in say . . . two hours if that is agreeable to you. Two of my PAs have cars we tow behind our caravan when we travel. I'll borrow one of them and meet you there."

Eleanor sighed so loud, the others simply stared at her. "That works for us."

Jonathan looked at the picture in his hand. "Can I keep this?"

"Of course. I have more on my phone that I took while he was with me. I'll be happy to send them on to you. The one I just gave you is what Ben looked like eight months ago. He's a sturdy little boy, gangly, all angles and planes but still sturdy. Smart as a whip, too. He has your mannerisms, from what I've just observed. He also has the same gap between his front teeth as you do. I told him we would work on that later, and he said no because he loves to suck spaghetti that way."

Jonathan laughed. It was a genuine sound of pure merriment. "That's exactly what I told my mother when I was growing up."

"I guess we'll leave now and let you do what you have to do. We'll meet you at the café in two hours. I do want to thank you for treating me far better than I deserve." Jonathan just nodded and turned away.

Back in the Range Rover, Eleanor climbed into the backseat and burst into tears even before the ignition turned over. Rita and Irene wisely kept silent, knowing Eleanor was crying tears of relief. They both knew it because their own eyes were misty with tears.

"Just drive around, Irene. Give us a tour of Sycamore, Mississippi, until it's time to meet Jonathan. He appears to be a fine man and certainly has his wits about him. What he's doing is phenomenal, and he pays for it all himself. Who does that? Not many that I know," Rita said. "I can't believe the three of us ever thought of him as a scalawag."

"You didn't. I did. It was all me. I convinced you both that I was right in doing what I did," Ellie said from the backseat. "What I can't believe is how I could be so blind."

"The past is prologue, Ellie," Irene said. "You've taken the first step in righting all your wrongs of the past. That has to count for something," she said reassuringly.

"I still have to live with what I did," Ellie said as she continued to cry into a wad of tissues.

"There's not much to see in this backwater. We're approaching what appears to be the main street. I'm basing this on the fact that there is a grocery store, a hardware store, and a small pharmacy. This road we're driving on appears to be the only paved road around here; all the rest are dirt roads. I see a post office there at the end, next to the café Jonathan mentioned. Once we drive to the end of the street, we've seen all there is to see in this town. We will be there in about thirty seconds. What do you want me to do after we get there?"

"Drive around and see if you can find a park or something where we can wait, till it's time to meet up with Jonathan," Rita said.

Eleanor continued to cry in the backseat.

A full half hour later, Irene veered to the right onto a dirt road. A sign stuck in the ground read BEST FISHING IN MISSISSIPPI.

"There might be a picnic area or something," Irene said as she reduced her speed over the bumpy road.

"I'm thinking that sign must be a lie. I don't see anyone fishing," Rita groused. "I do, however, see a fire pit and a picnic table."

"That's good enough for me. Park. I need to breathe some fresh air," Ellie said as she gave her eyes a final swipe before climbing out of the car.

"Not a soul in sight," Irene said.

"Right now, I see that as a good thing. We won't have to socialize," Ellie said, sitting down at the picnic table, which was warped and worm-ridden. She didn't care as she let her finger poke at a nickel-size knothole.

Overhead, a flock of birds took wing from their perches in the scraggly trees. The sky was still blue, but twilight was fast approaching. The few leaves left on the trees rustled in the wind, which seemed to be picking up.

"Do you think Jonathan will come back with us when we leave, which I assume will be tomorrow?" Rita asked.

"No, I don't," Ellie said. "He can't just leave all these people in the lurch. He will make provisions, possibly call in a few doctor friends who might or might not owe him a favor to take over his practice. He'll make sure he leaves everything in good hands. He knows that Ben is safe and sound, so a few more days aren't going to change anything. He'll do everything right. I think we all just saw that side of him, which just makes what I did so much worse." She held up her hands, palms outward. "I'm over that. At least for now. Also, I appreciate you two more than you will ever know. Having said that, please don't minimize what I did. I need the misery and the guilt to remind me what a fool I was and . . . and . . . other things."

"We hear you, Ellie," both old friends said at the same time, compassion ringing in their voices.

"How do you see this playing out, Ellie? Like how and when will you introduce Ben to his father? You know the boy better than anyone, so how do you think he'll take having a brand-new father sprung on him out of the blue."

Ellie bit down on her lower lip as she shook her head from side to side. "If you had asked me that four years ago, I would have said just fine. But he's been with the Ryans these last four years, so I'm not sure how living through that has affected him. He's older now, wiser.

"I hate saying this, but I can't call it right now. I want to believe Ben will accept him with open arms, but as I've found out over the years, wanting something doesn't necessarily mean you're going to get it. Whatever he does, I will just have to accept it. I don't see any other options."

"I think Ben comes out the winner here. He gets a real father, and he'll still have you, Ellie, along with Aunt Rita and Aunt Irene," Rita said. "To my way of thinking, that's win-win."

"From your lips to God's ears," Ellie said as she continued to pick at the knothole on the picnic table.

"This is a very lonely place," Irene said, looking around. "I guess that sign is some sort of local joke about this being the best fishing place in the state of Mississippi. Or else the fish have decided to go somewhere else, where they will not be caught."

"It's peaceful here, and that's all that matters right now," Rita said.

"It's too quiet," Ellie said. "I like background noise. When it's this quiet, my mind goes into overdrive."

"We could pick a fight with each other and scream and yell, but to what end?" Irene said. "Let's just go with it's peaceful and quiet here. We can commune with nature and think secret thoughts, make wishes in our heads and try to imagine what will go down days from now," Irene said.

"Sounds like a plan to me," Ellie said, her gaze dropping to the watch on her wrist. So many minutes until it was time to go. Her mind drifted to different scenarios of how it would go with Jonathan. She couldn't help but wonder what life would be like now if Diana had married Jonathan Philbran. The only thing she was reasonably certain of was that she would probably still be alive. The urge to cry was so strong, she bit down on her lower lip till she tasted her own blood. *Serves you right, you crazy old woman. Start thinking positive, start thinking that your grandson is going to be united with his real father. Start thinking how happy they will both be after they get to know each other. Think positive. There is no room now for negative thinking.*

Time passed turtle-slow until Irene said, "Okay, let's hit the road. If I drive slowly, we'll get there right on time." She looked over at Ellie. "Are you done with the crying now? Do you want to stay longer so you can make that knothole bigger?

"Smart aleck." Ellie grinned. "I'm done crying. And no, this hole does not need to get bigger. But I think I got a splinter in my finger."

"Serves you right," Rita said callously. "If you can't pull it out on your own, we are going to meet up with a doctor, so maybe he can help you. If not, he can always amputate your finger."

"Just drive, Irene. I want to get this all settled so we can head home where we belong. I for one can't wait to sleep in my own bed and take a shower in my very own shower."

Irene shifted gears and gingerly drove down the deeply rutted road.

Chapter 11

On any other day, at this time Jonathan Philbran's thoughts would be on the long list of patients he'd ministered to earlier. He'd recall every single patient, go over in his mind the diagnosis and the treatment and what if anything still had to be done. Whatever decisions he came up with depended how many more days he would spend at his makeshift clinic in whatever town he was in at the time. He never left the area until he was 100 percent sure he was leaving all his patients in better health. He made mental notes about the patients he had to do a follow-up on and later entered them into his computer. It was not unusual for him to backtrack to check on one of the patients. He did it all because he cared and was dedicated to his profession.

Today, though, his thoughts weren't on his patients but on a gap-toothed, curly-haired little boy with chipmunk cheeks and deep dimples who looked just like him. He had a son! That had to be right up there in the miracle department. His stomach felt like an active beehive as he climbed behind the wheel of an old Ford Bronco that had seen way too many miles but whose engine purred like a contented cat.

A son! Just knowing that changed the whole dynamic of

his life. From this point on, he was going to have to make life-altering decisions. Not just for himself but for his son as well. His thoughts were all over the map as he drove down the lonely road, his eyes peeled for the little café where he would find out everything there was to find out about his new son, so he could make all the right decisions.

What surprised him most about his current situation was that he held no rancor for Eleanor Lymen. She had had her own crosses to bear all her life. That she finally found the courage to right her wrongs was all that was important. And because she was Diana's mother and his son's grandmother, he could not deny her anything.

Jonathan's heart leaped in his chest when he saw the café five hundred feet ahead of him, along with the copper-colored Range Rover. He slowed and turned on his signal light even though no one was behind him. Rules were rules, and Jonathan always obeyed the rules.

As he got out of the car, he wished he'd taken the time to shower in the camper before leaving the site of the clinic. A shave would have gone a long way, too. *Too late now*, he thought as he loped ahead to the door that would lead him to the mysteries of his newfound son. His heart was beating so fast that he stopped in his tracks and took slow, deep breaths until he felt in control of himself. He could not remember ever being so nervous.

The three women were waiting for him, smiles on their tired faces. Eleanor's eyes were puffy and red, but her smile was the widest. He grinned back as he sat down. A young waitress, probably the owner's daughter, came over to the table. Jonathan pointed to the glasses of sweet tea already on the table. "I'll have the same."

"Dinner is either meat loaf, string beans, mashed potatoes, and gravy with biscuits, or stuffed pork chops with pan gravy, garlic pecan carrots, baked potato, and biscuits.

Coffee comes with the meal along with seven-layer choco-late cake. Doesn't matter which dinner you get. I'll get your tea and return to take your orders."

When the waitress returned, Rita said, "All three ladies are having the meat loaf."

"Make that four," Jonathan said to the waitress as she set his frosty glass of tea in front of him.

Eleanor opened her photos on her smart phone and handed it over to Jonathan. "There are hundreds of pic-tures of Ben, for the first four years. And some of Diana, too. I don't know how to transfer them to your phone. If you can do it, please do so."

Jonathan reached for the phone with shaking hands. The women spoke softly of the weather, the café, their up-coming meal, and the trip back home as they risked glances from time to time at Jonathan, whose eyes were misty as he stared at his newfound flesh-and-blood son.

When he finished uploading the photo gallery to his phone, he handed Eleanor her phone and grinned from ear to ear. " 'Thank you' seems inadequate."

"So you forgive me, Jonathan?" Eleanor whispered.

"Of course. The past is prologue. Let's all agree not to look back, only forward."

He watched as the three women's heads bobbed up and down. Having said that, he added, "What's *our* next move?"

"I think that pretty much depends on you, Jonathan," Irene said. "We're leaving in the morning to drive home. It's a two- or three-day trip for us. When do you think you can leave? There's no rush now because Ben is in safe hands."

Jonathan's mind raced as he thought of everything he would have to do before he could leave. "A week, maybe five days if everything goes well. I'll fly back and pick up a car when I get there. I know where to find you, but I'll call when I get there, so we can . . . so we can figure out the best way to . . . to introduce me to my son. Does that work for all of you?"

"It does," Eleanor said, just as their food arrived. After the first two bites, the foursome proclaimed the meat loaf the best they'd ever eaten. They made small talk, mostly about Jonathan's career and how much it meant to him.

Rita, a nurse when she was younger, asked the most questions.

"We all volunteer at two of our local hospitals and donate one day a week to the Red Cross," Irene said.

By the time the seven-layer chocolate cake and coffee arrived, the foursome said they were stuffed to the gills but somehow they would force down the delectable chocolate delight. Which they did.

And then it was time to say goodbye. The women openly cried when Jonathan thanked them for making him the happiest man on the planet. He ended with, "I know it isn't going to be easy for me to suddenly appear in Ben's life and to think things will be wonderful right off the bat. Just know that I am prepared for anything and everything because, from this day forward, my son is the most important thing in my life. I'll turn myself inside out if that's what I have to do."

"We'll help in any way we can, Jonathan," Eleanor said as she fought her surprise when Jonathan hugged her. She was so overcome with emotion she almost blacked out, but strong arms kept her steady on her feet.

It was full dark when Jonathan climbed into the old Bronco. The women watched until the red taillights were just pinpoints of light.

"Guess we should head on down the road to our digs for the night. Let me be the first to say that went much better than we had any right to expect. It's true, that old saying, to forgive is divine. There's more to that old saying, but I forget what it is," Irene said.

"To err is human, to forgive is divine," Rita said.

"We're forgiven, that's all that matters," Eleanor said as she took her turn at the wheel. "Tomorrow is another day, so let's get on with it."

Maggie crept quietly down the back staircase leading into Myra's kitchen. She thought she was the first one up, so was shocked to see Kathryn already seated at the table, coffee cup in hand. "What? No breakfast?"

Kathryn laughed. "You know I am the world's worst cook. I've been waiting for someone who knows how to cook to get it going. Ah, here she comes, Isabelle to the rescue. What's for breakfast?"

"How about whatever you come up with?" Isabelle quipped right back.

Maggie groaned. "Okay, okay, scrambled eggs and bacon. Let's nuke the bacon, it takes too long to fry it the way everyone likes it."

"Works for me," Kathryn said cheerfully. "I'll do the juice and the toast. Izz, the coffeepot is on you this morning."

Ten minutes later, all the sisters were assembled in the kitchen.

"I just peeked in on Ben, and he's still sound asleep, with all five dogs on the bed with him. They have him surrounded and are loving every minute of it. It's been a long time since there have been kids here," Myra said wistfully.

"I got a text from Eleanor this morning. She said they are on their way home. They left at sunrise. Jonathan will arrive in about a week. We need to decide what we're going to do here, ladies," Isabelle said.

"I think my plan is the best," Maggie said as she whipped the eggs in the bowl into a frenzy. "We go in teams and stake out the house for a day or so to get a feel for their movements. Then we make our move. We do not have a phone number for either Connor or Natalie, and Ben said he didn't know their cell phone numbers because he never had a reason to call them. Also, he didn't have a cell phone. We might have to get that from the Institute, which means Isabelle will need to get in touch with Mrs. Lymen, so she can call the Institute to tell them to give us what we need. Like ASAP." The frothy eggs went into the oversize frying pan.

"On it," Isabelle said, already tapping out a text to Eleanor Lymen.

"Bacon's ready," Nikki called out.

"Toast is being buttered," Alexis announced.

"Juice is poured," Kathryn added.

"Table set," Annie proclaimed.

"Another minute, and the coffee is ready, and Yoko's tea is brewing," Myra added.

"Here come the eggs," Maggie said as she slid the scrambled eggs onto a huge platter. "Have at it!" she said gleefully.

Forty-five minutes later, the kitchen was spick-and-span, and Ben's breakfast was ready for him in the warming oven.

The time was twenty after eight.

"Looks like today is going to be one of those splash-and-dash kind of days, so make sure you all take the appropriate gear," Myra said as she gathered up her rain slicker and umbrella. "Let's go over our assignments one more time before we split up."

"I'm staying here with Ben," Isabelle said.

"Yoko and I are going to stake out the house," Kathryn said. "We'll do our best to get the numbers of their license plates off their vehicles and follow them if they venture out."

"Alexis and I are going to go into town and see if we can find the places that Natalie patronizes. If we're lucky, we might find a few friends willing to talk," Nikki said.

"I'm going to the *Post* and dig into the archives and figure out how best to approach the couple later today," Maggie said.

"Myra and I are going to pretend to be real-estate agents canvassing the neighborhood to see if anyone is interested in selling their property for a quick sale," Annie said.

"When Ben gets up, I'll quiz him. He might know some things he's forgotten to mention. I do recall his saying earlier there is a landline but that neither Natalie nor Connor answer it because it's usually a bill collector," Isabelle said.

"Let's do it!" Nikki said.

The sisters high-fived each other, even Isabelle, who was staying behind.

Outside, before getting in their respective vehicles, Myra said, "Let's agree to meet up at the café Isabelle suggested. I think she said it's called Sara's View. She said it's just two doors from her office, so it should be easy to find. One o'clock okay with everyone?" Everyone said it was.

Isabelle watched until the last car whizzed through the open gate. She sighed when she saw the monster gates glide back to their home base. Safe and sound for now.

With nothing to do but stare at the four walls, Isabelle poured herself more coffee that she didn't want or need. What to do? Nothing, her mind shrieked. She stared off into space as her thoughts took her everywhere and nowhere. What seemed like a long time later, she turned when she heard the dogs thundering down the steps as they beelined for the back door. They barreled through like they were shot from cannons the moment she opened the door. They were good for a full ten minutes. She turned in time to see Ben, fully dressed, his curly hair still wet from the shower.

"Well, hello there, sleepyhead," she said, hugging him. "How did you sleep?"

"Great, even though the dogs took up most of the bed. They sure do keep a person warm. I hardly needed covers. I hope someday I can get a dog. Do you think that will ever happen, Izzy?"

"I absolutely do, Ben. I'll take that one step further and say I bet you get two or three. Dogs need dog company, not just human company. A human can't play with them twenty-four hours a day."

"That makes sense," Ben said seriously. "Okay, I'm marking down on my mental list to get three dogs. Maybe four, so I can name them Spring, Summer, Fall, and Winter," he added, and giggled.

"Sounds good to me. Ready for breakfast? Maggie cooked this morning, and yours is in the warming oven."

"I'm ready. I could eat a bear. Where is everyone? It's quiet here."

"Why don't we just say they're out on . . . um . . . assignment. They'll be back later this afternoon. When you're done with your breakfast, we need to talk. I have some questions you might or might not have the answers to. Be sure now to save a little of that bacon for the dogs."

"I know. I like it that I don't have to make my own breakfast even if it is just cereal because the milk always tastes funny. I could get used to this," he said, his eyes twinkling.

"I hear you! I love it when my husband brings me breakfast in bed on this really pretty tray we got as a wedding gift, and he always puts a flower on it even if it is an artificial one."

"He must love you very much to do that," Ben said.

"Yes, I think he does, and I love him just as much. I don't know if I ever told you this, but Abner and I were both orphans. Neither one of us ever had a real family. We grew up in a series of awful foster homes and orphanages. I guess that's what drew us together, so we each try to be for the other what we missed growing up. I also consider all my friends here at Pinewood part of my extended family. We're all like sisters to each other."

"That's very sad," Ben said seriously, "that no one loved you growing up. I had my grandmother, but I don't think that's the same as a mom and dad. But on a more positive note, look how good you turned out. And I'm doing okay, too. We can't be bitter because that just makes you miserable. You have to learn to make the best of a bad situation and look for the rainbow that's just around the corner. My grandmother told me that, and I think she's right, don't you, Izzy?"

He's only eight years old. "I agree," she said, walking over to the kitchen door to let the dogs back in. "Get that bacon ready, but don't give it to them till they have their own breakfast," Isabelle said as she set the dog's food bowls, which Myra had prepared before she left, down on the floor.

"Break each piece in half, and that way they think they're getting two treats." Isabelle grinned as she picked up the bowls and washed them.

"What did you want to talk about, Izzy?" Ben asked, getting right to the point.

"A couple of things, but first I got a text early this morning. Your grandmother, Rita, and Irene are on their way home. They did what they had to do and should be here in three days. Isn't that wonderful?"

Ben's closed fists shot in the air. The dogs barked, and Isabelle laughed out loud. "I love it when I have something to look forward to. You can count down the hours on your new watch."

"The questions?"

"I think you told me that you didn't know the numbers of Natalie's and Connor's cell phones, right?" Ben nodded. "Do you have any idea how we can get them?"

Ben pondered the question and started to shake his head no, then exploded in sound. "Actually, I do know how. You could call some of the restaurants they call into for delivery. You could pretend you called in an order and you never got it, then say what number do you have on file? Then you give them an entirely different number and say, that's where all the confusion comes in. They use Ling Chow for Chinese, Donatelli's for Italian, and Sweet Ribs for ribs. There are magnets on the refrigerator for all three plus a bunch of others."

"You know what, Ben, I never would have thought about that. You really are a genius, you know that?"

"I know." Ben giggled, a little-boy sound of pure mirth. Isabelle loved the sound.

"Do you know where Connor works?"

Ben closed his eyes as he scrunched up his facial muscles. "It's a glassblowing place in town. They have a showroom on the main street, but he works in the back of the property in their workroom. I'm not sure. I think the word 'special' is part of the name. He only works there a few days a week. He does his pottery and other stuff in the building behind the house. Is it important?"

"I'm not sure yet. Does he work the same days every week or does he rotate?"

"Mostly Tuesday, Thursday, and Friday. I think those are his favorite days. I'm not sure if he can pick his own days or if his days are assigned to him."

"And Natalie?"

Ben laughed out loud. "Natalie's job is shopping. And going out to lunch. I'm not making that up. That's what Connor says to her when they fight, which is pretty much all the time. They never say nice things to each other. And I cannot imagine Connor bringing her breakfast in bed, with or without a flower on the tray."

Isabelle laughed at Ben's witticism, as she was texting

Ben's information to the sisters. She knew that within minutes, they would all have Natalie's and Connor's cell phone numbers.

"So what should we do today, Ben?" Isabelle asked.

"I need to hit the books this morning. I don't want to fall behind, so if it's okay with you, I'm going to go into the study and work until noon. After that, I'd like to explore the farm if it's okay with you. The dogs can get a good run at the same time. I just love that old barn. I want to climb up to the loft and jump down into a pile of hay. Do you want to join me?"

"I don't think so. But I will catch you if you decide you want to slide down that glorious banister in the hallway. Now *that's* a whole other experience." Isabelle grinned.

"Okay, we'll do that first," Ben said, laughing at the thought of coming down the banister headfirst.

"What's with that *we* stuff? You do it. I catch you. End of story," Isabelle said, as Ben scampered off to the study, the dogs hot on his trail.

Isabelle cleaned up Ben's dishes and returned them to the kitchen cabinet. Since she had the morning free now, she had to decide what to do to while away the time. Nothing interesting came to her other than to call her office just to see what was happening. She supposed she could watch some stupid game shows or watch some talking heads on the twenty-four-hour cable news channel saying the same thing over and over about whatever was current on the news. She decided against doing any of that and sat down at the table, her eyes glued to the back door, where she watched a hurricane of autumn leaves swirl about through the glass pane. Her thoughts took her to the sisters as she wondered how they were faring in regard to Natalie and Connor Ryan.

Nikki and Alexis both felt their phones chirp at exactly the same time. Both looked down at Isabelle's text. "Well, okay, then," Nikki said as she stared across the street at Donatelli's Italian restaurant in the village. "Let's go play detective, Alexis, but first send off a text to the others that we have this one covered. If we come up blank or they don't cooperate, we can always try the Chinese restaurant over there on the corner."

An incoming text from Annie brought both women up short. Nikki read it and started to laugh. "Myra and Annie are going to pose as Realtors canvassing the neighborhood to see who wants to sell their house to some rich sheik from Dubai who is bringing his genius son to the Institute and needs a house for his son's staff. Money will be no object. Annie said they stopped at Staples and had some flyers printed to hand out. I don't think I would have ever thought of that, what about you, Alexis?"

"Nope. Leave it up to Annie to come up with something like that. It just might work. Greed is a powerful motivator. The big question is, will the Ryans open the door to them?"

Nikki shrugged as she opened the door to the Italian restaurant. The wonderful odors of garlic, basil, and cheese made her mouth water. She knew that if Maggie were with them, they would already be seated at a table and ready to order one of everything.

A rotund little man in a spotless white tunic and a cap on his head to protect his hair smiled at them. "We won't be ready to serve for another hour, ladies. My staff hasn't reported in yet. I hope you can come back."

"It's not a problem, sir. I'm here to . . . to ask you a question. My name is Natalie Ryan. Two days ago, I called in an order, and it was never delivered. I wonder if you would mind checking your call-in orders to see if you have the right phone number for me. I'm a regular customer, and this is the first time this has happened. I'm not complaining; I just want to know what went wrong."

"Certainly! Certainly! My apologies. Let's see," the rotund little man said, as his chubby fingers pecked at the keyboard. Yes, yes, I see that you are a regular customer. The number we have on file is . . . actually we have two numbers." He rattled them off, then turned the computer around so that Nikki could see the numbers that both Alexis and she memorized. "The last order placed was for baked ziti, lasagna with a double order for extra meatballs on the side."

"My last order two days ago was for three orders of spaghetti and meatballs, three garden salads, and a loaf of garlic bread and an order of garlic knots. And those two phone numbers are the right numbers."

The rotund little man looked perplexed. "I can't explain it. I am so sorry. The only thing I can think of is that my grandson was working two days ago, and if a pretty girl walks in, he forgets what he's doing. Teenagers," he said, throwing his hands high in the air as he rattled off a string of Italian that both women knew would not be good for the errant grandson when he showed up for work. "Will you accept a coupon for three free deliveries?"

"That's not necessary, sir. Mistakes happen. Remember when you were young and a pretty girl walked in?" Nikki smiled. "Thanks for your help, sir."

Outside, in the tsunami of falling leaves that the wind was whipping every which way, Nikki said, "That was almost too easy. We might as well head back to the farm since our job here is done. But first text those numbers to the others. I'll drive."

"I think we're on a roll here, Myra," Annie said as she read off Nikki's text. "I also think things are going to start moving rather quickly. I like these flyers. I think we made the right decision not to have a brochure printed up as opposed to just this one colored sheet. Less for someone like Natalie to read, easier to come to a decision, too. Ben did say she wasn't the brightest bulb in the chandelier, and the only thing she relates to is money."

"Ben is such an endearing little boy. I can't fathom how his stepparents could have treated him the way they did. He would have been much better off with his grandmother, who truly loves him. We need to do something about that, Annie. I'm talking about fighting for grandparents' rights. Put that on our list of things to take care of."

"We're going to make it right for Ben, Myra. In the end, that's all that will matter to that little boy. I don't care if he's a genius or is going to graduate from college in two months, he is still a little boy. I won't rest easy until we take care of those two bloodsuckers. They are or were planning on 'doing away' with that child. No matter what words you use, that's murder pure and simple. And all for money." There was such hatred in Annie's words that Myra flinched, even though she felt the same way.

"So, how are we going to do this? I think Ben said there are nine houses on their street. They are all big houses. Should we just put these bogus flyers in their mailboxes but actually knock on the Ryans' door? What?" Myra asked

"They might see us if they're window watchers, so we'll knock on doors to be on the safe side. You take one side of the street, and I'll take the other. If people are home, just hand them the flyer and leave, no conversations. We'll time it so that I finish my side and join you to hit the Ryan house at the same time. If they open the door, we start a dialogue. Does that work for you, Myra?" Annie asked.

"It does. Park behind Kathryn and Yoko. Send off a text telling them what we're going to do. Find out if there has been any activity so far today with the Ryans," Myra said.

Five minutes later, Kathryn's return text read: *Nada. No activity on the street at all. I think everyone works except for the Ryans. We've only seen one vehicle, and it was a*

UPS truck. The guy left a package by the door of number 909. He rang the bell, but no one answered, that's why we think everyone works.

It only took Myra and Annie seventeen minutes to ring every doorbell on the street, with, as they had hoped, no results. They stuffed the folded flyers in the mailboxes and headed for the Ryan house, where Annie gave the lion's-head door knocker a loud bang that reverberated up and down the street. When nothing happened, Annie banged the knocker again. And again with the same results.

"Keep banging it. Sooner or later, they'll open the door or threaten to call the police," Myra said as she looked up and down the street. "Maybe we should walk around the back. Ben said Connor has a shed or workroom where he works when he's home. It's possible they're both out there."

"Good thinking," Annie said, and turned and literally goose-stepped to the back of the house. She could hear the hum of a potter's wheel. She nodded to Myra as she headed for the little building, whose door was standing wide open. Both women could see a man bent over the wheel, his hands all muddy and sloppy.

"Mr. Ryan?" Annie called loudly. Connor turned, his eyes wide at the sight of the two women.

"Yes. What can I do for you?"

"It's more like what we can do for you, Mr. Ryan. I'm Martha, and this is Alice. We work for a private placement service that handles property for customers from other countries. I see that your hands are occupied, so I'll just put this flyer on the table, and you can read it later. But I can tell you what it says. We have a client who lives in Dubai. He's going to be bringing his son to the United States to study at the Institute, and he's interested in purchasing a house in the vicinity for the staff who will be seeing to his son's needs. He's willing to pay top dollar. The truth, is money is no object. We left flyers in all the mailboxes on the street because no one else was home, and the first one who makes an offer is the one we'll go with, because time is of the essence. Our client is a sheik with money to burn. Having said that, are you and your wife in the market to sell your house?"

"What exactly does 'money is no object' mean?" Connor asked as he shut down his potter's wheel. He dipped his hands into a bucket of water and washed and dried them.

"The sheik will pay just about whatever your asking price is, that's what it means. Or anyone else's price who calls us. We don't have time for a bidding war, so first offer gets the prize."

"What's going on here?" a shrill voice demanded as a woman bare of makeup and still in her nightgown marched across the lawn. "Who are these people, Connor? You're trespassing, ladies. Didn't you see the sign on the tree?"

"Actually, no, I didn't see a sign," Myra said as she handed the woman a colorful flyer.

"You want to buy our house?" the woman they assumed was Natalie demanded.

"Well, not us specifically. Our client is a sheik from Dubai. I just explained all that to your husband. Money is no object. First one on the block to make an offer is the one who gets to sell. As we told your husband, we left flyers in all your neighbors' mailboxes. You people appear to be the only ones home during the day."

"We wouldn't consider it unless the price is right," Connor said.

"According to the assessor's office, this house is appraised at one point seven million dollars. But real estate has recovered from the recession of late, so it is highly likely that, if you put it on the market, you could get something like two million or thereabouts, though it might take months for it to sell. The sheik is in a hurry to bring his child to the Institute, so as I said, we'll take the first offer that comes in."

"Can you give us a few minutes to discuss this?" Connor asked as he led his wife across the lawn and into the house.

"Gotcha!" Annie chortled. She looked at Myra. "They're going to go for it, and their magic number is going to be three point nine million dollars. The nine is wiggle room. Wanna bet?"

"I know a sucker bet when I hear one." Myra laughed. "But to answer your question, no, no bets. Ah, here they come. Try not to laugh, Annie."

"Okay," Annie said happily.

Chapter 12

Natalie and Connor Ryan stood in the open doorway of Connor's work shed, their eyes glazed as they watched Myra and Annie walk away. They barely noticed that the sky had opened up, and rain was falling in torrents. Both were speechless, which was a rarity, especially for Natalie Ryan. Connor was the first to break the spell. He simply walked through the doorway, toward the house, oblivious to the rain. He was soaked through to his skin. He barely noticed that, either. He was about to slam the kitchen door shut when Natalie pushed her way past him. He looked at her, thinking she looked like a drowned rat. What in the name of God had he ever seen in this woman?

They stood eye to eye, their soaking-wet clothes and shoes flooding the kitchen floor. The tension in the room was on the verge of going nuclear when Connor stomped off toward the stairs.

"Come back here, you weasel. We need to talk, and we need to talk *NOW!*" Natalie screeched.

"Go to hell and kiss my ass on the way down, you crazy lunatic!" Connor bellowed in return. "Your days of telling me what to do, when to do it, and how to do it are over.

Get that through your everything-is-fake head once and for all! Just shut up and leave me alone!"

"Or what? What are you going to do? Did you forget I have you on record?" Natalie snarled as she squished her way up the stairs behind him.

"Did you forget that I have a recording of you saying you wanted to do away with Ben? I'd say that's a stalemate. Now, get the hell out of my way. I won't tell you again," Connor said, his eyes blazing as he turned to confront his wife. Natalie had the good sense to back away.

Inside the master bedroom, the room she no longer shared with her husband, Natalie shed her clothes, dried off, and pulled on a silky, fancy designer sweat suit that did nothing to warm her chilled body. Her brain whirled and twirled as she made her way downstairs to the kitchen, where she brewed a pot of tea. Tea always calmed her down for some reason. All she could think about was three million dollars. Maybe even four million or five million, if they wanted to hold out. She was literally dizzy at the thought. She shook her head to clear it and to remind herself that you get more flies with honey than you do with vinegar, which meant she had to cool her jets and be nice to her husband. She knew he was a hothead, and that he simply withdrew into himself and refused to communicate when he was angry. Well, he was going to have to communicate with her now. This was an opportunity too good to pass up. The only fly in the ointment was the snot-nosed kid. Where the hell was that little shit? She closed her eyes, knowing in her gut that the kid, present or absent, could somehow queer this deal. Her spine stiffened. First order of business was to find the kid and get rid of him, once and for all.

Natalie's eyes narrowed. In a million years, she had never once thought Connor had the stones to tape her conversation. Well, blackmail was a two-way street. Like it or not, the two of them were in this together, and they'd have to work something out. Once the house was sold and the kid gone for good, they could each go their separate ways. But where was that damn kid?

Natalie's back was to the door as she spooned honey into her tea. She sensed Connor before she actually saw him. "Want some tea?" Her voice was almost as sweet as the honey she was spooning into her tea.

"No, I don't want your stinking tea. I don't want anything from you," Connor snarled, his voice full of hate, as he bustled around the kitchen. He emptied the coffeepot and cleaned it, something Natalie never did. He made a rude comment under his breath, but she heard it anyway.

"I heard that! I told you when we got married I was not Suzy Homemaker. You promised me a cook and a housekeeper. I don't see a cook and a housekeeper, do you? I was up front with you all the way. I never pretended to be anything other than what I am. You were the devious bastard, and look where we are now. Let's sit down at the table and talk like two grown-ups. Let's call those women and say we want five million dollars, and we agree right now. We split it down the middle, then you go your way, and I go mine. How does that sound, Connor?"

"Aren't you forgetting a little matter named Ben? Did you somehow magically forget that this is Ben's house, not ours? We're just allowed to live here in order to take care of him."

"What?" Natalie screeched so loud, Connor swore people in the next county could hear her.

"Don't 'what me,' you moron. Diana bought this house before we were married to get away from her mother and that damn Circle. For whatever reason, we were still living on the Circle when she died. Maybe she had forgotten all about buying the house. Who knows? She was like that, very forgetful, living on her own plane of existence.

"After she died, as you well know, Ben lived with his grandmother for a couple of years. I had to get an apartment to live in. Then, when his grandmother went to court to get permanent custody, I needed to do something not to lose the goose that would eventually lay golden eggs. Enter the ever-loving Natalie as wife and stepmother.

"Diana didn't even tell me about the house until a few days before she was killed, when, for some reason I could never understand, she finally decided it was time to move away from the Circle, and when she did tell me, she told me it was in her and Ben's name. I told you that. Don't go saying now that I didn't tell you.

"Let me repeat what I just said, so your minuscule brain can take it in. Diana bought this house *before* we were married. The key word here is *before*. Now do you get it? We do not own this house; therefore, we cannot sell it. End of story. Period."

"You adopted him, so that means you're in charge of his money, so this house is as much yours as his. Call a lawyer! Like now would be good, Connor Ryan. While you do that, I'm going to call those ladies and seal the deal before someone else beats us to it."

"Damn it, Natalie, it doesn't work that way! I knew you were stupid, but you are acting so far beyond stupid right now that even I am amazed. When they do the paperwork, they'll see the house is not in my name or your name. It was in the name of Diana and Benjamin Lymen. As far as I know, the deed was never changed. Since Diana is dead, the house now belongs to Ben and only Ben. Diana had no idea she was going to die, so there was no reason to change the deed. And that's the bottom line. This house is not ours to sell. For once, try to pretend you're at least a little bit smart."

"Forge his name. How's that for being smart? After I make the call, you and I are going back to that damn Circle, and we aren't leaving till we find that little snot. I know he's in one of those houses. We just missed him. He's there and in hiding. I saw those pantries in all three houses. There were all kinds of canned goods he could be living on. You said yourself he's resourceful. There is no place else he could be. Let's go, Connor. We're wasting time here. Unless you want to end up in jail, we have to be united on this.

"While you pull out our rain gear, I'm calling those women to tell them we'll take their offer for five million dollars, and we'll throw in all the furniture and all the contents. The sheik can move his people in and not have to do a thing. Move, Connor!"

Connor knew when he was beaten. No way did he want to end up behind bars. He felt sick to his stomach as he rummaged in the laundry-room closet for their rain gear. He had a bad moment when he saw Ben's slicker and raincoat hanging next to his. He almost lost it then. But a vision of him gripping the bars of a prison cell exploded behind his eyes.

Connor made a promise to himself at that moment. He would not lift a finger to harm Ben. If Natalie wanted him dead, then she would have to be the one who did the dirty deed. Yes, he would be an accomplice to murder, but he wouldn't get the death penalty. Hell, he didn't even know if Virginia had a death penalty. He'd probably get life in prison without the possibility of parole.

God Almighty, how did it come to this? The answer was greed. Pure and simple.

"You waiting for a bus, Connor?" Natalie shrilled.

I should just kill her right now, Connor thought as he made his way back to the kitchen. He could choke her to death, stuff her in the trunk of the car, drive away, and dump her body someplace in the mountains. He shook his head to clear it. He was no murderer. He wondered as he donned his slicker if Natalie was having the same thoughts he was having. There was no doubt in his mind she could kill him and not think twice about it. Except for the fact that she needed him. He felt himself shiver, not with cold but with fear.

His heart beating trip-hammer fast, Connor followed Natalie out to the car in the pouring rain. There was no turning back now.

Myra and Annie were the first to arrive at the café. They asked for a large table, saying others would be joining them shortly. Then they ordered coffee. Just as the waitress brought their cups and the carafe, Myra's phone pinged that she was receiving a phone call. She looked at the name on the caller ID and grinned at Annie. "They took the bait. Didn't take long at all. I'm going to let it go to voice mail.

"Oooh, here's a text from Kathryn. I'll read it to you. 'The Ryans are on the move. They came out dressed in rain gear, got in the car, and we're following them. This is just a guess on my part, but I think they're headed to the Circle. What do you want us to do? Nikki and Alexis have headed back to the farm, so it's just us. No word from Maggie. One of you call her. We have to pay attention to the road in all this rain if we go back to the farm.' "

"I agree," Annie said. "Like Kathryn, I think they're headed back to the Circle. As far as they know, Ben has no one to run to for help. To them that means he's holed up in one of the houses, so they must believe that their first search wasn't thorough enough. They won't have to break and enter this time because the doors haven't been fixed yet. How long are we going to make them wait till we respond to the voice mail? What did it say?"

"Just that they're willing to sell but they want five million dollars, and the entire contents of the house go with the sale. She asked we call her back as soon as possible. To me that means maybe later today or tomorrow. What's your spin, Annie?"

"I'm all for delays. They're riding high right now and have probably already spent the money a dozen different ways. Let them sweat."

Myra drained her coffee cup as another text came in from Kathryn. "She says she was right, they went to the Circle. They didn't follow the Ryans but parked at the Institute, so they can see when they leave. She wants to know if they should stay with the surveillance."

"Let's think this through. They can't do anything but watch. We have to assume it's going to take them at least two more hours to ransack all three houses. When they don't find the boy, they are going to head back home. So, no, tell them to come here, and we'll talk. Oh, look, here's Maggie," Annie said as she fired off a return text to Kathryn.

"I'm actually cold," Maggie complained as she slipped out of her poncho. "It's raining really hard. My feet are soaking wet."

"Sticky buns are on the way." Myra smiled as Maggie rolled her eyes.

"Fill me in on what's happened so far this morning." She finished her first cup of coffee in two long gulps, then filled it a second time. When Annie wound down, Maggie started to laugh.

"What's so funny?" both women demanded, their faces creased with worry.

"What's so funny is that the house is in the name of Diana Lymen and Benjamin Lymen. She bought the house before she married Connor Ryan and never changed the deed. She paid in cash, so there is no mortgage. The Ryans couldn't sell it even if someone really wanted to buy it. I don't even know if they know it's in Ben's name. It's a fact, I checked at the county courthouse. I even printed out a copy to show you all."

"We believe you, dear. Natalie Ryan called and left a voice mail a little while ago saying they were agreeable to selling for five million dollars, and they'd throw in the contents of the house. We haven't responded as yet.

"Right before you got here, Kathryn sent a text saying the Ryans left dressed in rain gear and headed out. They followed them as far as they could, and, of course, they went directly to the Circle. Kathryn and Yoko are parked at the Institute, so they can see when they leave. We told them to come here. We know where the Ryans are and what they're doing there. They are convinced Ben is still hiding in one of the houses."

"Wow! I called the police department and asked if any kids have been reported missing. They said no. So much for concern about Ben. Where are Nikki and Alexis?"

"They went back to the farm. They got us Natalie's and Connor's cell phone numbers, which is a real plus. It was young Ben's idea to call the take-out restaurants that the Ryans patronize. They lucked out; the owner gave them the numbers without any hesitation. I guess you got the same text, right?"

"I did," Maggie said as she eyed the platter of sticky buns. "That's going to make my job easier. By that I mean when I call to ask for the interview. I can do it after I finish off these sticky buns. I'm starving!"

The three women looked up when the bell over the doorway tinkled as Kathryn and Yoko entered, shedding their rain gear and hanging it on the post by the door, along with their umbrellas. "I feel like a duck," Yoko said, laughter in her voice.

A second platter of sticky buns appeared along with a

fresh carafe of coffee. The women tucked in, enjoying the warm, sugary delight. When the platter and carafe were empty, all eyes turned to Maggie, who already had her cell phone in her hand. She called Natalie's number and wasn't the least bit surprised when it went to voice mail. She hung up and pressed in the digits for Connor's number. He responded after the third ring.

"This is Maggie Spritzer from the *Post*, Mr. Ryan. The Lymen Institute gave me your and your wife's cell phone numbers. I hope that was all right." Before he could say yes or no, it was or wasn't all right, Maggie rushed on. "I just tried calling your wife, but the call went to voice mail. The reason for the call is we'd like to do a feature article on you and your wife and what it's like living with a child genius. This article will bring loads of attention to the Institute because a real-live sheik from Dubai has enrolled his own genius son at the Institute. He's the same age as your son, Ben. We thought it would be a great human-interest story."

Caught off guard, all Connor could think to say was, "Ben's sick, he's got some kind of stomach virus that is lingering on. I don't think he would . . ."

Natalie snatched the phone out of her husband's hand, and said sweetly, "This is Natalie Ryan. Connor is our shy one. Tell me what it is you want from us. I heard part of it because he had you on speaker mode."

Maggie went through her spiel again, ending with, "And, of course, we are prepared to put you up at the Hay-Adams for two nights and to give you a five-hundred-dollar gift certificate at Nordstrom to use for anything you want. What do you think, Mrs. Ryan?"

Natalie wanted to say this must be her lucky day, but she turned cagey. "Exactly what will it entail?"

"Well, this is about you and your husband, parents of a child genius, what it's like to live with him. We want you to talk about him, but we won't be interviewing him at all. We have all we need from the Institute in regard to your son, along with this year's class picture. We, of course, will want to take some pictures of you and your husband, and when the sheik from Dubai arrives, we'll interview him and run his interview alongside yours and, of course, with pictures of the two child geniuses."

All Natalie could think about was the five-hundred-dollar gift certificate at Nordstrom. "When?" she asked.

"Well, if tomorrow is convenient, we could do it in the morning, then you and your husband can check into the Hay-Adams. We'll send a limo for you, and, of course, we'll make sure you get a ride home after you check out. Will that work for you?"

Of course it would work for her. She would be at Nordstrom when the doors opened the day after she came home. "As long as you understand that Ben is not involved with this. We try to shield him from publicity, and right now, the little darling is in bed with a frightful stomach bug that refuses to go away."

"That's fine. I'll see you tomorrow morning at ten o'clock. I'll have a photographer with me."

Natalie agreed and ended the call.

Maggie's fist shot in the air. "She agreed, and I didn't even have to exert any pressure. I think the mention of the gift certificate is what did it. The minute they leave the house after the interview, I'll find a way to leave the door open so we can take over the house and wait for them on their return. By that time, Mrs. Lymen will be back and re-united with her grandson. At which point, I assume Ben's biological father will make an appearance, and it's happily ever after for that little munchkin."

"All right then," Myra said as she rummaged in her wallet for money to pay the bill. "We should head back to the farm. The roads are going to flood if they haven't already. What is up with all this rain we've been having lately?" she grumbled.

"Are you sure you don't want Kathryn and me to go back to the Institute to make sure, when they leave the Circle, they go straight home?"

"Where else could they possibly go in this miserable weather other than home? The two of them will be tearing their hair out and behaving like maniacs when they can't find Ben after they've completed their search. What better place than home to vent and plot and scheme?" Annie said. Everyone else agreed as they donned their rain gear and headed for their cars.

As the sisters headed out to the main highway that would take them back to Pinewood, Connor was demanding to know what his wife had agreed to. She explained it in great detail, daring him to say no. He didn't.

"The kid is not here. We have looked everywhere, and unless there is some kind of secret room, he is not here in Eleanor's house, contrary to your belief. I don't think he was ever here," Connor said.

"I agree. Now we go to Irene's house and check it out. Try to put some energy into it, Connor. This concerns you as much as it does me. Mess up, and I'll stomp on your neck until it's nothing but pulp. I do hope you noticed that while all three of those old biddies are gone, this pantry, at least, is well stocked with all kinds of canned goods, canned meats, fruits, and vegetables. The little snot could hide out for a year and not starve. I'm sure the other two houses are the same. Old people like to keep a lot of food handy in case they can't get out."

Connor didn't know if that was true or not, but he was done arguing. So he donned his rain gear for the slog next door to Irene's house. As he followed his wife out the door, his gaze fell on the butcher-block knife holder. How he'd dearly love to take the biggest and sharpest knife and plunge it into his wife's neck. Then he'd step over her and get in the car and drive till he ran out of gas.

But he wasn't going to do that because, at heart, he was a coward. He was glad they hadn't found Ben at Eleanor's house. His gut told him they weren't going to find him at Irene's or Rita's house, either. Where he was, Connor had no clue. Secretly, he was glad the little boy had eluded them.

Two hours later, the Ryans were back in their kitchen; Natalie was pacing around like a wild tiger. Her claws were out, and Connor cringed. "There must be some kind of secret room or something in one of those houses. Nothing else makes sense. He's in one of those houses, I'm sure of it. Think, Connor, where else would he go? Nowhere, that's where, so he's holed up there in some kind of secret hidey-hole only kids know about. Because if he was on the loose, he would have gone to the cops, and they would be here crawling all over the place." Natalie kicked at the kitchen cabinet as her right hand swept everything on the counter onto the floor in her insane rage.

All Connor could do was shrug. They had practically dismantled all three houses on the Circle without finding so much as a hair to indicate that Ben had been in any of them.

"And on top of that, those women did not return my call. I'm going to call again to see what the problem is."

"Do that and you'll appear too eager. Patience is a virtue, but I guess you don't have a clue as to what that means."

"Stuff it, Connor. The day has yet to arrive to signal you had a good idea. If I left it up to you, we'd be living in a tent and peeing in a ditch. You need to be preemptive and aggressive in this world or you get left behind. Now, which one of us is going to forge Ben's name on the contract?"

Connor threw his hands in the air. "You don't even know

if your offer was accepted yet. You don't even know if the women have checked their voice mail. And it is possible someone else came in with a lower offer. I can't talk to you anymore; you're simply too stupid."

"Oh, and you're so smart, is that what you're saying?" Natalie sniped.

"Damn straight that's what I'm saying. I'm going out to the workshop. Do whatever the hell you want to do. Take a suggestion and clean this house for your interview tomorrow, so you can convince that reporter what a loving wife and stepmother you are. For whatever it's worth, if she's any kind of reporter, she's going to see right through to what you really are."

Natalie picked up the jar of honey on the counter and heaved it at Connor, who expertly dodged it. The jar shattered against the wall, and honey dribbled everywhere. Connor laughed, an evil sound, as he barged through the door and out into the rain to head for the shed, where he hoped he could find some peace and quiet.

Left to her own devices, Natalie started to pace again, paying careful attention to the widening pool of sticky honey on the floor. Why hadn't the real-estate people called her back? What Connor said made sense even though she wanted instant gratification. She'd give them a few more hours. The big question looming now was whether she should tell them about the house being in Ben's name before they found out or wait for them to mention it. Somewhere, she had to find something with Ben's signature on it so she could practice copying it. Surely there would be something in his room, a workbook, a test paper, something where he signed his name. How hard could it be to copy a kid's signature? First, she'd practice tracing it, then try it freehand. She told herself that in a few hours, she'd be able to write the kid's name as well as she wrote her own. She stopped in midstride. What if the signature had to be notarized? How could she get around that? *Don't panic*, she told herself over and over as she continued to pace. There was a solution to everything. You just had to find it.

Where was that damn kid? What was his endgame? What did he think was going to happen by his hiding out? Natalie's face turned into a mask of hate as she envisioned choking the life out of her eight-year-old meal ticket. Frustrated, she cursed long and loud, making up words she didn't even know she knew.

Tired with all the pacing and worrying, Natalie headed for the second floor to shower and dress for the day. She needed to calm down, and a shower usually did wonders. Then and only then would she venture into Ben's room and get down to business.

An hour later, feeling a little less stressed, Natalie opened the door to Ben's room. She saw the unmade bed, his slippers at the side. His desk was neat, books piled up on both sides, his computer in the middle. She looked around. There were no pictures on the walls, no toys to be seen. No shelves on the wall to hold things. There was nothing in the closet except copy paper, a box of pens, and another box with paper clips. The dresser drawers had a few neatly folded tee shirts, some underwear, and some socks. A jacket hung on the clothes tree by the door. His book bag was gone. It was hard to believe this was a kid's room. It never occurred to her to blame herself for not fixing the room for a little boy. She started to paw through the books on the desk until she found a workbook with Ben's name on the inside of the cover. For a little kid, his penmanship was pretty decent, she decided, and wouldn't be too hard to copy. She sat down and reached for a clean yellow legal pad. Then she turned on the computer and was surprised to see that an hour and a half had gone by, with still no response from the real-estate women.

Connor's words ringing in her ears, Natalie fell to work. Two hours passed before she was confident she had Ben's signature down pat. She gathered up all her practice papers and left the room. Again, Connor's words echoed in her ears. Maybe she should freshen up the living room. At least dust it, and maybe run the vacuum cleaner. And then there was that mess in the kitchen with the honey she had to clean up. With no other options at her disposal, she fell to the task and finished up at three o'clock, with still no return call from the real-estate people.

Natalie peered out the back door. She could see her husband clear as anything as he worked the potter's wheel. Connor had the emotions of a rock. Maybe she needed to think about making a clean sweep when she took care of Ben. There was no doubt in her mind that she could do both and not break a sweat. If she did that, the whole five million dollars would be hers. The minute the check was in her hands, she'd book a flight to somewhere in Europe and leave this life behind her.

With nothing else to do, Natalie brewed a pot of tea and turned on the small television that sat on the counter. Time to see what was going on in the world. All it took was fifteen minutes of watching doom and gloom to make her change the channel to *The Golden Girls*. She gave that another ten minutes, then switched to the Shoppers Channel, where they were selling makeup. She watched, enthralled, as the makeup artist transformed homely looking women into showstoppers. She would have ordered it, but Connor, bastard that he was, had taken all her credit cards because they were maxed out. That alone was enough to reinforce her idea to take him out along with Ben.

The clock on the stove said it was four-thirty. Still no call from the real-estate people.

Call or not to call? She walked over to the door. Connor was still in his workroom, but now the lights were on. It was still raining. She should be thinking about dinner. Her days of ordering in or going out to dinner were long gone, so dinner was either ramen noodles or canned pasta, neither of which appealed to her.

Natalie could feel the rage building in her as she contemplated the nearly empty pantry shelves. This was not what Connor Ryan had promised her.

Not in a million years.

Chapter 13

The clock on the Range Rover's dashboard said that it was nine-fifteen when Eleanor Lymen parked the car outside her house. She was so tired, she could barely keep her eyes open. She was *almost* sorry she had agreed to drive straight through in their rush to get home from Mississippi. She looked around at all the service trucks, then at the Nissan Sentra that belonged to her housekeeper, Martha. Cleanup was under way. She turned and raised her voice. "We're home, girls! Wake up!"

Irene and Rita struggled to sit upright, their hair mussed, their eyes glassy with fatigue. "What's going on?" Rita asked as she looked around at all the service trucks.

"My house is being put back to order. I called Martha, and she called all these people to come and do the repair work. I've been on the phone with her ever since I took over the wheel. She told me this wasn't just a break-in. She said that whoever it was who invaded my house was full of rage and hate. She said they even pulled the chandeliers out of the ceiling. They weren't just looking for something; they were bent on destroying whatever they could. She assured me that everything would be taken care of by noon. Then they'll go to work on your house, Irene, and yours,

Rita. So in the meantime, until all that is done, you're staying with me."

Eleanor Lymen slid out of the driver's seat on wobbly legs. The cool autumn air was like a soothing balm to her, and she was wide awake instantly. "Come along, we might as well face it and get it over with. I know it was Connor and that *skank* wife of his who did all this. I just know it," she said vehemently. Irene and Rita agreed.

All it took was one look at the kitchen to send Eleanor flying back outside, tears streaming down her cheeks. "Dear God, I didn't know there could be such hate in a person! Why smash my great grandmother's dishes? Why throw pans at the refrigerator to dent it? Why smash the oven door? Who does things like that?" she cried.

"A very sick person, Ellie, that's who. I think you should call your friend Isabelle right now and tell her we're back. But before you do that, let's check in to the Holiday Inn, so we can take a shower, a nap, and put on some clean clothes. Ask her if we can drive out to wherever they are, so we can see Ben. I want you, and us, too, to be clicking on all our cylinders when we see our boy. It makes sense, Ellie," Irene said.

"Irene's right. All of this," Rita said, waving her hand behind her, "can be fixed. Right now, you feel like you've been violated, and you have, but that's all going to change and those . . . those two evil people will be made to pay. Get in the car. I'm driving," she said, taking charge. "Do. Not. Look. Back. Just get in the car."

Eleanor nodded and climbed into the backseat. "Whatever would I do without you two," she cried.

"It's a two-way street, Ellie. We wouldn't know what to do without you, either," Irene said.

"Together, we make a good team. So far, we're doing pretty good, so let's keep it that way," Rita admonished, tearing out of the driveway and heading for the ring road that would take them to the highway and the Holiday Inn three miles down the road. If any of them had been paying attention to the opposite side of the road, they would have seen Natalie Ryan at the stop sign, her face contorted in rage.

"No one is expecting us till sometime tomorrow, so we're ahead of the game. We can shower, take a nap, and dream about our reunion with Ben. Then we put on clean clothes and find someplace that will serve us a superior lunch. Finally, if Isabelle gives us the okay, we drive out to McLean for our reunion with Ben. Win-win!" Rita grinned.

In spite of herself, Eleanor laughed out loud. "I wish I had bought a present for Ben. We should have gotten him something. Little boys like presents. Why didn't we think about that, girls?" Her voice was fretful at this lack of foresight.

"Well, we didn't, so no sense dwelling on it. We have the rest of our lives to buy him presents. Ben isn't like other little boys, Ellie. Think about it. What could we have bought him? Action figures? I don't think so. Games? Nope. Trucks, cars? He's too big for those. Knowing what I know about kids today, we would have had to buy some high-tech gadget, and Neanderthals that we are, we probably would have bought the wrong thing," Irene said.

"There is that," Eleanor agreed as she thought about her friend's words.

"Okay, we're here. I hope this is the last time we have to live out of a suitcase and spend half our days at a Laundromat. When things get back to normal, whatever normal turns out to be, I am going to hang out in my nightgown for a solid week and eat nothing but junk food, take naps, and watch those soap operas we haven't had time to watch in the last six months. I'm not going to an-

swer the door, the phone, or look at mail, either. So there!"
Irene announced.

"Hear, hear. Well said. I think we're too old for contin-
uing adventures. What about you, Ellie?" Rita asked.

"I'm working on a plan," Eleanor said. And no amount
of cajoling from her two friends could make her share
what her plan was.

While the three old friends were showering and snooz-
ing, the sisters were waking up at Pinewood and doing
their thing, which meant making breakfast and going
through their plans for the day.

Yoko had griddle duty and was making pancakes while
Kathryn layered bacon on a special rack just for mi-
crowave ovens. Alexis squeezed orange juice while Myra
and Annie pored over a blank real-estate contract that
Nikki had provided. Maggie had coffee duty, while Isabelle responded to e-mails and texts on her smart phone.

Ben and the dogs had yet to make an appearance.

"So when are you going to call the Ryans and put them
out of their misery?" Nikki asked, her question directed at
Myra, who looked up and smiled.

"Right now. Stop what you're all doing so you can
hear; I am going to put the call on speakerphone. Let's
see how Mrs. Ryan responds to my little bombshell. Now
what name was it that you called me by, Annie? Do you
remember?"

"Yes. Do you think I would forget something like that?
I was Martha, and you were Alice. Now go ahead and
call, Alice."

"Okay," Myra said. All eyes were on Myra as she pressed
the numbers for Natalie's cell phone. It wasn't picked up
until the fourth ring. "She's playing hard to get," Myra
said, mouthing the words for the others. "You know she
just has to be standing there waiting for this call."

"Hello." Myra grinned.

"Hello yourself, Mrs. Ryan. This is Alice. I'm sorry it's taken so long to get back to you, but you know how it is when you're dealing with someone on the other side of the world. Sheik Abdullah has accepted your offer for five million dollars. All furnishings convey. As you agreed. There is one problem, however."

Myra strained and thought she heard Natalie Ryan suck in a deep breath as she waited for whatever the problem was. "What kind of problem is that?" Natalie asked coolly.

"The house is not in your name or your husband's name. That's the problem."

"Really? Oh, pooh, that's not a problem. Why ever would you think that would be an obstacle? Ben is more than agreeable to selling this huge house. We talked to him at great length yesterday about the possibility of selling it and putting the money in a trust for him. He understands things like that.

"That child is like a mini financial wizard. My husband says if he wanted to, Ben could give those boys on Wall Street a run for their money. But I digress. We, Connor and I, are Ben's legal guardians because Connor adopted him. Everything was done legally and aboveboard. We have all the paperwork.

"I don't know if you know this or not, but Ben will graduate from college in December. He wants to take a year off and do nothing before he registers at the Institute for his master's the following year. He was the one who suggested we should downsize. When he registers for his master's, he plans to live in the dorms with the other students at the Institute. At that point, he seems to think turning ten years old means something special. Who are we to argue with a genius like Ben? What that means is that we won't really need this big house. We'll get a smaller one in a nice neighborhood where Ben can make friends this next year. So what is the problem?" The edge in Natalie's voice did not go unnoticed by the sisters.

"I'm not exactly sure, Mrs. Ryan, but our attorneys said they will need to speak to your attorney before we can go any further. We're dealing with a very wealthy man who isn't familiar with how Americans do things, so we have to be careful. My bosses don't want to get sued for doing something wrong or possibly illegal."

"Wrong? Illegal?" Natalie had to fight to control the rage that was slowly beginning to creep into her tone.

"I didn't mean that the way it sounded. We just have to make sure all our i's are dotted and all our t's are crossed. The only way that can happen is if lawyers are involved and are on the same page. After all, five million dollars is an awful lot of money. I'm sure all it will take is for you to take Ben to the lawyer's or have the lawyer talk to Ben. For what your attorney charges an hour, I'm sure he'll make a house call. You did say Ben was sick. How is he feeling, by the way? Better, I hope."

Natalie's mind raced. Part of her knew she was screwed. The other part of her refused to believe it. She looked at Connor, who was staring at her with hate-filled eyes, knowing she was going to go down for the count. Like hell. "Thank you for asking. At first we thought Ben might have appendicitis, but that was ruled out." It wasn't exactly a lie since she'd made it up to begin with, so she could rule it out just as easily. "I'm thinking he has chicken pox, because he has these red blotches all over his stomach and chest. Also, he's got a fever, so no, we are not taking him out. He's sleeping right now, and I'm not about to wake him up."

Myra looked around at the sisters, and quietly mouthed the words, "She's quick on the uptake."

Natalie clenched her teeth and decided to take a gamble. "I'm sensing something here that's bothering me. It's almost like . . . like you don't trust me and my husband. Maybe we should just forget this. We're not in a hurry to sell. You did come to us, if you remember. Until yesterday, we were just in the thinking stage of selling. It's all up to Ben. Connor and I can live anywhere. It is what it is. If it's meant to be, we'll find the right buyer when the time is right. Ben is my top priority right now. I'm going to have to cut this conversation short because Connor and I promised to do an interview with a reporter from the *Post*, and I have to get ready. Thank you for calling me back, Alice. Bye."

Myra's face registered shock, amazement, then anger. "She called my bluff! Do you believe that! Now what, ladies?"

While the sisters debated Myra's conversation and what should be their next move, Connor Ryan's jaw dropped to the floor with the same shock, amazement, and anger the sisters were feeling. "What the hell was that all about? What are you up to now, Natalie? Do you have any idea how asinine you sounded? If that woman didn't think you were crazy before, she's certain of it now."

"You are so stupid sometimes, Connor. I can smell a rat a hundred miles away. And this reeks of *eau de* rodent. I think those two women were trying to set us up. It's all about Ben. It's not about us or the sale of this house. Let's see if they call us back and accept our signatures on the contract. You think about all that while I get dressed for the interview. By the way, when I went to the Krispy Kreme for our bagels and coffee, guess who I saw!"

"Stop with the games. Who did you see?"

"Those three old biddies. They were on the opposite side of the road going away from the Circle. I saw them, but they didn't see me. You need to call the lawyer and tell him Eleanor Lymen is back in town and have her arrested. There's a bench warrant out for her arrest, which was never enforced because she and her friends had left town in the middle of the night. She needs to pony up that money the court ordered her to pay us."

Connor digested his wife's words. If Eleanor Lymen was back in town, that had to mean she knew where Ben was. It also meant she was probably the one who snatched him and had him someplace no one would find him. She was also probably the one behind his disappearance to begin with. Damn, this was all going south so fast, he felt like he was on a greased slope with nothing to break his fall. *Go now,* his brain shrieked. *Go now! Right now! Don't wait. Now!* Despite what his inner coward was telling him, his feet remained rooted to the floor.

Where would he go? How far would he get? He had no money to speak of. And the world wasn't exactly crying out for glassblowers or for him to craft a one-of-a-kind piece of pottery. Like it or not, he was stuck. And inner voice or no, he knew it all too well.

Natalie returned, dressed in designer jeans and a camp shirt. Connor eyed her suspiciously. "What's with the getup? I thought you'd be dressed to the nines since you said this would be a photo op, along with the interview."

"I'm canceling the interview. Nothing about this is feeling right. First, the deal with the house out of the blue, then the interview out of the blue, then out of the blue I just happen to see those three old biddies on the road driving to God knows where. I don't think you need to be a rocket scientist to figure out this is all about Ben and the fact that we didn't report him missing. Don't you smell a rat, Connor?"

"All I smell is that shitty perfume you're always wearing. I never smelled a rat, much less saw one, so I have no clue how they smell. Right now, I am all for packing up and leaving. You can do whatever the hell you want."

Natalie looked at her husband with a jaundiced eye as

she tapped out Maggie Spritzer's cell phone number. The moment she heard the reporter's voice, she said, "I'm sorry to call you on such short notice, but I have to cancel our interview. I'm sorry for the inconvenience." She immediately broke the connection and looked at Connor. "Okay, this is where we fall back and regroup."

"You need to get real, Natalie. Ben is gone. And with him, all our leverage. We have nothing. By now, wherever he is, he's talking up a storm and telling anyone who will listen what his life has been like with this loving family. We need to leave, and we need to leave now, before the cops come knocking. I'm going, with or without you."

Connor's cell phone took that moment to chirp. He looked down at the name of the caller: Lymen Institute. He clicked on, and said, "Connor Ryan."

"Good morning, Mr. Ryan, this is Dr. Evan Phillips, the Institute's administrator. I'm calling to give you a heads-up. Dr. Emily Banks is on her way to your home with Ben's assignments. She also needs to pick up his finished work and to talk with him. She should be ringing your doorbell momentarily. I hope Ben is progressing well. We miss him here at the Institute."

"Yes, well, that might pose a bit of a problem, Dr. Phillips. Ben appears to have chicken pox and is really under the weather. Right now he's sleeping, and I do not want to wake him. I can accept his new work assignment, but I can't give you anything in return because I truthfully don't know if Ben has done any work or not. He's been quite sick, as you know."

The silence on the other end of the phone bothered Connor. Maybe Natalie was right. It was all closing in on them. He waited, fully expecting Dr. Phillips to agree to simply dropping off new work for Ben. He almost jumped out of his skin when he heard Dr. Phillips say, "In that case, I'll send our in-house physician and nurse to take a look at Ben and report back to us. We are responsible for Ben and his well-being and have been since the day his grandmother entrusted the boy to our care."

Natalie turned as white as the wall she was leaning against. She grabbed the phone out of Connor's hand and said, "This is Natalie Ryan, Dr. Phillips. That will not be necessary. We have our own doctor looking after Ben, and he is on the mend. He doesn't need any more poking and prodding by your people or anyone else. We're his parents, not you or the Institute, and I do not care what your paperwork says. If you want to bring this to a test, I will call the news channels and let the world see what you people up there on the hill are all about. Do I make myself clear, Dr. Phillips? Oh, and one last thing: If I have anything to say about it, Ben will not be returning to your precious Institute once he completes his studies in December. Without Ben, what do you think Mrs. Lymen's endowment will mean to you? Now, I have a sick child to see to. Call your messenger and tell her to leave Ben's work by the front door."

Natalie stared at the phone in her hand before she handed it back to her husband. "Now do you believe me?"

Connor sat down at the kitchen table and dropped his head into his hands. "What do you want to do, Natalie?"

Natalie busied herself at the stove as she brewed a pot of tea. The truth was she didn't know what to do. Connor was right. He was finally accepting the fact that it was all closing in on them. She closed her eyes, then let out a yelp of pain when the bubbling water bounced out and splashed on her hand. An omen? The wonderful rich and rewarding life she'd been promised, which had never materialized, and all her hopes for it were now going down the tubes. And it was all because of that smart-assed little snot, whom she hated with a passion. He had outsmarted her. Connor was oblivious, and she secretly thought he had a soft spot for the little snot, whereas she hated the kid's guts. All that money wasted on an eight-year-old! It was totally obscene. She needed a plan.

Natalie poured two cups of tea and liberally spooned thick yellow honey into both cups. She plopped one down in front of Connor, who was staring off into the distance. She snapped her fingers in front of his face, and he didn't even blink. "Snap out of it, Connor. We need to talk and . . . we need to do something. Like now would be good, Connor. Look at me, you idiot, or I'm going to dump this tea right in your lap. Now, I'm not going to tell you again, look at me!" she screamed at the top of her lungs.

To make her point, Natalie grabbed her husband by the shoulders and shook him until he fell off the chair he was sitting on. She gave him a kick for good measure. "Now are you ready to talk to me?"

Holding his side with both hands, Connor struggled to his feet and gingerly lowered himself back onto the chair. "There's nothing to say, Natalie," he said wearily. "We need to pack up and leave as soon as possible. Otherwise, I see a whole bunch of police coming to cart us off to jail. Is that what you want?"

"No, it is not what I want. We're missing something here. There has to be *something* we can latch onto. It can't end like this. It just can't. He's still your son, you legally adopted him. We are his parents. We have rights. Ben was not mistreated. All his needs were met by us. That's our bottom line. What can they do to us? He ran away in the middle of the night. Kids run away all the time."

"And when they do run away, the parents contact the cops, and we did not do that. Why not, we'll be asked. And what do we tell them? Because we were afraid that if you found him, he would tell you that my wife intended to kill him? Not calling the cops was our mistake, Natalie."

Connor actually enjoyed the look of fear he was seeing on his wife's face. "You want to know something, Natalie?" Not bothering to wait for her response, he rambled on. "I think the reason Ben ran away was that he heard us talking and heard you say you wanted to do away with him. If you remember, he said, I stress the word *said*, that he was asleep in the laundry room waiting for his clothes to dry. I don't think he was asleep at all. I think he was in there cowering in fear, and I think he heard us. He heard you announcing that he needed to be eliminated. And like anyone on the verge of getting a college degree, he understood exactly what you were saying. After all, you don't need to be a genius to figure out what you were talking about. He waited till it got dark and ran. Same night. That tells me he heard us, and he was afraid. He's smart, you have to give him that. Wherever he is right now, you can rest assured he is either telling them what transpired or he has already told them. That's why, in my opinion, which being as stupid as you are, you never listen to, that offer came in on the house, the interview you canceled was scheduled, and, on top of all that, you spotted Eleanor Lymen, who is suddenly back in town. There is no such thing as coincidence, at least to my way of thinking.

"You can talk now, Natalie. Let's see you figure this one out. While you're doing that, I'm going to pack my gear, and I'm leaving. You can do whatever you want."

Natalie gulped at her tea, which was no longer hot. "Then why haven't they done something already?" she shrilled to her husband's retreating back.

"I can't talk to you because you're too stupid. What do you think has been going on? I'm not waiting for you, so if you're coming, move your butt."

Natalie sniffed. Like she was really going to do anything her husband suggested. He was the reason she was in the

predicament she was in right now. He wasn't going anywhere, not if she had anything to say about it.

There had to be a way out of this. There just had to be.
What she had to do was find it and act on it.

With nothing else to do, Natalie brewed yet another pot
of tea. She looked at the jar of honey and was dismayed to
see that it was empty. That had to mean she would have to
use the sugar substitute that Connor preferred, which always left a bad taste in her mouth.

"Make do, Natalie, make do," she said to herself as she
nursed her blistered hand.

What was that old Yogi Berra saying? Ah, yes—"it ain't
over till it's over." And she had miles to go before anything
was over.

Chapter 14

Sitting on the shoulder of the road, Maggie Spritzer watched cars and trucks whiz by on the highway. She switched her gaze to the cell phone in her hand. She could not believe it. Natalie Ryan had just canceled their interview! Unbelievable! First she'd dissed Myra and now her. She looked around to make sure she was far enough off the highway to be safe before she sent out a text to the sisters apprising them of this latest development. She ended the text with, *I think the Ryans are going to make a run for it. What do you want me to do?*

The incoming response came in less than a minute from Kathryn. *How far away are you? Stake out the house. Park where Yoko and I parked. We're on our way.*

Maggie's return text read, *App ten klicks. Will do.*

"I can do that," Maggie muttered under her breath as she waited for a break in traffic before she pulled onto the highway. Her thoughts were all over the map as she pondered what her next move should be. If the Ryans left while she was surveilling them, should she follow them? Should she brazenly go up to the door and say she really needed the interview, maybe increase the Nordstrom gift certificate? Her gut told her that nothing would work. The rats were about to abandon ship. Better to just stay undercover and wait for the others to arrive. With strength in numbers came power.

From all she'd been told, and granted, most of that knowledge came from Ben Ryan, an eight-year-old, Natalie Ryan was not someone to mess with. Since he was old beyond his years, Maggie had to give credence to his assessment of the woman. And he'd lived with her for four years, so he had to know just about everything there was to know about his stepmother's behavior.

Something had to have spooked Natalie Ryan. But what? Maggie gave herself a mental slap to the side of her head. Ben's disappearance was the first part of the answer. Ben, the golden goose, the meal ticket, the path to riches. The second part was Myra's telling her that Ben would have to be there in order to transfer ownership of the house to the fantasy sheik. Put the two together, and you ended up with a rat big enough for anyone with Natalie's background to smell.

Maggie slowed for a traffic light. She was less than two blocks from the Ryan house. She could see the Institute on her left, high on the hill at the top of the Circle.

In the bright autumn sunshine, the building looked like a beautiful academic campus. The only thing missing was students loaded down with backpacks as they chatted up their friends, strolling about. Ah, to be that young again. And to know what she knew now back then. She shook her head to clear her thoughts as she maneuvered her car into the same spot that Kathryn and Yoko had parked in. Was it just yesterday? It seemed like an eternity now.

Maggie turned off the engine, unbuckled her seat belt, rolled down the window, and settled down to wait. With the window down, she noticed what looked like a book bag hanging off the Ryans' front doorknob. She frowned. Was it Ben's? What would a book bag be doing hanging on the door? Ben had had his bag with him when Isabelle brought him to the farm. Because she was an investigative reporter, hence used to solving mysteries, Maggie surmised that someone from the Institute had delivered books, assignments, or workbooks to the house because they believed the boy to be ill. When no one opened the door, they had just left it hanging from the doorknob. It was the only thing that made sense. She felt satisfied with that explanation.

Maggie itched to get out of the car and march up to the door to demand to know why the Ryans had canceled the interview. If she did that, against orders, she would at least be able to take a peek inside the backpack. But even if she did that, what good would it do? Ben wasn't there, so the problem was moot. Better to stay right where she was and wait for reinforcements. She absolutely hated stakeouts. Hated them with a passion. There was so much she could be doing instead of wasting time sitting on her duff waiting for something that would or would not happen. Hours and hours of wasted time. Team player that she was, she sighed and kept her eyes on the Ryans' front door.

Then a horrible thought suddenly struck her. If the sisters were on the way, who was going to stay with Ben? She quickly fired off a text, one eye on the Ryans' house and the other one on her phone. The response came a minute later from Nikki: *Isabelle stayed behind with Ben because Eleanor Lymen and her friends are on the way to the farm.*

That's a good thing, Maggie thought. She felt sad that she wouldn't be there to see the grand reunion of grandmother and grandson. How wonderful that was going to be for Ben. Isabelle would tell them all about it, but it wouldn't be the same as witnessing it herself. She smiled to herself when she thought of the brilliant, precocious little boy and how fortunate it was for him that he'd found Isabelle. Sometimes things actually worked out the way they were supposed to. Sometimes.

Maggie had to fight not to doze off. Things were just too quiet. Only two cars had passed her on the street since she'd arrived. No one was mowing their lawns or raking their leaves. Where was everyone? It was almost like ghosts lived on this street and only came out after dark.

Ten minutes later, after she'd chewed her nails to the point where her fingers hurt, Maggie heard the unmistakable sound of Yoko's delivery van. It pulled up behind her, but no one got out. Instead, Maggie's phone chirped with an incoming message that was one word, *Report*. To which Maggie responded. *Nada. No activity*.

Maggie heard the door of the van slide open. She looked in the rearview mirror to see Myra and Annie advancing toward her car. "We're going to brazen it out and go up to the house. We'll go around back, where Connor has his shop, and see what we can do. We brought the bogus contract with us," Annie said, waving a bright green folder in the air. "Give us at least ten minutes, then follow us. Hopefully, by that time we'll be in the house and in control of the situation. Then it's game on."

"Good luck," Maggie said as she looked down at her watch. This was going to be the slowest ten minutes of her life. She could feel her adrenaline spike. She took deep breaths and waited as she watched Myra and Annie make their way to the Ryan house, and, instead of going to the front door, turn right and walk around to the back of the house. The minute Myra and Annie were out of sight, Maggie's hand flew to the door handle. She eased it open so she could bolt the moment the ten minutes were up. She knew the other sisters were doing the same thing she was.

The minutes crawled by. She wished she knew what was going on. Had the Ryans opened the door to Myra and Annie, or were they still there banging on the door?

Annie gave one hard, ferocious knock to the door, and shouted, "Mr. and Mrs. Ryan, it's Martha and Alice here with the contract on your house. Our attorney faxed us a notification that it is okay for you to sign for your son, Ben. We just have to have your signature notarized, and we'll have a deal. Alice and I are both notaries. Hello! Are you in there? We don't have much time. Two other people on the street called and are interested in the offer, but before we canceled you out, we wanted to make sure that's what you really want. Hello," she shouted again.

Inside the kitchen but out of sight of the paned windows on the back door, Natalie looked at her husband, and said, "Maybe I was wrong. What do you think, Connor?"

"I don't think anything," he said in an angry whisper. "This is your show entirely, so do whatever the hell you want. I'm still leaving."

Natalie felt her eyes narrow as she lasered in on her husband. "Does that mean I get to keep the whole five million dollars? Say it, I want to hear the words come out of your mouth."

Connor just laughed. "Yeah, Natalie, you can keep the whole five million. That's if you ever get it."

"What's that supposed to mean?"

"It means whatever you want it to mean." Connor laughed out loud as he walked over to the kitchen door and opened it.

"Ladies," he said by way of greeting, still chuckling.

"Oh, my," Myra said. "We thought you might not be home. We were just about to leave. I'm so glad we were persistent. This is such a wonderful deal for you both. And for us, too. Business has been slow lately, no one wants McMansions these days. You should consider yourselves lucky on this deal. I have the paperwork right here. All you have to do is sign where the X is. And on the line where Ben's signature should go, you sign his name, initial it above your signature, and we have a deal. My partner will notarize everything, give you a copy, and in three weeks you'll have your money. Does that work for you?" she said cheerfully as she held out a pen to Natalie, who was looking at it like it was a snake about to strike. Connor stood behind her, his face expressionless.

"By the way, there appears to be some kind of bag hanging on your front door. We noticed it on our way around the back. Looks like it might be your son's book bag," Annie said.

"In a manner of speaking it is Ben's bag. One of the professors must have dropped it off when I was in the shower and didn't hear the doorbell. I'm sure it's just his assignments. Connor, why don't you get it?"

Connor obediently trotted off and returned with a bright blue Oakley rucksack packed to overflowing. The name RYAN was stenciled in stark white on the outside flap. He plopped it down on the kitchen table.

Myra wiggled the pen in her hand. Natalie reached for it just as the kitchen door opened, and the sisters piled into the room.

"What . . . what . . . who . . . ?" Natalie stammered as she stared at the women, then at the pen that was suddenly in her hand.

"Think of this as a home invasion," Nikki said, as the women surrounded Natalie and Connor. Myra and Annie stepped back to complete the circle.

"Told you," Connor whispered into his wife's ear. She glared at him, then at the women, as she tried to figure out what her next move should be.

"What do you want? We don't have anything worth stealing."

"Sure you do. We want the boy," Nikki said. "Where is he?"

Natalie fixed her gaze on Myra and Annie. "You're part of this, right?" she said, waving her arm about. "There never was a deal with a sheik to buy this house, right?"

"Told you," Connor whispered in her ear yet again.

Natalie couldn't help herself. She knew she should keep quiet, but she said, "And the interview for the *Post,* that was all part of this . . . whatever *this* is, right?"

"Yes," Kathryn barked loud enough that Natalie flinched.

"Where's the boy?" Yoko asked.

"He's not here," Connor said quietly, surprising everyone.

"Where is he?" Myra demanded.

"We don't know," Connor responded just as quietly.

"We've been trying to find him. We've looked everywhere, but he's gone," Natalie said desperately as she eyed the steely-eyed women surrounding her.

"Did you report him missing? He's only eight years old. We did not see or hear about any Amber alerts," Alexis said.

"No, we did not report him missing," Connor said. "My wife insisted he could take care of himself and knew how to survive, as he is very resourceful. That's the best excuse I can come up with. Let's cut to the chase here. What is it you want from us?"

As one, the women laughed long and loud. "What do you think we want?" Annie finally asked when everyone had stopped laughing.

"We don't know; that's why my husband asked you," Natalie snapped. "So we screwed up. Parents screw up every day, and their reward isn't a home invasion. I'll ask you one more time, what do you want from us? Just because we screwed up this once doesn't mean we aren't good parents."

"Nothing, nothing at all," Nikki said. "There is nothing you could give us that would change things at all."

"We're here to make you pay for what you did to young Ben while he was in your care. We're going to ask you some questions. You would be wise to answer them quickly and truthfully. But first, rest assured that Ben is safe and sound, and he's told us all about both of you and his life in your care. His grandmother is back in town, and just about right now, the two of them are being reunited. In addition to that, Eleanor Lymen finally located, after six long months of searching, Ben's biological father, who, by the way, knew nothing about the boy's existence. They also will be reunited shortly," Annie said.

Natalie swallowed hard at Annie's words. Connor was right; it was over. She should have listened to him and left last night or at the very latest early this morning. Good God, why hadn't she listened? It was over, and she had to accept it. Like hell! She'd go down fighting. *At this point, what do I have to lose?*

"Tell me what kind of mother you were to Ben?" Nikki asked.

"I was a good mother," Natalie lied through clenched teeth.

"How many nights a week did you cook dinner for him? Remember now, we have Ben's side of this, so you get points for being truthful," Nikki said.

"I'm not much of a cook. We mostly ordered in or brought home takeout. Ben liked to make his own sandwiches at lunchtime because it made him feel grown-up, and he also liked to do his own cereal in the morning for the same reason," Natalie continued to lie.

Kathryn made an ugly sound in her throat. "Are you sure it wasn't because you couldn't get your lazy ass out of bed in the morning to make him breakfast and left it up to him to scrounge for his own lunch?" Natalie chewed on her lower lip but didn't respond to Kathryn's accusations.

Nikki made a check mark on her list.

"How often did you do Ben's laundry?"

"The boy did his own laundry," Natalie said curtly. "He felt grown-up doing it."

"He's only eight years old," Nikki said. "And he was

only four years old when he was forced to come live with you." She made a check mark on the pad she was holding in her hand.

"When it rained or snowed, how did Ben get to the Institute? Did you drive him?"

Natalie sucked in her breath. "He rode his bike. He had a poncho for rain. Boots for snow."

Nikki made another check mark on her list.

"How many times did you take the boy to the doctor or the dentist?"

"He wasn't sick. There was nothing wrong with his teeth," Natalie said.

Nikki made another check on her list.

"How many birthdays did you celebrate with him? How many cakes did you buy or bake and what kind of gift did you get him?"

"Okay, okay, so I'm a rotten mother in your eyes. Motherhood is a work in progress. I get it that I'm not up to your standards. The kid is healthy as a horse. He's smarter than everyone in this room. He didn't need me; he made that clear from day one."

Another check went on Nikki's list.

"How often do you buy fresh fruit and vegetables for Ben? You know, oranges, apples, bananas, string beans, carrots?"

Natalie tried to look away, but Yoko grabbed her by the arm and jerked her around, so she was almost eyeball to eyeball with Nikki. "Answer the question, damn it!"

"The market is on the other side of town. Ben could get all that at the Institute if he wanted it."

Before Nikki could place another check mark on her list, Kathryn's fist shot out, hitting Natalie dead center in her mouth. Chips of her teeth, resembling white Chiclets, flew in all directions, and her lips seemed to deflate right in front of their eyes. She shrieked in pain, her hands flying to her mouth. Connor cackled in glee as he clapped his hands in approval.

"Moving right along here, how much money did you save in an account for Ben from the allotment you got each month? What was his allowance? Don't bother to answer that, the answer is zero to both questions. He never received an allowance of even a quarter a week."

Another check mark went on Nikki's list.

"How much do you and your husband owe in bills? I think it's close to a quarter of a million dollars. Is that about right?"

"That's a damn lie!" Natalie screeched, her voice sounding like mush without the pricey caps on the stubs of her original teeth. She was howling in pain and outrage, to her husband's delight.

"No, it isn't," Connor said quietly. "Actually, it's a bit more than that. Natalie is the one who spent the money, not I."

"You bastard!" Natalie screeched again.

Another check mark found its way to Nikki's list.

"Tell us about Christmas. What kind of gifts did you get the boy? Did you put up a Christmas tree for him, decorate the house?" Nikki asked.

"They had a Christmas tree at the Institute. The staff gave all the students a gift," Natalie whined. Nikki's eyes narrowed to slits as she watched Natalie crumple. She turned to the group and asked where Alexis was.

"I'm right here," Alexis said as she appeared in the doorway, holding a pair of strappy black leather shoes. "Lookie here, ladies. See these shoes! I have lusted after them for a whole year, but no way could I ever afford them, and even if I could, I wouldn't pay sixteen hundred dollars for a pair of shoes. But this lady did. Look! Look! Brunello Cucinelli! And there were five more pairs in her closet."

As one, the women stared at the shoes dangling from Alexis's hand.

"And you bought all those obscenely priced shoes with Ben's money when he was wearing underwear that was so tight it was cutting off his circulation," Kathryn roared, as her fist shot out and landed squarely on Natalie's nose.

Connor clapped his hands. "There goes ten grand down the tube for the nose job. Bravo! Bravo! Whatever your name is. I've wanted to do that so many times, I've lost count."

Yoko, her face a mask of rage, moved at the speed of light to get behind Natalie. She reached out, grasped her hair, and pulled. The sisters gasped, and Connor Ryan burst out laughing as he stared at Natalie's hair extensions in Yoko's hands. "They cost nine hundred dollars. If you keep on going, you can add up the tab for the contact lenses, the nose job, the caps on her pearly whites. They cost enough to retire on. Lip injections. Breast augmentation. Tummy tuck. The list goes on and on."

"What's with this guy?" Myra hissed in Annie's ear. Annie just shrugged. The sisters stared at him as they, too, tried to figure it all out.

Connor Ryan threw his hands in the air. "I want to go on record right here and now that I never, ever laid a hand on Ben. I'm not father material. I admit that. I agreed to adopt him because that was the only way Diana would marry me. I married her for her money. I admit that, too. I also admit to picking up this skank," he said, pointing to Natalie, "in a bar. I was drunk at the time; you need to know that, too. This was when Eleanor Lymen decided that just having Ben living with her was not enough and filed for custody of Ben. I knew he was my meal ticket even if, for the sake of convenience, I had let him live with his grandmother after Diana died. So I fought it. I enlisted Natalie's help, so we could present a family unit for Ben to live with. It worked. Eleanor is an old lady, and grandparents have no rights. That's my story. Hers is different.

"On my phone, I recorded her saying she was going to do away with Ben. Unless you have another definition for 'do away with,' that means she meant to kill him. It's all there. And she has me on her phone asking her to marry me so we could fight Eleanor in court. I admit it. It will be up to you who you believe. Now, having said that, I think Ben can pretty much verify everything I said. And for whatever it's worth, I'm truly glad you found the boy's father. The kid needs a real father. I hope he steps up to the plate. And you won't get any resistance from me. I'll sign whatever you need me to sign to make it easy for him going forward."

The sisters found themselves in what Nikki said felt like never-never land. Nikki looked over at Maggie, and said, "Watch these two; we all need to talk."

"Sure thing," Maggie said happily.

Natalie was getting some of her gusto back. She looked at her husband and said, "You can't testify against me, I'm your wife. You agreed to everything. Don't try to weasel out of this now."

"No, I never agreed. I simply went along, waiting for my chance to split. I didn't want to end up dead at your hands, and I suspected that was your ultimate goal. I recognize that I'm weak, a *wuss* if you will, but I draw the line at murder. I don't give a hoot in hell what happens to me as long as you pay for what you were planning. I hope you got all that, you bitch!"

In the dining room, with the door to the kitchen open, the sisters heard every word Connor Ryan uttered. "What are we going to do with him? I don't see us meting out the kind of justice to him we have planned for his wife. Do we let him go? Do we do . . . *something* to him to make our point?" Myra said angrily.

"Ben never said anything really bad about Connor. Yes, he was greedy. The worst thing he did in regard to Ben was neglect and ignore him. No harm came to the boy through Connor. Right now, he's stone-cold broke, in debt up to his ears, and he has no money in the bank. This house, even the workshop in the back, belongs to Ben. We could turn him loose and let him go the homeless route. Or we can do something else as soon as we figure out what that *something* is. We need to take a vote on it," Annie said.

"We get him to sign off on everything, so Ben's new father doesn't have a fight on his hands. I can do all the legal work right here and right now. Then we can relocate him somewhere far, far away via Pearl's underground railroad," Nikki said.

"Do we really believe he would not have harmed Ben? I think that's what we need to agree on. Would he have helped Natalie? Would he have stood by and watched her do it? Or would he have found a way to split or stop her?" Yoko asked.

"It all comes down to two words. Harm or neglect? That's what we have to agree on," Alexis said. "A vote will go a long way right now," Alexis said. "Just a reminder. I brought my red bag. It's in the car. Someone text Maggie and ask her what her vote is in regard to Connor."

Myra fired off a text and held up Maggie's response, which was *Let him go*. The final vote was six to one to send Connor via Pearl's railroad to never-never land. Nikki was the lone holdout.

"Majority rules," she said bitterly. She looked at Kathryn and nodded. The look meant call Pearl and make arrangements for Connor.

Kathryn grinned. She loved going up against Pearl and took it as a personal challenge.

"Okay, then. Alexis, fetch your bag. Kathryn, you're in charge of Connor. Don't give him the shot until Yoko puts him to sleep. Back up Yoko's van to the garage door, and we'll dump him in there. Just to be on the safe side, use the Flexi Ties on his hands and feet. Do you need any help, Kathryn?" Annie asked.

"Nope! I got it," Kathryn said happily.

"Okay, ladies, let's do it!" Myra said jubilantly. She looked around at Alexis, and asked, "Seriously, were those shoes really sixteen hundred dollars?"

"Yes, ma'am," Alexis said smartly.

"Six pair in total, eh?"

"Yes, ma'am." Alexis grinned.

Myra smiled, an evil smile. "Pack them up in a bag, dear. But first, take a knife and slash each one so that it is unwearable. We're going to let Mrs. Ryan take them with her when she . . . um . . . goes on her final journey, but not with them in a condition that would let her sell them to give her a financial start."

"Oooh, I love the way you think," Alexis cooed before she ran out of the room to grab a knife and go up the stairs to Natalie's closet. She slashed each shoe until it was unwearable, then dumped the pricey shoes in a laundry bag that was lying on the floor. She looked around at the shoe racks and felt dizzy at what she was seeing. She shook her head to clear her thoughts and raced down the steps.

"I'm ready, my dears!"

"So are we!" the sisters shouted in return.

Chapter 15

Isabelle watched as the massive iron gates opened and a dusty, muddy Range Rover sailed through the wide opening and came to a stop. She opened the kitchen door and ran out to greet Eleanor Lymen and her two friends. They hugged and laughed and swiped at their eyes as Isabelle led them inside to Myra's homey, warm kitchen, where a nice fire was blazing, and the scent of fresh coffee permeated the kitchen.

"You guys look exhausted. Sit down, have a cup of coffee, we'll talk for a bit, then . . . you get to hug your grandson! He is going to be so happy, Ellie. You're all he talks about."

"Where is he?" Ellie asked.

"In the barn. He loves climbing up to the loft and jumping down into a bed of hay. It takes us hours to pick it all out of his hair and off his clothes. The dogs, too. He is in his glory, Ellie. I don't think that child has had so much fun in a long, long time.

"Myra has four barn cats, and he plays with them, he talks to the horses, rubs them down, feeds them apples and sugar cubes. The dogs, all five of them, think he's their personal playmate. He's being a little boy, Ellie, and loving every minute of it."

"I don't know how to thank you and your friends for taking him in and caring for him. I've been so worried. Tell me the truth, Isabelle, is Ben upset with me for leaving him? Even though there was nothing I could do legally, I was still there on the Circle for him."

"Not one little bit. He understands. He is such an amazing little kid. Just when I think I have him figured out, he throws me a curve. I love him so much. We all do. We're going to miss him when you all leave. I hope you'll let him come to visit, call, write, whatever."

"Of course we will. What's the story on Connor and Natalie?" Rita asked.

"You know what, Rita, let's leave Connor and Natalie till later and not spoil what is going to be a wonderful, happy reunion, which is way too overdue," Isabelle said, not unkindly. The women nodded, knowing she was right.

"You're right, of course," Ellie said agreeably. "Is Ben still doing his schoolwork?"

"Yes, every day. He is very conscientious. Just this morning, before he went out to the barn, he called his professors and sent off his work through the computer. I'm a real Neanderthal, so I don't understand how that works, but he does, and that's all that matters. He did say he was up to date on everything and ahead by a week on his future assignments, but he has to take two oral quizzes this afternoon. He said he will graduate in December as planned. Isn't that amazing?"

"It certainly is," Ellie agreed as she finished her coffee. "Can we see him now?"

"Sure. But let me call him on his new phone. He loves to get calls. I bought him this phone called a Jitterbug. He thinks it's the best thing since peanut butter and jelly."

Ellie laughed. "We all have the same phone. Big numbers, easy to use, and that 5* thing in case of trouble. Okay, call him," she said, excitement ringing in her voice.

Isabelle laughed as she pressed the numbers for Ben's phone. He shrieked a greeting as all the dogs started barking at the same time because of the zippy ring tone.

"Hey, kiddo, there's someone here to see you! Hurry up!"

When there was no response, Isabelle opened the door and motioned for the three women to go outside. "This is your chance to see a real live streak of lightning. He knows it's you. *Go!*"

The three women ran as fast as their elderly legs would allow. Ben barreled out of the barn at full throttle, the five dogs barking and yelping as they thundered their way to the running women.

"Granny!" Ben screamed.

"Ben!" Eleanor Lymen screamed in return.

Fifty-two pounds of pure boy threw himself into his grandmother's waiting arms. Rita and Irene circled them as much as the dogs would allow.

"You're killing me!" Ben gasped. "But it feels good."

"I think you cracked my ribs," Eleanor howled.

"Are you going to keep me?"

"You better believe it!" Eleanor said, meeting Isabelle's eyes. Isabelle just nodded.

And then they were all back in the house. Isabelle busied herself pouring a glass of milk for Ben and setting out a plate of brownies. She handed out treats to the dogs, then withdrew to the family room to call the sisters for an update, leaving Eleanor, her friends, and Ben to their privacy.

Forty minutes later, Ben poked his head in the door, and said, "Izzy, I have to go upstairs and call the Institute. I have to take two oral quizzes. You remember I told you that, right?"

"Sure do. I'll just visit with your family until you're done. We'll be here, Ben, waiting for you."

Back in the kitchen, the three women stared at Isabelle,

their eyes moist. "I'm out of words, Isabelle," Eleanor said.

"None are necessary. Did you tell him about his father?"

"No, not yet. I have a favor to ask you. Your . . . um . . . people, you said they're at the Ryan house taking care of things, right?" Isabelle nodded.

"Can you call them and ask them to do something for me?"

"Sure. No problem. What is it you want?"

Eleanor cleared her throat. "Jonathan, Ben's father, told me that when he was seeing my daughter he bought her a string of pearls. He said Diana loved them so much, she never took them off. Never. When he found out about her death, he researched the robbery, and he said there was a picture of . . . of . . . Diana, and she was wearing the pearls. I myself never saw that picture. At the time, I was in a black void somewhere. He said, and he didn't go into detail, that while he had a robust trust fund, it was stipulated that he had to also work to have access to it. So he worked his way through college and med school by waiting tables, pumping gas at stations over the weekend. Yet he managed to save enough to buy Diana the pearls. He said he paid ninety-four dollars for them at a pawnshop. He'd like them back because in case he ever has a daughter he would want her to have them. Is that possible?" Tears dribbled down Eleanor's cheeks as she tried to wipe them away.

"Absolutely, I can do that. Listen up."

Annie clicked on on the first ring. She listened to Isabelle, her face tightening into one of hot rage. "I'll take care of that right now."

"Who was that?" Myra asked.

"Isabelle." Annie looked at Nikki, whose face was contorted in anger as she continued to grill Natalie Ryan.

Annie held up her hand for Nikki to stop the interrogation.

"What?" Nikki bellowed.

"That was Isabelle. She asked us to do something. Can I have the floor for a minute?"

"Sure."

"Mr. Ryan, what did you do with the pearls Diana was wearing when she was killed in that bank robbery?"

Connor Ryan wore the expression of the proverbial deer caught in the headlights. "Ah . . . the coroner gave me her belongings in a bag. I brought them home and . . . and . . . I put them on a shelf in my closet."

"Alexis, go get them," Annie ordered.

"They . . . they . . . aren't there anymore. Natalie found the bag and threw everything away but the pearls. She had them. They were just cheap pearls. Not real. At least they didn't look real to me," he said lamely.

Natalie's mind raced. At last, a bargaining chip. Maybe if she gave up the pearls, they'd let her go. If she could just remember what she'd done with that shitty string of beads. They were probably in what she called her overflow drawer, with all the makeup, perfume, and other junk she no longer used but was too lazy to clean out.

"I'll only ask you once. Where are the pearls?" Nikki demanded. "If you don't give us the right answer, I'll let Kathryn have another go at you. I bet she could pop those silicone implants in your boobs in less than three minutes. You might bleed out, but then, there is no one in this room who would care. So where are the pearls?"

All it took was one glance at the murderous look on Kathryn's face, and her clenched fist, to warn Natalie to cooperate. "They might be in my junk drawer in the vanity," she lisped, as pink drool dribbled down her chin. She swiped at it with the sleeve of her shirt. She knew she was beaten, that her options were all gone.

Alexis was already on her feet and headed for the second floor. She returned fifteen minutes later. "That drawer alone has close to several thousand dollars' worth of makeup and perfume. But I found the pearls!" She handed them to Annie like they were the queen's jewels.

Annie, in turn, called Isabelle. "We. Have. The. Pearls."

"Time to get this show on the road," Myra said. "We've been here too long as it is. The neighbors might be returning soon. I heard a few cars go by a while ago."

Nikki looked at Alexis. "You got your bag and everything you need?"

"Good to go."

"Load Mr. Ryan in the van so we can get started here," Nikki ordered.

"You might as well cooperate, Mr. Ryan. Otherwise, you'll be sporting some serious bruising and undergoing a lot of pain," Yoko said as she tightened the Flexi Ties on his wrists and gave him a push forward. Kathryn and Annie propelled him toward the garage. They waited until they heard Myra back Yoko's van to within an inch of the opening before they popped the garage door open. The back of the van rose slowly, and Connor Ryan was shoved inside before it reached the top, only to come down a second later. The garage door closed with a bang. By the time they were back in the kitchen, Myra was walking through the front door.

"It's all in the teamwork," Myra said, laughing.

All eyes were on Alexis as she made a production out of rummaging in her red bag of magic tricks. "What . . . what?" Natalie lisped.

Kathryn wagged her finger under Natalie's nose. "Shut up!"

"It's a given she's going to scream her head off," Yoko said. "Somebody tape her mouth shut!"

"I'll be happy to do that," Annie said as she dug around

inside Alexis's bag for a roll of duct tape. "I didn't know they made duct tape in color these days. I really like this purple color. Kind of girly, if you know what I mean." The sisters all laughed as Annie peeled off a long strip and slapped it around Natalie's face and on top of her real hair.

"That's going to hurt like a bitch when it has to come off." Nikki grinned.

"Who said it's coming off?" Myra chirped.

Natalie fell off the chair in a dead faint. Kathryn and Yoko hauled her back up and taped her to the chair.

Annie filled a pot with cold water from the sink and dumped it all over Natalie. "We want you alert here, so stay awake."

"I think we should start, dear," Myra said.

Alexis whirled around, the remaining unslashed pair of Brunello Cucinelli shoes dangling from her hands. She whirled and twirled them around for all to see.

Nikki leaned over. "We're going to make you pay for those shoes and the other five pair you had upstairs. We're going to make you pay for every miserable, stinking, lousy thing you did to that little boy to satisfy your own greed. Do you understand what I just said? Blink twice if you do." Natalie blinked twice, tears flooding her eyes.

"She's finally getting it. Okay, Alexis, light it up!" Nikki said.

When Alexis turned around a second time, she had an acetylene torch at full bore. She handed it to Nikki. "Careful, that baby's hot."

Natalie slumped in the chair. Annie dumped a second pot of water all over her. She gasped as she shook her head like a dog caught in the middle of a rainstorm.

"You waiting for a bus, Myra? Take off her shoes and roll up her pant legs," Annie ordered.

"Okay, okay," Myra said as she yanked off Natalie's Ferragamo flats. She tossed them across the room. "Nikki, the only way this is going to work is if we prop her feet up on a stool. She still has free mobility. Maggie, tie her ankles together."

Moments later, everyone stepped back as Nikki reached for the torch. "We're going to burn your feet right down to the bone. Take a good, long look at those classy shoes and know from this point forward you will be walking on your knees." With that, she swiped the torch across Natalie's feet.

"God, that smells," Kathryn said.

"She blacked out again," Alexis said.

"Hit her again, that's barely a first-degree burn," Annie said. Nikki happily obliged as she recited almost verbatim all the questions she'd asked Natalie earlier. She realized that Natalie couldn't hear her, but she didn't care. She kept swiping the torch across her bare feet, which were now blistered, with the flesh turning black. "And this is for not cooking for the boy, and this is for that and that and that."

"Enough!" Myra said ten minutes later. "Fix her up and get her loaded into the van. Kathryn, call Pearl and tell her we can't wait for darkness on this mission. Tell her to meet us at the depot and be ready to roll within the hour. Do not take no for an answer. Explain about Natalie's condition and what she's going to need. Yoko, give her a shot. Alexis, wrap her feet in that medicated blanket and make sure you have an extra one to give to Pearl. We're done here, ladies. All we have to do is tidy up and hope the smell goes away sooner rather than later. I seriously doubt anyone will come looking for these two, but you never know."

Yoko was the first to leave, Kathryn right behind her. "We'll meet you back at the farm," Kathryn called over her shoulder. "Someone call Isabelle."

Nikki had the phone to her ear. "Izz, we're done here. The Ryans are on the way to the depot, where Pearl will take over. Annie has the pearls. Sorry you missed the fun. We avenged Ben. I hope he never finds out. It's enough that we know, and his grandmother. I'm hoping for clear skies for him from here on in." She listened a moment, and said, "It was brutal, Izz, but she deserved it, plus more. I won't have a bit of trouble sleeping over this. We'll see you in a bit."

Nikki turned around. She stared at Alexis, Maggie, Myra, and Annie. "I will never ever understand how a person can harm a child or an animal. Never!" Tears gathered in her eyes as she stared at her sisters, who gathered around her, murmuring soft, caring words of compassion, words that only women seemed to know for some reason.

"Time to go home," Maggie said happily.

"Yes, it is time to go home," Myra said. "Our work here is done."

The sisters linked arms and walked out of the Ryan house into the bright October sunshine.

Another mission successfully completed.

Epilogue

Eleanor Lymen handed over the potato peeler to Rita and said, "You need to do this. I'm so nervous I'm going to slice my fingers off if I keep at it." Rita reached for the potato and the peeler and shooed Eleanor over to the table.

"Sit!" she ordered. "Irene, make her a cup of coffee."

Irene did as ordered. "Calm down, Ellie, it's all going to work out just the way it's supposed to. Jonathan is going to arrive, and he's going to meet his son, and everyone is going to live happily ever after. Get with the program here, will you," she said, not unkindly.

"I should have prepared Ben. God in heaven, why didn't I do that, girls?"

"We talked about this for hours on end, Ellie. The three of us decided this was the best way to do it. Jonathan agreed with us, so will you just relax already?"

Eleanor gulped at the coffee in her cup just as Ben made an appearance in the kitchen. "Boy, it sure does smell good in here. Don't tell me, I know what you're making for dinner." He ticked the menu off on his fingers. "Roast chicken, giblet gravy, and stuffing. Lots and lots of stuffing, lettuce salad with hot bacon dressing, creamed corn, those bright green peas I hate, homemade dinner rolls, cranberry orange sauce. And for dessert, red velvet cake with real whipped cream. Did I get it right?" he asked anxiously.

"You did," Eleanor said, using both hands to hold her coffee cup. "Your job is to set the table. The dishes are on the counter. Careful with them, Ben. We're eating dinner in the dining room this evening."

"Wow! Two welcome-home dinners. The spaghetti and meatball one was enough that first night, but two! I'm not complaining, but . . . there's an extra plate here," he said, looking quizzically at his grandmother.

"Yes. We're having a guest today." Eleanor wanted to say more, but one look from Irene stifled the words in her throat.

"But the food is all your favorites. I'm sure our guest will like it as much as you do."

Ben picked up the plates and headed for the dining room, calling over his shoulder, "Who is it? Do I know them?"

"Uh, no," Eleanor said. "He's what you might call a new friend. We really like him."

"Well, if you all like him, then I guess I will, too," Ben said, coming back for the salad plates and silverware. "You said 'him.' It's a man, then?" Eleanor nodded as she stared into her empty coffee cup, which Irene hastened to refill.

"When is he getting here?" Ben asked.

Eleanor looked down at her watch. She wanted to say "any minute," but instead she said, "Soon."

Five minutes later, Ben was back in the kitchen. "Table's

all set. Do you need me to do anything else? If not, I'm going back up to my room. My finals are on Monday, and I want to make sure I have everything down pat. Dr. Andrews said if I pass them all, I don't have to go back till graduation day. Oh, did I tell you, Dr. Andrews told me this morning I could pick my graduation date if I pass everything with an A. A piece of cake," he said, grinning from ear to ear.

The doorbell took that moment to ring. Eleanor almost jumped out of her skin. Rita and Irene stopped what they were doing. Eleanor's voice sounded so strangled that she barely recognized it as coming from her own mouth. "Do you want to get that, Ben? Be polite now, and bring our guest back to the kitchen."

"Sure," Ben said, running to the front door. He opened it and looked up at the giant standing in front of him. "Hi! I'm Ben. Grandma said to bring you back to the kitchen."

The giant spoke as he held out his hand. "And I'm good at following orders. I'm Jonathan Philbran."

"Who are you? Grandma said you were a new friend."

The giant dropped to his haunches so he was at eye level with Ben. "It sure does smell good in here. But to answer your question, I'm just a guy with three yellow buses, a job, and some money in the bank. Your turn." He grinned, showing the same gap between his front teeth that Ben had. "Whoa, whoa, what's that look of sudden panic I'm seeing on your face?" Jonathan asked, alarm written all over his face.

Ben backed up a step, then another, as Jonathan rose to his feet.

"Your . . . your hair looks like mine. Actually, you look like . . . you look like me!" He turned and ran screaming, "Granny, Granny!"

Eleanor Lymen closed her eyes as Ben flung himself at

her. Irene and Rita immediately closed ranks as Jonathan Philbran stood outlined in the kitchen doorway. He looked at his son, then at the three women. He threw his hands in the air. "Obviously, we should have given more thought to my introduction."

"I think I know who you are," Ben said. "You're my father. You look like me. That's why Granny left, to find you. Am I right?" he blurted, in full panic mode.

"Yes, that's right, Ben. Remember in my letter to you I said I had to do something because I had made a serious mistake, and I needed to make it right?"

"I remember," Ben whispered, never taking his eyes off the man who had just said he was his father.

"I sent Jonathan away. I thought he wasn't good enough for your mother. I had no right to do that, but I still did it. That's what I had to make right. Ben, look at me and listen very carefully to what I am saying. Jonathan never knew about you. When he left, he had no idea that your mother was pregnant. And I never knew who he was. Back then, he was using a different name. None of what happened is his fault. I am totally to blame for your not having a father and for what happened to you after your mother died. Please tell me you understand what I just said."

Ben's eight-year-old brain tried to fathom what he'd just been told. He had a real father, and his father's name was Jonathan Philbran. He had three yellow buses, was just a guy with a job, and had some money in the bank. He left willingly when his granny said he wasn't good enough for his mother. What kind of person would do that? In a flash, he started to remember all the parts and bits of conversations he'd heard between his granny, Irene, and Rita that had made no sense at the time. His mother was ... was mentally challenged somehow. He was a child genius, and he had no idea what his real father was. Maybe somewhere in between. What did they want him to say? More to the point, what did *he* want to say? Clearly, they were all waiting for some reaction from him. But as he grappled with what to say, his father spoke quickly.

"What your grandmother just said—it's true, but what she didn't tell you is I was going to leave anyway. Your mother . . . I dearly loved your mother. I want you to know and believe that. I loved her with all my heart and soul. But . . . your mother didn't love me the same way. She cared for me, that much I knew. But when I wasn't with her, she forgot about me. Even forgot who I was. No one, not your granny, not Rita, Irene, or I wanted to admit that Diana, your mother, had mental issues. When I finally realized it, and this might surprise you, but I'm a doctor and I was a doctor then, I knew I had to let her go and move on with my life. It was at that point that your grandmother approached me and told me to hit the highway. I didn't argue or fight with her, I just left, then went to a friend's house and had a total meltdown. To this day, I love your mother as much as I loved her the day I walked away. I had no idea she was pregnant. If I had known, I would have stayed. Nothing could have taken me from her side. I would have been there for you every step of the way."

"Do you understand, Ben?" Eleanor asked softly. Ben nodded. "Can you forgive me?" Ben nodded. "And your father?" Ben nodded again.

"What's going to happen to me now?"

"That's totally up to you, Ben. Jonathan and I agreed that whatever decision you come to, we will accept."

Ben squared his thin shoulders and looked around at the four people in the world who totally loved him. He could see it in their eyes, and he swore later that he could feel the love. He was smart enough to know he was about to make the most important decision of his eight-year-old life. "I think I would like to take some time to think about all this," was the best that he could come up with at that moment.

"Of course you do. I think I would be disappointed if you'd said anything else," Jonathan assured him.

Ben tilted his head to the side. "So what do you do with three big yellow buses?"

The tension in the room evaporated like magic with the question. Jonathan sat down at the table as the three women started to bustle about the kitchen.

"I'm a doctor, but not the kind of doctor who has an office in a building. My office is the buses. I travel around the country, mostly to poor rural areas, with my staff, and we work out of tents. When I said I had some money in the bank, what I meant was I have a lot of money that was left to me by my grandparents, and I use that to fund what I do and to pay my staff. That's how your grandmother and her friends finally found me. I was in Mississippi when they did. I would have been here sooner, last week, actually, but I had a couple of sick kids I wanted to make sure were on the mend before I left. I hear you're ready to graduate from college in December. That's awesome!"

"About as awesome as what you do," Ben quipped. "You really do look like me."

"I'm going to take that as a compliment," Jonathan said, a big grin on his face.

"Can you suck spaghetti through the space between your front teeth?"

"Are you kidding? That's one of my major accomplishments. Can you?"

"I'm pretty good at it," Ben said shyly. "Going forward, what am I supposed to call you, Dad, Pop, what?"

"Good Lord, no. A man has to earn the right to be called Dad. That's a serious title and one to be taken seriously. Maybe someday you'll think I earned it, then you can make the decision. For now, Jon is good. That's what all my colleagues and friends call me. Well, some call me Doc."

"How's all this going to work?" Ben asked curiously as he found himself warming up to the giant man sitting across the table from him.

"Your grandmother pretty much explained that it's up to you. I can tell you what we came up with, but that doesn't have to mean you need to go along with it. We all meant it when we said it was up to you."

"What did you all come up with?" Ben asked. His hands folded under the table in his lap, Ben crossed his fingers.

"My plan was to take a year off and go out to my ranch in Montana. Your grandmother, Irene, and Rita decided that they'd like to join up with my team. Rita is a nurse, so that's a big help right there. They'll keep doing what I've been doing since . . . well, for a long time. We thought that you might like to go to Montana with me. I'd like you to be a real kid, to catch up on all the years you missed, doing what kids do. I get to learn right along with you. I can teach you to ride a horse, we could go mountain climbing, snowboarding, ice-skating, swimming, shoot baskets. I even know how to use a Hula-Hoop. I know how to do all those things, and I'd love to be the one to teach you; and you can teach me how to be a dad. A year. I didn't get past that in my thoughts, to be honest with you. How does that sound to you?"

Ben closed his eyes for a moment until they started to burn. He hoped he wouldn't cry. This was the stuff he had always dreamed about but never talked about. When he opened his eyes, he saw everyone staring at him. He thought they were all holding their breaths, waiting for what he was going to say.

"It sounds pretty darn good to me, but I still want to

sleep on it. What's my name going to be? I've already had two," he said with a grimace.

"I already started the paperwork. Like it or not, kid, your last name is Philbran, and guess what! My middle name is Benjamin."

Ben's face lit up like a moonbeam.

"Dinner's ready!" Eleanor called out, happiness ringing in her voice.

Ben turned to his father. "You are absolutely going to love this dinner. It is my favorite, and Granny made it just for me, and I suspect you, too. Plus, we're eating in the dining room, and that's just for special occasions; plus, on top of that, we're eating off the good dishes. The downside is that you and I have to clean up." Ben giggled.

Jonathan laughed out loud as he wrapped his arm around his son's shoulders and led him into the dining room.

"Ben?" Eleanor said.

"It's my turn to say grace," Ben said, bowing his head. "Thank you, Lord, for what we are about to receive, and thank you for bringing Jonathan to our table today."

"Dig in," Eleanor said, tears glistening in her eyes.

And dig in they did.

It was the day after Thanksgiving at Pinewood. Much to the sisters' chagrin, their men were off again on another project, and the women had all had Thanksgiving dinner at Pinewood. Now the sisters were all clustered in the kitchen, admiring each other's attire. Today was Benjamin Andrew Lymen Ryan Philbran's graduation day.

"I think we'll make young Ben proud," Myra said, "and we all smell good in the bargain. This is exciting. I've never been to a graduation where only one student graduated, much less an eight-year-old. Remember now, no crying. Everyone swear not to cry."

Everyone swore they wouldn't cry, and not a single one of them believed she would be able to keep that promise. This was Ben they were talking about, the little boy who had stolen his way into their hearts and refused to leave.

"I'm driving," Maggie said. "I brought the *Post* van. Let's go, or we're going to be late, and it looks like it's going to snow any minute. Chop, chop, people!"

An hour later, Maggie parked the van just as snowflakes started to fall from the sky. "I wonder if that's some kind of omen or something," she muttered under her breath.

"Ellie said to just go in, turn to the right, go to the auditorium, and sit on the right side. The left side is for the professors and any students who care to attend," Isabelle said.

Jonathan Philbran was waiting for them in the small lobby. He was dressed in a dark suit, pristine white shirt, and red power tie. He had a fresh haircut and smelled like a woodsy glen. He smiled, but it was a nervous smile. "Hurry, ladies, it's about to start. I feel like my heart is going to bust right out of my chest."

"That's not going to happen," Eleanor Lymen said, coming up to them and ushering them into the auditorium. The minute they were all seated the music to "Pomp and Circumstance" filled the room as Ben, dressed in his cap and gown, strolled down the center aisle. He was grinning from ear to ear as he made his way up to the stage, then climbed up three steps so he could reach the lectern. He had no notes.

He waved his hand and said, "Welcome to my graduation, ladies and gentlemen. Since I am a class of one, I am the valedictorian. That means I should give a speech, but I'm not going to do that because whatever the future holds in store for me is too far down the road for me to speculate. I want to thank all of you for coming. I want to thank all my professors for all the help they've so generously given me and how they were always there for me when I needed them.

"I want to thank my grandmother, Rita, and Irene for enrolling me here at the Institute. There is one other person I want to thank. I wouldn't be standing here talking to you today if it wasn't for her. You people on my right don't know her, all those on the left know her as Isabelle. Because she's my friend, she allows me to call her Izzy. Thank you for finding me, thank you for being my friend, and thank you to all your friends who took care of me when I needed help the most. I hope I made you proud today.

"That's the end of my speech. Oooh, wait a minute, there is one other person out there I need to thank. See that big guy in the back row who towers over everyone else. That's my *dad*!"

With that, Ben hopped down, ran off the stage, and threw his cap in the air. Everyone clapped. Everyone wiped at their eyes, even some of the attendees on the left.

There was a ton of laughter, hugs, more tears, and more hugs.

"Refreshments are being served in the cafeteria, and a table has been set up with gifts for the graduate," the dean said over the loudspeaker, as the crowd made their way to the cafeteria.

"We're sorry, but we have to cut this short," Jonathan said thirty minutes later. "Our flight leaves in an hour, thanks to Countess de Silva, who graciously provided us transportation to Montana. We need to say goodbye now. But first, I want to give Ben his graduation present." He looked at Isabelle, who was carrying one end of a large basket. Maggie had hold of the other.

They set it down in front of Ben, who let out a whoop

so loud it could be heard in the next county. Two golden retriever puppies stared up at Ben with soft, adoring brown eyes. Each wore a bright red collar. One said JAM. The other said JELLY.

Now everyone was crying, as Ben laughed and cried himself as he struggled to hold both puppies, who were licking him to death.

"Okay, we're outta here, everyone," Jonathan said as he reached for one of the puppies.

Ben stared around at his new family. He allowed himself to be kissed and hugged. When it was Isabelle's turn, she bent low and whispered in his ear, "If I had only one wish, Ben, it would be to have a son like you. You have a good life now, you hear. And please, please, don't forget me." In spite of all the promises she'd made to herself, she was crying like a baby.

Ben leaned forward. He whispered in return, "Izzy, if I only had one wish, it would be that you could be my mom. You take care of yourself, and don't you forget me, either."

"We're never going to get this show on the road," Jonathan shouted as he scooped Ben up under his arm and literally ran from the room, the two puppies yipping and yapping.

"Okay, people, enough with the tears. All is well that ends well. Let's all retire to the Dog and Duck, where we can drown our sorrows. Myra rented the whole place just for us," Nikki said.

The room was suddenly blasted with sound as someone from the Institute turned the recording of "Pomp and Circumstance" to the highest decibel level possible.

Fists pumping in the air, tears rolling down their cheeks, the sisters, along with Ellie, Rita, and Irene marched out of the building.

The tears were replaced with smiles and high-fives as they walked out to the van through the falling snow.

"Now this is what I call a truly happy ending," Annie whispered to Myra.

"As always, my friend, you are spot on," Myra said with a laugh.